Grandpa's
Last
GIFT

SONYA TUCKER-POINDEXTER
& JEFF MILLER

To Dad, our prayer warrior! Thank you for everything, but most of all, thank you for teaching us how to pray and always have faith!

Table of Contents

Chapter 1

It was a beautiful morning, blue-bird skies, bright sunshine shimmering down, and enough gas left in the tank for Hazel Grace Jackson to push herself to jog at least one more mile. A brilliant red cardinal flew right in front of her, a little too close for comfort, Hazel thought. She watched the majestic creature circle again as if to taunt her and then fly away. She couldn't help but think of her grandpa's love for the bird and one of his favorite verses Psalm 104:12, *Beside them the birds of the heavens dwell; They lift up their voices among the branches.*

A persistent noise slowly brought her out of her trance. She realized it was the ringtone for her mom. Hazel frantically groped for the device while trying not to slow her pace.

"Hey mom."

"Did I wake you?" Came her mom's words in a thick southern accent.

"No…I'm out jogging. A cardinal just flew right in front of me. It reminded me of Grandpa. How's he doing?"

"That's actually why I called," her mom said. "I wanted to let you know that he is pretty sick. Doc doesn't think he will live much longer." Her mom sounded kind and sad, but also with the hopeful resignation of those who have had plenty of time to mourn what was coming and had to watch a beloved father deteriorate in mind and body for way too long.

Wilbur Lee Tucker had been a strong, energetic lover of God, family, and country. He was the kind of patriarch who left a legacy of believers who were doing their part to make the world better and expand the kingdom of God. Grandpa had called it "taking territory." Hazel Grace loved her grandpa and Jesus. She was a leader in her campus ministry and served in the praise band of one of the local churches in her college town of Norman, Oklahoma.

As her mother spoke, the last three years came flooding back to her like a movie on fast forward. At a routine doctor's appointment, his physician had shown concern about some clogged-up arteries, carotid artery disease, he had called it. "Your risk of stroke is incredibly high, Wilbur. If we don't get you a bypass this week, it could be very serious for you."

After multiple tests, they decided surgery couldn't wait, and they prepped him for what turned out to be a quadruple bypass. Hazel would never forget what happened next because it was an event that God used to bring her back to herself when she was at her lowest point, sophomore year.

Hazel was saved and baptized when she was six years old. Some people say little kids can't possibly know what they are doing at that age. And it's true, many times, it is an eager mother who *prays the prayer* with her child and then tells them they want to get baptized. But Hazel knew that there was a moment. She was reading the kids' Bible her grandpa had given her when she was suddenly overwhelmed with emotion. She didn't understand it, but it felt like love. She prayed, "God, I love you."

Something made her rush into the room where her mother was and tell her excitedly that Jesus loves her. They talked for a good long while, mom asking questions and Hazel answering like a six-year-old, but genuinely. They met with the pastor, who, as a rule, wouldn't baptize children, but he made an exception, saying, "This is the real deal!" It was Grandpa Tucker who baptized her with tears in his eyes. She can still remember his broken-up voice saying, "Hazel Grace, I baptize you in the name of the Father, the Son, and the Holy Ghost!"

She went down into the water, and when the strong hands of her Grandpa pulled her up, she knew God was with her. She was full of the Holy Spirit, but again, it just felt like love. She loved her momma, her daddy, her Grandpa, and, well, the whole world! She was genuinely made a new creation, not by her baptism but by her faith.

But sophomore year of college, she had simply slipped. Away from her home, her family, her church, her Christian friends, it had taken almost the whole freshman year. Still, by the end of the year, she had become what she calls the typical college student. Little by little, she had become like the girls who had horrified her in her first days at school. Partying, drinking, dating the wrong kind of boys, all of it was new and exciting.

At first, it had felt liberating. Any pangs of conscience were shoved way down deep. A small part of her knew that someday there would be a reckoning, but she had been too sheltered, she decided, and every girl needed to experience life. What started as liberation and freedom was eventually revealed to be bondage and slavery. She was lying to her mom about attending church. The low point came when her parents visited, and she took them to a church she had never been to.

She should have chosen a mega church because the pastor spotted them, and before Hazel Grace could usher her parents out quickly after the service, he greeted them warmly.

"We're Hazel Grace's parents. I'm Sarah, and this is Russell. We prayed for a great church like this for her while she was away at school. Thank you so much."

"Oh, you're welcome," said the pastor. "I hope she will like it here." And then to Hazel, "You should meet our college pastor and some of the other students."

"I would love that!" Said Hazel Grace, frantically pulling her parents to the door.

Her mother was puzzled by the whole experience. "You've not met the other students?"

"I guess they must go to the other service," she lied. Fortunately, her parents had no idea that Hazel Grace would lie to them. She knew they'd be crushed, and after they left for home, she sat in her dorm and began to spiral downward. For the next several weeks, she became more and more depressed. Partying most nights was now a way of life. If she resisted, her friends persisted until they prevailed, and she would go out again.

Eventually, her parents caught on and began to worry about her. Her grades were slipping, her phone went unanswered often, and she even forgot to call her Grandpa on his birthday, something that had never happened before. A part of her was telling her to go back to that church, to find some new friends, and to go back to Jesus. Still, that voice was overcome again and again by this new way of life and the terrible feeling that she was too far gone. She wanted out of it but felt no power to change. So, she just got more and more unhappy, depressed, ashamed, and finally, she had to admit that she hated herself. She never stopped believing in God, but she was convinced by some dark voice that God had to be mad at her. How could she go to him now? This is the state she was in when her dad arrived to take her home because Grandpa was having heart surgery and might not make it.

The heart wing of the hospital had a full waiting room. Almost everyone there was part of the family that she had loved all her life. Just being with them had a double effect. At once, she was uplifted by being with them, but she also felt the shame of her secret plunge into darkness in the presence of all these good people; aunts, uncles, cousins, all of them Christians. They were praying, encouraging one another, and seemed generally hopeful.

"I feel like God told me dad is going to be OK." This was Aunt Michelle, smiling sweetly. Everyone knew to take it seriously when Aunt Michelle said the words, "I feel like God told me…". She had a reputation for being a woman of prayer and a friend of God. "You want God to do something? Get Michelle praying," was what her dad had always said.

"I hope so, Aunt Michelle." Hazel Grace was greeted warmly by everyone, and she even forgot for a while that her life was falling apart. "How long has he been in?"

"Surgery started about a half-hour ago." Michelle showed Hazel Grace a screen with a short list of patient numbers and the status of the procedure. Grandpa's number had just moved from prep to surgery. The docs expected it to take between three and six hours. *Oh boy,* thought Hazel, *that's a long time to avoid telling anyone about what is going on in my life.*

Hazel managed to get through the hours by turning all the questions back onto her relatives. "How's business?" "How did your flowers do this year?" "How do you like your new horses?"

Around 2 P.M., the surgeon came in before the

number moved on the screen, so they were surprised to see him already. "Mr. Tucker is in recovery. I'm sorry, but it didn't go the way we had planned. He went into cardiac arrest. We were able to get his heart going again, but he went without oxygen to the brain for more than two minutes." The surgeon looked gravely at as many eyes as he could find. "It is very likely that his brain is not going to function properly when he wakes up."

"Doc, are you saying he could be brain dead?" Asked Uncle Will.

"That is a distinct possibility. Maybe not, but I want you to be prepared."

The air went out of the room. Hazel Grace simply would not believe in a world without her Grandpa. She refused.

Her Grandma, Connie Tucker, was sitting across the room. She had not greeted her yet, because she saw that she was engrossed in comforting one of Hazel's cousins. She'd talk to her as soon as she could.

Even at sixty-eight, you could see that Connie had been the beauty of the county. She still was. Wilbur loved to talk about the miracle that brought them together. He used to say, "The Lord opened the eyes of the blind, but he blinded the eyes of my Connie, long enough for us to get hitched, and then it was too late!"

The truth was that Grandpa was as handsome as Grandma was beautiful. Neither one of them knew it, except through the eyes of the other.

"Normally, we wouldn't let anyone in until he is awake, but he made me promise to let you all come in and pray for him as soon as possible. Go on in. He's in room 246."

Of the fifteen family members, three had to go let out animals or go to work, and so when the family crowded into the recovery room, there were twelve, including Hazel Grace. Tears filled her eyes seeing her Grandpa in that setting. She had never even known him to be sick, let alone lying weak and pale, his mouth and nose filled with tubes. It was impossible. But here he was, and here they all were, doing what this family always did. They prayed. The twelve of them held hands and prayed. Hazel wasn't sure, but she would swear she could see him smiling behind all those tubes. It was in the lift of his cheeks. But that was impossible.

The doc said he wouldn't wake up for quite some time yet. Wherever he was, it wasn't here. The family prayed with great conviction. Some college kids might be bored by that, but Hazel was home, and she knew it was right where she wanted to be. Soon, she found herself praying along with everyone else, asking God to heal

Grandpa and speed his recovery, and thanking him in advance for what he would do. They cried out to God to heal Grandpa's brain and to give him back to them. They were not ready, they said, for Jesus to take him.

That day in the hospital was powerful and went a long way in bringing Hazel back to herself, but God really moved in her heart the next morning when she and her mom were praying with Grandpa.

Though they prayed for healing, the prayers were bringing Hazel Grace back to God. Each minute, she moved closer to him. In one moment, she asked God for a sign that he was healing Grandpa, and immediately, the hand she held closed around hers for about two seconds. Hazel Grace was filled with the same love she'd felt as a little girl. It was love for Grandpa, her mom, her whole family, this world, and Jesus. Outside she wept and prayed for her Grandpa. Inside she repented and came home to God.

Hazel and her mom went home when Michelle and Will came back for a second shift, bringing Grandma some clean clothes and a new crossword. Sometime in the morning, the miraculous news came that Wilbur was awake, alert, and his normal self. The doctor came in mid-morning to check in on him. He seemed shocked and happy to see Wilbur telling silly jokes to the nurses and good-naturedly complaining about the "service around here," with his customary wink. The nurses loved it and were as happy as anyone to see the old man doing so well.

Hazel and her mom arrived while the surgeon was checking up on him. Grandpa seemed thrilled to see Hazel Grace. He said he'd been praying for her a lot lately and had been praying that he would get a chance to see her soon. Then, the story he told them rocked her mind and completed the change in her heart.

"It was touching how you all were praying for me," said Grandpa in a croak. They had only just taken out the tubes that had been down his throat. He was still dried out and thirsty, and he sounded like it.

"Oh, you heard about that?" Asked mom.

"I saw it."

"What do you mean you saw it?" Asked Grandma, puzzled. Hazel Grace, who had been holding his hand again, leaned in, interested.

"I mean, I saw all of you. You, Will, Michelle, Dee, Amy, Hazel Grace, Sarah, and your sisters - Debbie, Evelyn, Katherine, and Carolyn. Oh, and Bill was there too. It was touching for you all to pray together like that."

Grandma, Mom, and Hazel Grace were stunned

into silence. "Dad, that is not possible. You were unconscious." Hazel Grace remembered that she thought there had been a smile on his face when they were praying.

"I guess I was, but I remember all of it," said Wilbur, starting to get riled up. "And you, Doc, I appreciate the way you held on to my heart like that. But I suppose if you hadn't squeezed on it the way you did, I probably wouldn't be here."

The doctor nearly dropped his clipboard. "Wilbur, you're messing with me. Who told you I had to manually pump your heart?"

"Nobody! I saw it with my own eyes!"

"Wilbur, that is not possible. Your chest was wide open, and you were under anesthesia."

"Well, I don't know how, but I saw your hands wrapped around my heart. I saw it clear as day!"

"Calm down, calm down. You need to rest. It's just that what you're saying is extraordinary." Hazel Grace could see that the color had left the doctor's face. He was shaken. She had no way to process this, but mom had an answer.

"I guess you had one of those out-of-body experiences, Dad. I think scientists call them NDE's near-death experiences. I've read a lot about them but definitely haven't known someone with first-hand experience. That's pretty incredible!"

"Well, I don't know about all that," replied Grandpa, "but I guess God isn't finished with me yet." Sarah and Hazel Grace looked at each other, smiled, and said Wilbur's favorite quote in unison, "God has a plan!" Wilbur smiled and nodded, "indeed, he does, never doubt it."

By the time Hazel Grace returned to school, she was done with her downhill slide. She went back to the church where she had taken her parents, and she got involved in the college student ministry. Soon, she was leading a girls' Bible study on campus and singing in the praise band at church.

"I want to come home," said Hazel.

"I think you should. Do you want daddy to come to get you?" Her mother still hated the idea of Hazel Grace driving by herself that far from college.

"I'll drive."

"Ok, get here as soon as you think you can. Do you think your teachers will understand?"

"They will. I'll get assignments and bring them with me. Might need something to do in the waiting room at the hospital."

Wilbur had recovered from his bypass a few years before but then began a deterioration that was culminating in this final week. First, it was his mind. He had always been one of those brilliant country boys. People constantly underestimated him because of his accent and bumpkin colloquialisms. But to underestimate the mind of Wilbur Lee Tucker was a mistake. Now, though, things had changed. Not long after the heart surgery, he had begun to show signs of dementia. When he got a little confused, it made him anxious. This was scary for all them because Wilbur had been such a rock.

Little-by-little, the family became accustomed to the new reality and started the process of coming to terms with the evidence that Grandpa/Husband/Dad/Uncle Wilbur would not always be there. They started to live more and more in a world without him. It wasn't that they didn't have him, but this was a new Wilbur, one who had to be watched more carefully.

When Hazel Grace visited, she had learned from her mom that when Grandpa got confused, she could just ask him to tell her some story from the past. Sometimes he told it, literally believing that it had happened just the day before. Eventually, he couldn't remember names and could hardly put together a sentence. He would string together some words that did not go together in any intelligible way, but the earnest look on his face told them that he knew exactly what he was trying to say, and why didn't they?

But sometimes, he couldn't even do that. He would stutter, get one word out, realize it wasn't the word he wanted, and then he'd just look at you, terrified, or even sad…asking your name and asking where he was. He would cry out that he just wanted to go home, even though he was home. It was so painful for his family to watch. So many times, a person in that situation will begin to be abandoned in some nursing home. Family members who just can't cope will find more and more excuses to stay away, showing up at holidays or other days of obligation. But that is not what happened in Wilbur Lee Tucker's case. God bless her family, thought Hazel Grace when she thought about their devotion. As far as she knew, everyone hung in there right up to now. He was a burden that everyone seemed eager to take on, knowing it was their calling in life for as long as he lived to give to the great man who had given them so much.

After all, taking care of those in need was what he had taught them.

Hazel Grace found that when Wilbur was at his worst, he could always be calmed down with Scripture or a favorite hymn. He may not have spoken a comprehensible word all day, but start a Bible verse, and he could finish it. They really had no idea the scope of his Bible knowledge until these final years.

Chapter 2

Hazel Grace hoped she would not be pulled over as she sped home. The sense of urgency that she felt pushed her on faster and faster. *Calm down, Hazel*, she told herself. Nobody's got time for a wreck or a ticket. But she did make it home in record time and went straight to the hospital. She already knew she would find her mom and Grandma there, and one of her cousins was just leaving. There had been a nonstop steady stream of family. (Wilbur Lee had five daughters and a son.) When Hazel Grace saw her mother, she could see that this time was indeed different.

"Mom, how long have you been here?"

"Oh, I don't know. I spent the night last night."

"She spent the last two nights here," said the nurse, who Hazel had not noticed until now. They had spent so much time here lately that Nurse Jenny was part of the family. Grandpa and Grandma had shared Jesus with her when they were first getting to know her, and she had accepted Christ when she prayed with him. In that way, she was added to a list that was as long as only

God knew. Hazel Grace suspected it was in the thousands.

"Mom, you need to go home and rest. I can stay here with Grandma." Hazel knew that it would be useless to try to send her Grandma home. She would go occasionally, but only if she wanted to.

"Ok, honey, your aunts Michelle and Dee are coming to spend the night tonight, so you come home when they get here. I'll have some dinner for you. Momma, do you need anything?"

"No, dear. I'll see you tomorrow. I love you." She got up, and the two women hugged Grandma, kissing her "little girl" on the cheek.

"Ok, Mom. I love you, too." Mother stood and looked at Grandpa for a minute. Hazel Grace wondered if she was worried this was her last time to see him. Looking at him herself, Hazel wondered the same. He looked about as bad as she had ever seen him. His face was pulled tight, and it seemed to Hazel Grace that his eyes had sunk an inch deeper into his head. She made herself look at him, painful as it was. She knew she would not get many more chances. She talked with her grandma for a while and caught up on school and family gossip. Family "gossip" is not the right word for it. There was nothing juicy or wink-worthy in Grandma's gossip. She loved her family and had taught her children and grandchildren that you don't say anything about a person that they wouldn't like you saying. Grandma, who was known over town as a master flower gardener, was also known, only to her family and intimate friends, as a master poet. She loved words and took them seriously, always saying they could be used for blessing or cursing, and she would always choose the former.

Hazel Grace thought her grandma was holding up well, and she mentioned the fact, "It's just that I know where he is going. It's the same place I'm going to someday. My Wilbur has had a full life, and he is ready. He always prayed to make it to the very end, and he has. It gives me joy. Honestly, I know I'll grieve mightily when he finally goes home to be with his Lord, but for now, God has given me a Spirit of rejoicing."

Hazel Grace remembered that as long as she had remembered, her Grandpa said, "To live is Christ, and to die is gain." It comforted her to be with this woman, and she was glad that she seemed fit as ever. Hazel Grace imagined that there were many seasons of flowers yet to be grown. After a while, Grandma drifted off to sleep in the chair next to Grandpa. The nurse came in and tip-toed around the room, checking this and that. She patted Hazel Grace on the knee with a knowing and comforting look before shutting the door behind her.

After the nurse left, Hazel Grace sat in the dark listening to the blips of the monitors and the steady rhythm of the ventilator. She sat, and she remembered. Having lived right next door to her grandparents, she had spent so much time with Grandpa Tucker as a child. That little girl would have never understood that he wouldn't be around forever. Now, she regretted not spending more time at home in the last few years. One memory came flooding back in the darkness of the room.

"Grandpa, Grandpa!"

"Do I know you? You look mighty familiar," asked Grandpa, scratching his head.

"Silly! It's me, Hazel Grace!"

"Ohhhh, yeah, didn't we go to high school together?"

"NOOOOO!"

"Wait a minute, I know. You used to cut my hair."

"No, Grandpa, I'm the daughter of your daughter."

"Which one, Michelle?"

"NOOOO!"

"Dee?"

"NOOOO!"

"Amy, Claire?"

"No silly, your other daughter!" Hazel Grace must have been about five years old when they first had this conversation, which would be a regular feature of their relationship, even up to her late teenage years.

"Ummm, another daughter, you say…? OH! Gertrude?"

"No, silly, you don't have a daughter named Gertrude!"

"Penelope?"

"No!"

"June? Calypso? Venus? Jezebel? Delilah? Zipporah?" Grandpa would usually make up new names every time.

"Calypso, Grandpa?" That was a new one. Hazel Grace smiled at the memory.

"I know you, dear Hazel Grace. How could I ever forget you? You are named after my dear mother, and you are as precious to me as my finest horse," said Grandpa, slyly.

"Grandpa!" This usually ended in a big hug. Hazel learned to crave the smell of Stetson aftershave. Away at college, she bought a bottle for $5.48 at Walmart just so she could smell it when she missed home. She made a note to go to his house and get some to bring back to the hospital.

Eventually, Hazel fell asleep, and when she woke up, she was with Aunt Michelle, always at her Sudoku. "Hi, sweetheart."

"Hi, Michelle. How're you doing? Where's Grandma?"

"I'm fine. I asked her to please take a walk. She's with Dee somewhere in the hospital. How's school?"

"Busy, but I'll survive."

"Are you missing much this week?"

"Yes, but my professors understand. I'll get caught up. I brought some stuff home to work on."

They went on this way for a while, and then eventually, Hazel headed home in time to eat dinner with her family. Her dad, the other "best man she knew," was in the garage at his "tinkering." He was one of the most prominent lawyers in the small town, but she knew he'd rather have been a tradesman. Russell Jackson was one of the most respected men in their hometown. At fifty-five years old, he was still fairly trim, exercised with weights three days a week, and seemed to have strength to last for another fifty-five years. "Hey, Dad." She had snuck up on him.

Turning with only a mild start, which gave way to delight, "Hey sweetheart!" He put down the screwdriver and mechanical apparatus he had been working on and wrapped his arms around her, right up until his fingers, which he kept in a fist to keep from getting grease on her shirt. "How's Grandpa today? Mom said he slept all day."

"Still sleeping. Hasn't made a peep."

"Well, I guess that's better than being awake and in pain," said Dad.

"I think they have him pretty drugged up."

"I think so. Let's go see if dinner's ready." Dad grabbed a Diet Coke from the garage refrigerator for each of them on the way inside. They kicked their shoes off and went into the kitchen to wash their hands and help her mother finish putting stuff on the table. Hazel's sister, Jillian, was clearing schoolbooks from her dad's end of the table, where she had been finishing homework.

They sat down to eat. While there was a dim sorrow about the occasion, the knowledge that two and a half years of suffering was ending very soon lightened what would have been much heavier. Hazel Grace often wondered if it would always be this easy for her to come home. When the campus minister, Janie, who helped her get back to Jesus after Grandpa's heart surgery, was talking to her about the prodigal son, it was the analogy of salvation to "coming safely home" that made the most sense to her. As they ate and talked, she found herself praying that she would have these people to come home to for a very long time.

The next few days went by quickly. Any hopes that Wilbur would rally were slowly diminished. Without anyone talking about it, each family member shifted from praying for recovery to praying for God to take him home peacefully.

Several cousins her age had come home and were waiting in town for the inevitable memorial service. Hazel Grace wondered if there would be a whole lot of people at the funeral, considering that Grandpa had been fairly shut-in for the last two years. Would people have forgotten him in that time? At the very least, all her family would be there. Her mother had already asked her to read from the Bible at the service. At first, she had refused because how would she be able to get through that without falling apart? But then, she thought of Grandpa, and she remembered when he read Romans

8:35-39 at his brother Jack's funeral. So, painful or not, Hazel Grace would read the same powerful verses. She found herself praying that she could read the verses with the force of the Holy Spirit, *unction*, Grandpa would have called it, and could lead someone to Jesus that day.

On Friday evening, the family decided to move Grandpa home for the duration. The hospital could send in-home hospice nurses to care for him. Hazel's mother set up his room, and they got him into bed. The whole family just camped out in the house, much more comfortable than the hospital waiting room. Hazel Grace spent almost every minute in his room, which, as far as she could tell, had remained unchanged for her whole life. There were some updated photographs along with all the old ones. Family pictures, school pictures, sports team pictures. The funniest of Hazel Grace was the second-grade school picture in the thick-framed glasses and the toothless grin. The haircut was a sight to behold. "What were we all thinking?" She thought as she looked at it.

Hazel Grace prayed a silent prayer of thanksgiving for her family. However, it felt sad that the passing of time and this man would inevitably change things some. She prayed for her Grandma. She was so strong and even showed some joy, but Hazel Grace knew that was for the sake of her family. She had always been strong, but Hazel knew she had drawn much strength from her Grandpa, who was her rock.

Grandpa hung onto his earthly life until the Lord's day. Daddy led a church service for the family and a few of Grandpa's friends in the house, and then around 9 A.M., they began to sing. Uncle Will brought out his guitar, and they sang so much that Grandpa's pastor, Pastor Tim, had to take over while Will rested his fingers. Hazel could not think of a single hymn that they had not sung. Someone pulled out the old hymnal from the bookshelf and found the more obscure ones. When they ran out of those, they started over with the list. Hours went by that way. Grandpa's dog, Dodge, a loyal and protective Great Pyrenees, who had been by his side until the whole family crowded into the room, was outside the window. Even he participated, adding an occasional bark or a howl.

While they were going on this way, everyone could see that Grandpa's breath was coming in slower and slower rhythm. At one-point, Hazel Grace believed he had breathed his last. She had involuntarily begun praying that Jesus would open his arms for him when he opened his eyes in a gasp for air. A great hush fell over the family, and after a brief pause, he said, "I am washed in the blood." He closed his eyes again, and the family felt such a sweet Spirit in the place. Uncle Will took it as instruction and began to sing, "Washed in the Blood." When the song was over, Grandpa opened his eyes one last time, looked at everyone, and squeezed Grandma's hand more firmly than one would expect. Then he smiled.

Dodge pressed his face against the window and howled. Though the air had been still on that cloudy day, there was suddenly a gust. The wind chimes sang, and a ray of sunshine broke through the clouds and into the room. Wilbur Lee Tucker, beloved husband, father, grandfather, friend, pastor, and so much more, took his final breath on this earth and went to his heavenly home.

Chapter 3

Wednesday at 9:45 A.M., mourners began to arrive. The family was in awe of the crowd that had started to gather. Wilbur's second home, The Church of the Nazarene, opened the doors wide and welcomed those who had come to know one of their most faithful members, Wilbur Lee Tucker.

Looking out into the room, Hazel could see that they had underestimated the love and esteem people still had for her grandfather. Her heart was full to bursting at the respect and love shown by the crowd. This was a major event in the lives of many, as had been the decline of Wilbur's health and mind. Of course, they would come for a chance to say goodbye and express their best wishes to the family of their great-hearted friend.

Aunt Michelle had to send the funeral director out three different times to ask people to scoot inward to the middle of the pews and make room for those standing in the aisles. Michelle was a "Martha" type, and when troubles came, she coped by getting busy and "getting useful."

Grandma Connie was looking beautiful on the front row in her blue dress that was Grandpa's favorite. She looked serene, and her eyes were wet but focused. Hazel Grace went over to sit next to her, and before she could put her arm around her grandma, it was her grandmother who put her arm around Hazel Grace. Intending to comfort, Hazel Grace only just realized that she was the one in need. The gesture caused Hazel to break down for the fiftieth time that day.

People spoke softly and greeted one another, some reconnecting with long-lost friends. Above the chatter was the sound of the organ playing three songs on repeat: "Through It All," "When We All Get To Heaven," and one that Wilbur wrote, "Jesus is A Friend of Mine." The last one would be sung later in the service by her Uncle Will. The words were:

Oh, when I think of my life down here
I dreamed of wealth and fame
I worked so hard to gain it all
Just finding guilt and shame
But then I met this friend of mine
Yes, Jesus is His name. He filled my heart
With joy divine, then He called me by His name

Oh, since I met this friend of mine
It's never been the same, I found what
I was looking for, yes, Jesus is his name
Now I'm walking in the light of God
I have His peace within, this very
Special friend of mine, yes, Jesus in his name

Now he's walking with me day-by-day
Along life's narrow way. Oh, I'm so glad
This friend of mine is showing me the way
If I could work a million years
I never could repay, the debt I owe
This friend of mine, yes Jesus is His name

Oh, since I met this friend of mine
It's never been the same. I found what
I was looking for, yes, Jesus is his name

Right around 10:05am, the pastor began the call to worship. After some initial opening words, he began to talk about Wilbur's love of people. He spoke about the miracles that Wilbur witnessed and played a part in and how God used him throughout his life to lead people to Jesus.

"As Christians, we are all called by God to share the Good News of Jesus Christ," said the minister. "Just before Jesus left this earth to sit down at the right hand of his Father in heaven, he told his followers that they should 'go and make disciples of all nations.' Wilbur Lee Tucker took those words to heart. I've heard story after story from people who were personally led to faith by the man whose life we are here to celebrate today."

"I'd like to try something. If you are in this room today and you were personally led to Jesus by Wilbur Tucker, would you please stand?" Hazel Grace and her mother stood up. They were on the front row, so they did not see it until a collective gasp made them turn around and look. There may have been a hundred people standing up behind them. "If you were led to Jesus by someone who is standing up right now, you go ahead and stand up too." Another hundred or so stood up, and at this, the room burst into applause as the crowd realized just what a miraculous legacy they were witnessing. The applause went on for at least a minute, and then the pastor held up his hands and invited everyone to sit back down.

As Pastor Tim continued to speak about Wilbur's legacy and the Gospel that Grandpa believed and preached, Hazel fingered the old leather King James in her lap. Her mother had given it to her that morning just before they got into the car to drive to the church. There was an envelope in the Bible with Hazel Grace's name on it. She had felt a simultaneous urge to open it and read it right away and to never open it so that it could always be anticipated. She had decided to leave it in her room to open later that night when she had adequate time to appreciate whatever was inside. Now she noticed the pastor looking at her and nodding.

Hazel Grace stood up and made her way up to the microphone. She opened the old Bible gently. Had Grandpa left any word without an underline, a circle, or a box around it? Was there a margin without some personal note or some prayer for a loved one written in it? She had the page bookmarked, and she opened it to Romans 8:35-39 and read, just as her grandpa had done at his brother's funeral.

35 Who shall separate us from the love of Christ? Shall tribulation, or distress, or persecution, or famine, or nakedness, or peril, or sword?

36 As it is written, for thy sake we are killed all the day long; we are accounted as sheep for the slaughter.

Something came over Hazel Grace as she read. She believed the words as never before and her hope manifested in tears. The room was coming apart as others all around were moved similarly.

37 Nay, in all these things we are more than conquerors through him that loved us.

38 For I am persuaded, that neither death, nor life, nor angels, nor principalities, nor powers, nor things present, nor things to come,

39 Nor height, nor depth, nor any other creature, shall be able to separate us from the love of God, which is in Christ Jesus our Lord.

"Grandpa…Wilbur Lee Tucker is much more than a conqueror today," said Hazel Grace through her tears and broken voice. "He is where he wants to be, with Jesus, his brother Jack, his mom and many others he loved." Something else came over Hazel Grace, as the Holy Spirit seemed to compel her on.

"If any of you…*any*…don't know this grace, this love of God that makes you more than a conqueror, my Grandpa would think I was horribly remiss if I didn't say that you can know Jesus. He loves you and wants to be your Lord and your Savior. No matter what you have done, whether you are ashamed…if you think you are beyond God's love, or his ability to save you, you're wrong. Don't believe that. Grandpa would say it is a lie. God loves you!" Hazel Grace felt the love and presence of God in a way that she never had quite experienced. She queued Uncle Will to start singing, and as his melodious voice rose and filled the church, the power of the Lord took over. Some sang along. Others prayed or murmured Amen and Praise God. It would have been difficult to find a dry eye in the room. Pastor Tim closed with a final prayer asking for peace and comfort for all.

After everyone left Grandpa's house, Hazel suddenly remembered the letter that Grandpa had left her in his Bible. She grabbed it and then locked herself into the spare bedroom to discover what Grandpa wanted her to know. As she carefully opened the envelope, she got panicky at the idea that there may have been some funeral wishes contained inside.

Her fears were abated, and she forgot them as she was soon engrossed in what she was reading. It was a sermon. There was a sticky note on it that said, *"Give this to Hazel Grace…My last sermon."* She read it with eagerness. It was quickly evident that the sermon was also an autobiographical sketch by one of her favorite people in the world, now out of the world. Story after story, some of which she had heard before, others she had never heard, told of his life, ministry, and of God's faithfulness to Wilbur Lee Tucker, and his dedication to being used by God in whatever way God desired. Her Grandpa had been a boilermaker by trade, which caused him to travel a lot for jobs, but his passion was ministry and evangelism. The stories told of his faithfulness and his great effectiveness at his calling.

Her heart was, for the umpteenth time that week, bursting with fullness as she reached the end of the eight pages. The thought was beginning to formulate in her mind, "Someone should really write a book or a movie about this remarkable man." Just then, at the bottom of the page in Grandpa's handwriting was, "Zachary Stone, the ghost."

What in the world, thought Hazel Grace. Who was Zachary Stone, and what did it mean that he was a ghost? Hazel Grace sat on the bed, thinking. This makes absolutely no sense. Grandpa did not believe in ghosts. Angels, yes. Ghost, no. Why would he have written about this ghost, Zachary, and why leave this to her?

Hazel Grace went into the dining room where Grandpa had kept his computer. She sat down at his chair, which brought a wave of fondness, longing, sadness, and joy all at once. The smell was distinctly Grandpa, Stetson, and goodness. Anyone with a good-smelling Grandpa would understand. She pushed the feelings aside after a brief pause and then turned on the computer. "Hmm…Grandpa, what was your password?"

Jesus…

Password…(it was worth a try).

Hazel Grace…

Wilbur…

Wilbur Lee…

Wilbur Lee Tucker…

Connie…

Connie….

Connie Tucker…

She had a sudden idea that felt promising, *Sweet Connie Tucker.* Bingo. Grandpa always used to talk about Grandma that way. The fan in the computer began to whir, and with a "beep," the desktop came to life. She opened the browser and typed in "Zachary Stone obituary."

There were several, but none of them seemed to spark an idea. It could be anyone. Was this an old friend? Why did it say, "ghost?"

She tried typing in, "Zachary Stone ghost." This yielded a result, a website. "Ghostwriters Guild" and a profile of one of the writers, "Zachary Stone."

Ahhhhhhh…Nice picture, thought Hazel Grace. She was happy to have solved the mystery so quickly but was now perplexed anew. *Why was Grandpa connected to a ghostwriter?* It didn't really seem like Grandpa to want to write a book. The writer's name attached to the sermon with his life story in it only pointed one direction. Hazel Grace found herself praying that God would show her what it all meant.

She looked again at the picture. *Oh my,* she thought, *he's definitely easy on the eyes.* Dark hair, blue eyes, a tall slim figure. *Why this guy? Why Zachary Stone?* She searched his name and found another picture that seemed to be attached to a social media account. There wasn't much there. He hadn't added any post or picture for three years. Hazel sat back in her chair and thought a while as the sun went down outside the window. She turned to watch it disappear over the horizon and prayed once again that God would help her figure out what Grandpa had wanted her to do when he left her this stuff.

"That's very mysterious," said her mother. "Did you ask Grandma?" It was the next morning, and Hazel was waiting for bacon and eggs while she nibbled at one of her mother's famous biscuits, which had been her grandmother's famous biscuits, and her great grandmother's famous biscuits before that. If Hazel sat and imagined any of those women, the image of them rolling out the dough for a batch of biscuits would characterize any of them perfectly. This was a staple food for the Tuckers and the Jacksons—none of the women ever bought flour except by the twenty-pound bag. The smell of the bacon made Hazel Grace's stomach ache with hunger and craving.

"I did," answered Hazel Grace. "She had never heard of him. Have you ever heard of this guy? Did he ever mention him?"

"I don't recall anyone by the name Zachary Stone." Mother had stopped scrambling the eggs to think. Hazel smiled at the comforting reminder that her mom never spoke while she was doing something else. Most people could keep stirring eggs while they thought and had a conversation. Still, Mom was an extremely focused person, a uni-tasker, and whatever she did, she was all in. Hazel decided not to speak until the eggs were done, so they would not burn. When they sat down next to each other at the bar to eat bacon, eggs, and more biscuits, she resumed the conversation, again allowing her mother some space between questions, so her mom's food would not get cold.

"I do seem to remember the name Stone, but I don't recall from where. I'll keep thinking about it and let you know. I can't imagine that Daddy would be acquainted with a young writer. Why don't you try to find him?"

"I'm planning to. I just wanted to see first if you knew anything about him. Maybe I'll check with Michelle."

"That's not a bad idea," said mom, and she began in earnest on her breakfast. "I probably shouldn't cook my eggs in bacon grease, but I can't help myself." Hazel Grace smiled. Her mom was not in bad shape at all. She was more active than the average lady of her age, and Hazel Grace knew she enjoyed teaching a water aerobics class at the Y. She had attended once. She thought it was super cute seeing her mom, a dozen older ladies, and Mr. Johnson, who was a tiny ninety-year-old who looked and acted like he wasn't a day over sixty-five, well, maybe seventy-five. He had first come with his wife ten years prior, but she had passed away. No one thought he'd keep coming to the class, but to everyone's delight, he continued to show up faithfully and probably could have led the class.

"Who knows, Mom, tomorrow they'll be saying bacon grease is the new tonic of eternal youth," said Hazel Grace.

"That's true! You never know!"

After helping her mother to clear the dishes, Hazel Grace went back to her Grandpa's house to get back on the computer. *OK, Zachary Stone, who are you, and how do you know my Grandpa?*

She went back to www.ghostwritersguild.com and read Zachary's bio before clicking "contact."

Zachary Stone is a versatile writer with an MM from The University of Illinois in creative writing and a BA from the University of Texas In English Literature. Mr. Stone writes primarily sports autobiographies but often branches out to other nonfiction subjects…

There was more there, but Hazel was stuck on "sports autobiographies." This really did not make any sense to her. She clicked on "contact," and the email page appeared. "Here goes nothing…" she said out loud to no one.

Dear Mr. Stone,

My name is Hazel Grace Jackson, and my grandfather's name is Wilbur Lee Tucker. Recently, my grandfather passed away and left me his Bible. Inside was an old sermon and a sticky note with your name on it. I think it is pretty likely that you are the Zachary Stone that he had in mind because it said, "Zachary Stone, ghost." My question is this, do you know my grandfather? If so, how? Thank you for your time with this. I am eager to solve this mystery and see if there is anything my Grandpa wanted me to do for him. Maybe a book based on his sermon??? Please let me know if you can help me in any way.

Thank you very much,

Hazel Grace Jackson

She paused only for a moment before sending the message into the mysterious World Wide Web, and she wondered how long she would have to wait or if she would hear anything from the guy at all.

Five hundred miles away, sitting in an old beat-up truck, an old man turned down Hank Jr. on a tape player and redialed the number. It rang for a long time before he heard a woman's recorded voice, "I'm sorry, the owner of this number has not set up the voicemail for this account. Please try again later."

The man sat for a moment, closed his eyes, and prayed. The truck sat in the parking lot of a liquor store, and the man had watched people going in and out for a half-hour before he tried making the call. He was still in his only suit, and he picked up the program from the funeral he had attended the day before. As he sat, he scolded himself that he had never gone to visit his old friend, though he had intended to. If it hadn't been for him, he'd be in that liquor store right now, if not dead somewhere. He'd been sober for fifteen years, but lately, it started to feel hard. When he first got cleaned up, that is, when Jesus first cleaned him up, he was full of excitement to go home and be the dad that he had never been to his two kids. But now, his son was too old and too jaded. Now, he'd heard he was a drinker like him.

He thanked God that he did not desire to go into the liquor store. He didn't know why he did this, but he did it often. Sitting in his truck in the parking lot of a liquor store, any liquor store would suffice, reminded him that he was totally free. He liked to pray for the folks going in and out, and occasionally, when he saw a true hard case, he'd get out and go talk to them. He prayed about this and liked to think it was the Lord directing him. Either way, he had a knack for knowing who would want to talk to an old stranger. He had once been an angry man, but now he was kindness personified.

He was just about to drive away when he saw a car pull up and hit the curb a little too hard. *This poor guy is already drunk.* He got out of his truck and reached the man just in time to catch him as he stumbled. The man looked at the old codger whose strong arms held him up, and he looked grateful. He himself had been the angry kind of drunk, this was the other kind. He had the look on his face of a happy fool.

"Hey brother, what's going on?"

The man looked as though he were working something out. "Do we know each other?"

"No, no," said the old man. "I'll be Frank, and you be Earnest. I was sitting over there in my truck and couldn't help but notice that you seem like you've already had a few."

"Yeah, but not enough," answered the drunk, "I ran out of beer. You have some?" The man was good-natured, but barely able to stand.

"I don't, but how about you give me your keys, and I'll take you back home."

"Oh, I'm not going there. She'll be so mad at me." The drunk looked frightened.

"Your old lady?"

"My mother." The man was at least forty-five, maybe fifty.

"Well, my name is Billy. How about we head over to my place, and you can take a nap on my couch. I was about to watch a ball game."

"I thought you said your name was Frank," said the man, confused.

"It was just an expression, but my real name is Billy."

"You got any beer at home, Billy?"

"I'm afraid not, but I do have some Coke."

The man was alarmed, "I'm not into that."

The old man chuckled, "I mean Coca-Cola, Earnest."

"Who's Earnest?" Asked the man, bewildered.

"Ha ha, come on," laughed Billy.

He locked the man's car and helped him to his truck. He pushed away his hard hat, tie, a worn-out Bible, and his coffee thermos so that the man could sit. He helped him with the seat belt and then started up the pickup and drove two miles home.

Chapter 4

Dirty fingernails typed at warp speed.

The boy raced down the hill and back up again. He had been so full of nervous energy that running was the only thing he could do. Would making his heart race faster help him to get it under control? The air was cool, but he was a sweaty mess. Did she really say that she liked him as much as he liked her? Did she say she wanted to be his girlfriend? He yelped and took off down the hill again. As he approached the bottom, he stepped on a small log that he had not seen, which sent him rolling. He got up straight away. "Love makes me a Superman! I cannot be hurt!" But then he remembered that he was to see his father today. Just then, an actual cloud drifted in front of the sun, and the sky went gray. He felt suddenly cold and achy from his fall.

The dirty fingernails were attached to a pair of strong hands at the end of strong arms. Zachary Stone sat looking at what he had written. He was astonished at himself because he had had no intention of introducing a dad issue into the story. This always happened. Zach pressed the "backspace" key, meaning to delete the dad stuff, and just deleted the whole thing.

He took out his earbuds, and the coffee shop sounds, espresso machines, blenders, and superfluous conversations brought him back to reality. Looking at the clock on his phone, he saw he was going to be late again. He threw his laptop into the backpack, grabbed his work gloves and goggles, turned his hat back around with the words "Lawn Guyz" on the front. His phone showed him the bad news that his boss had tried calling him. The man had told him yesterday that he needed to set up his voicemail.

Zach tossed his lunch trash into the bin and hit the door hard. He was going to get reamed when he got back, but they would not fire him. When he was working, he was a machine, if he wasn't hung over. Today he was not and had decided to take a chance on writing. It had been two years since he'd left the University of Illinois and started the great American novel. Two years of failure. He now had developed eleven characters and no story. What was he thinking? He'd been offered a job at a publishing house in New York, but a big part of him knew that if he'd taken it, he would never write a book. He turned down his buddy who'd offered the job at least a dozen times. As he got out of his truck and pulled on his gloves, he felt more tempted than ever to take that job.

True to form, Matt was ticked off. "Stone, what time is it?"

"Matt, I'm sorry. I lost track of time."

"You're about to lose track of a job. Get out to the back lot and get on the weed whacker." This was punishment. Zach, like the rest of the crew, liked riding the lawnmower, and Zach was often picked to ride. For all his flaws, he had some favor with his crew leader, Matt, who was a lifer. As a crew, they took care of eight large apartment complexes. This one was the ritziest. It was so nice that Zach liked to fantasize about living there when he was working. Maybe he would publish something and make some money.

It's not that he had not written anything. He had fed himself with ghostwriting for a while, but ghostwriting wasn't really what he wanted to. He wanted something he could put his name on. He did not mind at all that he wrote for no credit. It felt good to get paid for writing, but he also wanted to take responsibility for his words. Maybe that was putting too heavy of a spin on things, but he believed in creative artwork as an expression of a person. If he could put his name on something he was proud of, well, that's why he got a creative writing degree, which he was still paying for, and with landscaping wages, would be paying for until he died.

He reminded himself that he needed to disable his account with the Ghostwriters' Guild. He hadn't checked his email from there in weeks. Not that he would have anything. He did get a steady number of inquiries but rarely did one turn into a legitimate job. Plus, he would not write for himself if he took on a ghost project. He adjusted his goggles, pulled the cord on the weed whacker, and got lost in work for the next three hours, stopping only for new-line and gas. He had to admit that this gig wasn't so bad, especially when it was cool like this.

It was three more weeks before Zachary Stone got around to checking his email with the Ghostwriters' Guild.

Hazel Grace was back at school. After she had tried and failed to track down Zachary Stone, she got wrapped up in finishing her last semester. Insanely busy because she always tried to cram too much life into too little time, she had forgotten about Grandpa's mystery.

Three weeks went by, and just before passing out in bed after cramming for exams, having started that late after her women's Bible study on campus, she checked her email. She had resolved only about seventy-five times before *not* to check email before bed if she wanted to get good sleep, but…what's a girl to do?

Amazon, junk, Old Navy, junk, Valvoline, junk, Payless, junk, Walmart, junk, Alumni Association, *not even graduated, and they want my money. Sorry, no money yet.* She was starting to doze, this was good. But suddenly, she bolted up, wide awake. A message from Zachary Stone, ghostwriter!

Dear Ms. Jackson,

Thanks for reaching out. I'm interested to hear more about your grandfather, although I'm sorry to say that I have never heard of him. If he knew me, I did not know him. Let me know if I can be of any service to you.

Well, she wasn't going to sleep now, not yet anyway. She got back out her grandfather's sermon and reread it. She finished reading it, her head full of the amazing stories of his life and her mind beginning to formulate a picture of all the possibilities before she determined that she would do whatever it took to see a book written about her Grandpa's life. She would meet this Zachary Stone, and she would get him to write this book. She still had no idea whatsoever about who he was or why her grandfather had picked him. Why hadn't he ever contacted him? How did he know him? She knew that it could not have been random, but hopefully, time would tell.

An hour later, she finally drifted off to sleep, planning to write him back in the morning. She wondered where he lived and if she would have to travel to see him. She was nearly unconscious when she heard her own voice in the back of her mind saying something that she wouldn't have dared conceptualize awake, "I wonder if he is a Christian. I wonder if he is single…"

Ugh, thought Zach. *I guess I'd better wait and see how this pans out before I disable my account.* He didn't actually think that he would hear back from Hazel Grace Jackson, but you never know. He also wasn't sure he really wanted a project right now. It couldn't hurt to talk to her, though, just in case, and there was never a time that he did not need the money.

When his mother died while he was in college, she left him a lot for a college student, but not that much in the grand scheme of things. It could have paid for most of his graduate degree, but he'd taken loans instead and then lived off the inheritance for the first year after graduation. He'd lived high on the hog when he got back to the Tulsa area. For one year, he'd enjoyed a luxury apartment that he reasoned he needed to write his novel. One year later, the money was gone. The fact was, he was surprised, even disgusted with himself for coming back home. The University of Illinois was nice and far away, but not even halfway to where he'd thought he would end up, New York or Boston.

Deep down, though, Zach realized that it was true what they say, *wherever you go, there you are.* If he was going to get away from his past, it wouldn't be by trying to run from it. He was better off running toward it. That way, he may have a chance of fighting it. If he saw it, his past, that is, he could kick it in the teeth and knock its head off. But so far, he just drank. He was still running but just not going anywhere. When he drank enough, his past took shape, and the head with those teeth he wanted to kick in belonged to his father. Dammit, why did he have to think about him, ever, at all?

Zach sat on the couch in a house that was owned by a sharp young college kid. The kid had saved up enough money in high school, stocking grocery shelves and mowing lawns to buy a house built for a family of four, and then he converted it to a house for seven bachelors. Zach doubted that it was legal. Zach lived in the attic with a jolly kid named Steve, who mostly played video games and went to his job as a tech support person for some or other insurance business. Steve was easy to get along with, but he did have a certain smell that took getting used to. For $160 a month rent with utilities included, Zach got used to the smell.

For a house with seven bachelors, the sharp young college kid ran a fairly tight ship and kept it tidy. There were some house rules, which everyone more-or-less obeyed, and Zach found that most of the men kept to themselves and were hardly ever around. No one brought girls home overnight, probably from embarrassment and because it was against the college kid's rules. Zach had seen him throw out at least two guys for being late on rent and for failing to keep up with their fair share of the chores. Zach appreciated the orderliness, while his own life was completely out of order.

He'd had a few beers already when he decided to see if that girl had emailed him back about her grandfather's book. He had decided that if she wanted him, he'd go ahead and take the job. His own book was going nowhere, and landscaping would wind down soon with the cold weather. He pulled his laptop from where he had last left it, plugged in under the couch.

Mr. Stone,

Thank you for getting back to me. I'd love to talk to you on the phone. Is there a number where I could reach you? Mine is 555-555-5555. I hope to talk to you soon.

Hazel Grace

Most of Zach's clients, surprisingly, did not ever ask to talk or to meet in person. He could see from her phone number that she was local.

Sure, I'll call you tomorrow at 10 A.M. unless I hear from you that it's not a good time.

Zach opened social media for the first time in weeks. He looked at old friends, pictures of his mom, photos of himself on other people's pages, and he looked at his own account. He had posted nothing for three years. What is there to say? He looked around the house. He thought someone else was home, but he wasn't sure. He was alone in the room. He was far from drunk. He was numb, but not from drinking. He was empty. He would write this book for this Hazel Grace Jackson, but he felt neither here nor there about it.

Would he ever write his novel? Probably not. *Ok, Zach, what will you do instead?* That was certainly the question. There was no answer anywhere inside him. Just emptiness and silence. What time was it? 12:30 A.M. He was off tomorrow, but he had to call this book lady. He should go to bed soon. He sat and drank for another hour, then dragged himself to the attic and went to sleep, kind of drunk.

At 11:30 A.M. the following day, Zach woke up to his phone. He drifted into consciousness and looked at the phone, 555-555-5555. *Aw dang.* He sat up quickly, rubbing his eyes.

"Hello?"

"Hi, is this Zachary Stone?" For some weird reason, he considered saying no, but instead, he fessed up.

"This is Zach. Is this Hazel?"

"Yes. Did I wake you?" She was not sure she should have called him. When 10:00 had come and gone, her first thought was, *do I want to put up with this guy? What will this be like if he's already missed our first phone appointment?* But "Zachary Stone," written in her Grandpa's handwriting on a sticky note, told her she had to give him at least a few chances.

Zach, for his part, knew how to be ashamed before a woman. He was raised by his mother. He loved her dearly, and while it was his father who got all his hatred, he had to admit that his mom may have done a number on him. He'd dated as much as the next guy, but he had yet to solve the puzzle of being with a woman or even dealing with them. He had a compulsion to be with someone, to love someone, and be loved, but he could never make it work out for more than a month. He always wanted to please them and derived a great deal of self-esteem from someone finding him attractive, which happened often, but then the same thing always happened. He fell hard in love in the first week, turned up the heat, promised her the world, and then got tired of it when she fell for him.

It didn't help that he always seemed to end up with drama queens. Most of his relationships began with white-hot love and ended with bitter hatred. Lately, there has been no one. He didn't know many women, wasn't around them and was never good at picking up strangers. He wouldn't know how to approach one in a bar or on the street, but if he were working with a woman and seeing her every day, he'd find a way into her heart, convinced it was where he wanted to be, only to find that it was too hard, leaving in shame some broken-hearted girl who had no idea what just happened.

What was wrong with him that he honestly believed he was in love after knowing someone for five minutes? Then once he won her over, his love turned to hatred? Maybe that's what he should write about.

Perhaps then he could figure himself out. But anytime he toyed with the suspicion that his mom had some part to play in how he was, he felt guilty and drove the thought away. The poor woman was dead, and she did not die easily. It was a slow death from cancer. His mom was a saint...for the most part. She did everything for him. She gave Zach and his sister everything she had. She was the dad and the mom for them.

Zach pushed down for the hundredth time a suspicion that her body gave out from the pressure of carrying the family. His mother had truly sacrificed everything for them. She could be forgiven if she mentioned as much every now and then. Boy, could she make him feel ashamed of himself. But that was her way of getting him to do right. And it pretty much worked. Still, sometimes he had thoughts about her, negative thoughts, and it made him even more ashamed now that she'd died so painfully. The truth was that it was his father's fault. That bastard. If he had been around, she wouldn't have had to be such a bitch all the time. Oh man, he couldn't believe he just thought that. What the hell was wrong with him? His mom was right. He was ungrateful.

"Maybe I got the time wrong, but I thought you said you were going to call me at 10. Maybe I was supposed to call you? If so, I'm sorry." Said Hazel, though she had the email right in front of her. *Come on, Hazel Grace, don't let this guy off the hook.*

"No, it's my fault. I overslept. Please forgive me. How can I help?"

Hazel Grace described her grandfather and the sermon he had left her in his Bible and that she had ascertained that he had intended to have a book written. She told him again that his name had been written on the note, and so she assumed Grandpa wanted him to write it. They talked for a bit about the process and agreed to a six-month timeline. Since Hazel Grace lived only twenty-five minutes from Tulsa, where Zach was, he suggested that they meet on occasion so that she could fill in some more information about Wilbur.

"I'm at school for another three weeks, but I graduate at the end of the summer term and will come home then."

"Where is school?"

"OU, of course!" Here was the first chance for a rapport.

"What? I figured you for a Cowboy girl." She could hear the grin in his tone and decided to play along. Anyone from Oklahoma knows that to a Sooner, those are fightin' words.

"Now I know you must be insane. Maybe I got the wrong guy after all." Zach laughed.

"It's much worse than that. I went to UT!" This was too much.

"O Lord, I know my Grandpa could not have known that." They continued the good-natured banter about that for a few minutes before agreeing that Hazel Grace would scan the sermon and share the file with him. She would also start writing down anything else that might go in the book.

"I think it should be about his life, but also it should expand on some lessons that can be drawn from it."

Pensively, Zach said, "OOOkay…"

"Don't worry. I'll come up with that if you can't. I'm assuming you're a Christian?"

Zach wasn't sure what to say. He decided on, "Yeah, sure, isn't everybody in Oklahoma a Christian?"

"I don't know, you tell me." She had him there.

"Honestly, I went to church some as a kid, but not now. I believe in God, though." *Do I? Or am I just saying that because I'm starting to want this job? Hmm. Better be honest.*

"To be exact, I have a problem with God. But don't worry about that. I'm a ghostwriter. This is your book, so we can say whatever you want. I went to Sunday school, so I can probably find some Bible lessons to put in. But...yeah, it would be best if you let me know whatever you're thinking and want in it."

Hazel thought it was too bad that Zach was obviously not a Christian, but her Grandpa had specifically seemed to want him, so she would go with it. They settled on a price, which was no surprise since his prices were on the website, and they made an appointment for three and a half weeks later when she was home.

Chapter 5

Zach sat at his computer, willing himself to write the great American novel.

The girl was not sure what to think. Surely this wasn't the first time that someone had rejected Mike. Now that he was threatening to hurt himself, she wondered why she hadn't seen his issues sooner. Should she call someone? Was this an empty threat?

"Mike, you don't mean that," she said, hopefully.

"I do mean it. I don't want you to misunderstand me. It's not one of those, 'if I can't have you, I'll kill myself, so don't go,' situations. I want you to go. I don't know why I thought this could work. I'm a mess. Just get out of here. I'm probably fine. I just need to think."

She didn't think she should go. "I'll tell you what, let me stay here with you for a little while, and you can tell me everything. I know we've only known each other for a couple of weeks, but I'm a good listener." It wasn't that the girl was above being a "fixer" who ended up with the wrong guy thinking she was all he needed to get it together, but that wasn't what this was. Mike was nice. She had no real feelings for him except compassion. "Go ahead. I'm listening."

Mike started talking. He determined that he would try to tell his life story but leave him *out of it. She saw right through it.*

"Are you very close with your dad?"

"Ugh!" [DELETE]

Today would not be the day for Zach to get traction on his novel. He had wanted to see if in the three weeks he had before his meeting with Harriet, no, it wasn't Harriet. No one was named Harriet in real life. It did start with an "H," though. He smiled at himself as he thought, *Henrietta.* It was not Henrietta. Wait, Hazel, like witch Hazel. He remembered the mnemonic device he'd learned as a kid for memorizing names. He needed something crazy to associate with the name. He imagined a woman flying on a broom, like Witch Hazel. The broom had to be crazy big, though, so the ridiculousness of the picture would stay memorable. What he needed was a face. His laptop was still in his lap on the couch, and he opened his social media account for only the second time in forever, with a plan to search for her.

There were about thirty messages, and he hadn't even looked at them the last time he was on. The oldest unread message was from eight months ago. His sister had written, "Earth to Zach…come in Zach." They had talked since then. [DELETE].

The next three were from Jennifer, his last, or maybe second to last girlfriend in grad school at the U of I. They had not talked since then, and he had no intention of talking. [DELETE].

The next said, "Hey dude, so are we going or what? I have my ticket, my sunscreen, and my grass skirt." This was from his best friend, in undergrad at UT, Chad. He had put off his own trip to Hawaii for almost a year, hoping Zach would get it together and come along. Zach had scraped out a living in that time and had no extra money for a trip like that. Chad finally went with someone else. [DELETE].

"Hey Zach, hope you're well, we've been thinking about you. Let me know when you can come see us, Aunt Linda." He decided to save that one and write back later. He would like to visit his aunt and uncle in Pittsburgh. Maybe after this novel.

"Hey man, that's ok. The job is yours anytime you change your mind." This was his best friend from grad school. He saved it too. Zach wondered what he was up to, so he stalked his page for a while. It looked like Brad was having a good time in New York. He seemed to attend a lot of work parties. It looked like he had a fun life. Zach thought it might not be so bad to join him. Steve had come home and was loading two plates of food from his personal pantry to take up to their attic room. Zach was in no hurry to get up there.

Two hours later, he knew everything his friends from grade school, middle school, high school, college, and grad school, plus what family he had, wanted him and the rest of the world to know about their lives. He wondered how they were really doing and then briefly considered making his first post in three years. Nah, what could he say? He didn't feel like he could put a positive spin on his life right now. He shut the laptop, and it wasn't until hours later that the thought of a witch on a giant broom. *Dang, I still don't have a face to go with the name…Hazel Grace. She's probably a plain Jane church girl.* He spent his last waking hours imagining her without trying. His Witch Hazel on a giant broom looked homely in the face and was skin and bones. He would have to look her up tomorrow.

Hazel Grace and Russell Jackson were in Tulsa at a brand-new driving range and restaurant, hitting golf balls off a rubber tee on the third-floor tee boxes.

"This is just what I needed." Hazel Grace was on the golf team in high school and routinely beat her father, who played a lot of golf but was terrible. The only thing Russell had going for him was that, occasionally, he could crush a drive. One in ten went straight and far and kept him paying his dues at the country club. He'd played the eighteen-hole course every week on average for twenty-eight years. Hazel Grace thought that if she had a real job by next Father's Day, she would buy him some lessons with the new pro.

"Anybody interesting in your life?" Whap! This was the one in ten that made him feel like a golfer.

"Not remotely, Dad." Hazel had been home for three days. There had been an interesting graduate assistant at OU, but she decided to turn him down when he asked her out. She couldn't say why. It just didn't feel right. She had gone on some dates with two different guys at her church, but there was something about the ones who were still single. It was sad, and she had Christian girlfriends who would have settled for them, but she wasn't going to force herself to be attracted to someone she didn't have any chemistry with. Janie, the campus minister, had encouraged her to look for character above looks, but she wasn't even sure about their character. Maybe she shouldn't judge, but just because a guy goes to church in the Bible Belt doesn't really make him a strong believer. Plus, the Christian guys she knew were weird about dating. Someone was giving them bad advice. In fact, they did not date. They "pursued a wife." Maybe if she got "pursued" by someone she was attracted to, it would be different, but when she was being pursued, she had so far managed to escape capture.

"I don't know what it is about the church guys at school." Her dad was always calm on this or any other topic. She knew he dreamed that when he gave her away at the altar, he could truly "give her away," having cared for her up until then. He had always treated her like a lady. Even when she was a little girl, if he was dropping her off or picking her up at a friend's house, he always got out of the car and walked her. She knew he wanted her to expect a man to be a gentleman. She was moving back home, and she knew that was more than all right with him. He had wanted her to stay local for college, but she had insisted. He couldn't help but relent, being a proud Sooner himself. He was far from controlling, but he was protective.

"Well, sweetheart, when you do meet the right guy, try to remember to let him win at golf." They both laughed at that. "Seriously, you know what we have always said."

"Right, focus on God and what he is doing in my

life, and he will bring the right guy at the right time. But honestly, I really did hope to meet someone in college."

Hazel Grace didn't know what she was going to do next. Her department had offered her an assistantship to come back for graduate school in education administration, having gotten her undergrad degree in elementary education. But Hazel also had flirted with the idea of a career in the medical field since her Grandpa's time in the hospital. Maybe hospital administration, or nursing school, or even medical school. She doubted she had had enough biology and chemistry, and whatever else were the prerequisites, but she knew she could get them locally if she needed to. She had promised herself to wait a month or two before deciding anything. Meanwhile, she was running her dad's law office while the woman who usually ran it was across the country helping her daughter with her new baby for a month. When she got back, hopefully, Hazel would have a plan.

"Gracie, just be patient." Russell briefly thought about the new associate at Mills, Mills, and Goldstein but put it out of his mind. He instantly disliked anyone he could imagine dating his daughter.

"I know. Pray for me."

"I always do," he said, and she knew that it was true. She knew that he was also the problem. Who is going to compare to Russell Jackson? He would have liked to know she was thinking that since that had been his very goal her whole life. What she didn't know was that he feared her standard was the mature Russell Jackson, not the cocky punk of a law student that her mother married. He supposed they both might have to compromise at some point when she finally did bring home her own "cocky punk."

They had dinner and went to the mall to get Christmas presents for Mom and Jillian and each other. She wasn't sure if she had properly hidden the record she had bought him at the large book and music store, the last of its kind. He seemed to be hiding something from her as well. She knew she would also get a bunch of cash from her parents, who had also hooked her up for graduation. She wondered if she would need it for the book about Grandpa. She also knew her dad liked to get her and her mom and sister jewelry. Nothing too lavish. Some cute earrings, or maybe a bracelet.

Three weeks later, Zach still had not put a face with a name until right at this moment. Every time he considered getting on Facebook to look her up, he just couldn't take the thought of confronting the past through the posts and profiles of former friends. Maybe they were still friends. It wasn't like they had some kind of parting of ways but is someone your friend if you haven't thought about them in a year? He would need to give this some thought at some point. Maybe he could cut his "friend list" from 1472 people down to a reasonable 500 or so. Now he was face to face with his new boss, Hazel Grace, and he silently apologized to her for assuming too little about her appearance.

She had blonde hair and brown eyes, which was, he would find out in time, a family trait. He stared at her eyes as she spoke to him about her project. He assumed they would be hazel, but there was no reason they should be. Still, there was something in them. He normally thought that if eyes were to sparkle, they'd have to be blue, but he corrected his mistake as he looked at her. He didn't know how, but he knew at a glance that she was at once an old soul, but with a timelessly young-looking face. Another thing he would find out later is that this too is a family trait, not just with the women, but even with the men. Any one of the Tuckers, Jacksons, and two-thirds of the extended family looked at least ten years younger than they were by the time they were thirty.

"Here is the sermon he left. I made copies, so you can have this one. I'll email the doc as well, so you'll have it there too." The packet was about twenty pages thick, and Zach speed-read through it enough to see that Wilbur Lee Tucker was a preacher and a tradesman.

"So, what kind of book are you looking for, a novel, a biography?" Zach asked the question and took a sip of his coffee, still too hot for the gulp he needed this time of day. They were sitting at a booth in Tulsa at a cafe that he had suggested, Tally's Cafe on Route 66. Hazel Grace had not touched the cinnamon role that the waitress had suggested. The place was decked out in 50s style and looked to be a tourist hotspot. "If it was lunchtime, I'd insist you buy me some chicken fried steak. This place is known for having the best there is."

"You obviously have not been to Silver Dollar in Collinsville," countered Hazel, with mock defensiveness.

"Nope, heard of it though. I feel like I had a friend in Collinsville."

"I'm sure I know 'em. They're probably family of mine. But yeah, maybe a biography. I also think he wanted there to be Bible lessons scattered throughout the book." The slightest hint of a frown flattened the corners of Zach's mouth, *his rather cute mouth, in a rugged sort of way,* thought Hazel.

"You don't feel comfortable with the Bible lessons?"

"Well," said Zach, "It's not really my thing, but if you'll get me some hints at what you're wanting…"

"I think some of them should be obvious by the stories he tells. For instance," she reached for the papers and flipped the pages until she came to what she was looking for. "Here, he talks about getting in trouble on the construction site for singing hymns all day. I thought maybe you could talk about what the Bible says about singing to God and praising him all the time." She could tell Zach was uncomfortable with any talk of the Bible. "Well…maybe I can help with that part, but…"

Zach interrupted. "Hazel Grace…by the way, do people call you Hazel or Hazel Grace?"

"Most people call me Hazel Grace. When I was about eleven, I thought it would be more sophisticated to go just by Hazel, but no one went for it. Then when I was thirteen, I tried to get people to call me Grace, but the closest anyone came to it was my daddy, who still usually calls me Gracie, at least half the time."

"OK, Hazel Grace, what would you think about writing this as a fictional biographical story? We'll use his real life, but write it like a novel?"

"I'm listening."

"Well, I just think it looks like an interesting enough story to make into a novel. I guess we could still have some Bible lessons in it, maybe at the end?"

"Or maybe at the end of each chapter," she offered?

"Yeah, or maybe at the end?" Zach didn't want to see the story broken up by the study questions. But they could negotiate that later.

"Ok, we'll decide as we get closer to publishing it," said Hazel Grace.

Zach said, a little too cynically, "How are you planning to publish it?"

"By faith," smiled Hazel Grace as she chewed her first bite of cinnamon roll, "Wow, this is amazing!"

"I told you," said Zach, self-satisfied, "but you'll need more than faith to publish a book."

"Just wait. God wouldn't have me doing this if he didn't have a plan for how to publish it." Zach was amazed at her confidence but also cynical.

"I've seen the publishing business. I don't think God is in it," Zach countered.

"You don't think so? What is the longest-running book on the bestseller list?"

Zach looked beaten. He knew that the answer

was obviously the Bible. "You got me there! OK, OK, I'll work on writing the thing. You go talk to God about getting published. One thing though, there seems to be some pages missing."

"No, they're all there." Hazel Grace looked troubled as she reached again for the papers. Sure enough, she didn't know how she'd missed it. All the pages were numbered, and there were two missing toward the end, but they weren't the last ones. Looking, she could see how she missed it—page seventeen to twenty made sense grammatically. Hazel Grace said she would go to her grandma's to look for the missing pages. They both agreed that Zach had plenty to go on for getting started. They made plans to meet again in a month, and Zach promised to make major progress by that time.

"Why don't we meet here thirty days from now," he suggested.

"Better yet, you can come to Collinsville and see the town where our family lives."

"OK, that's fine. Name the place."

"1927 Meadowlark Lane," said Hazel Grace, surprising herself.

"Where is that?"

"That's my parent's house." Hazel Grace did not

know what she was thinking. Was this even appropriate? She studied his face as he took a little too long to answer.

Finally, she exhaled when he said, "Yeah, OK. What time?"

"Come for dinner. I mean, you should meet my parents and Wilbur's wife, I mean, my grandma. Don't authors like to do research?"

Zach did think this was unusual, but was it inappropriate? He guessed not, although this had never happened before with other jobs. And despite himself, the thought of seeing her again was not unwelcome. "OK, dinner. Can I bring anything?"

"NO! I mean, no, my mom and grandma would not have it. They like cooking." Zach wondered if Hazel Grace also liked cooking. Then he snapped out of it.

"OK, great. I'll see you around…"

"Six. Oh, and I can already tell you it is going to be uncomfortable for you. OU plays Texas, and the game *will* be on." With the way the season was shaping up for his precious Longhorns so far, he thought that could be unpleasant. He also noted that she knew the game schedule a month out.

"All right. I'll see you then in my Longhorn gear."

"You better not, or my dad won't…" What in

the world was she about to say?! Hazel chided herself as she felt her ears getting hot.

"Won't want me to write the book?" Zach said, oblivious. "That's weird. You guys really hate Longhorns!"

"Yep! We sure do! OK, I got to go now. Let's talk soon."

Hazel grabbed up her bag and the papers. "Didn't you say I could keep those?"

"Oh yeah! Just…here you go! Bye!" She practically threw him the papers and made for the door. When she left, Zach finished the last two-thirds of her cinnamon roll, wondering what the heck just happened.

Hazel Grace got in the car and took a minute to calm down. She said out loud, "Hazel Grace Jackson, you like this boy!" Her tone to herself said, "Shame on you!" Hazel Grace had promised her parents and her extended family her whole life that she would marry someone who loved Jesus more than she did. She could not even pretend that Zach Stone *liked* Jesus, let alone *loved* him. She started her mother's car, more reliable for driving in Tulsa than her own. As she backed out, she noticed Zach coming out of the restaurant, and she tried to look as though she had not noticed him. He waved, but she did not wave back.

Chapter 6

"All right, gentlemen. Let's look at one more." Billy was flipping gingerly through the pages of a well-worn out Bible. The cover was tough since it was thoroughly duct-taped, but he was flipping gingerly because some of the pages were unattached. The man, "Earnest," from the liquor store was in an old, padded rocker in the corner. Earnest was named John, and the other man in the room happened to be really named Ernest, which ended the nickname for John, even though Ernest went by Ern. Billy, Ern, and John shared a frozen pizza while they read the book of John. Billy chuckled to himself as he realized that he was having John the drunk, ex-drunk, that is, read a passage about John the Baptist, written by John the Disciple.

John the ex-drunk was quite erudite, and he read John 3:33-36 with feeling from his very recently purchased *New King James Version* of the Bible, which was the same one Billy read: "He who has received His testimony has certified that God is true. 34 For He whom God has sent speaks the words of God, for God does not give the Spirit by measure. 35 The Father loves the Son and has given all things into His hand. 36 He who believes in the Son has everlasting life; and he who does not believe the Son shall not see life, but the wrath of God abides on him."

John looked up at Billy. "What does that mean that 'the wrath of God abides on him'?"

"Good question," said Billy. "What do you think it means?"

"Well," said John, "It says, 'He who believes in the Son has everlasting life,' so, I'm thinking that the 'wrath of God' must be for anyone who has not believed in the Son."

"Exactly, what do you think, Ern?" Of the two of them, Billy thought, Ern seemed like the hard case. Billy had been delighted to see how hungry to know things John was. Billy didn't know if God was saving him yet or not. John had come to live with Billy after he sobered up, and in the month since they'd met, as far as Billy could tell, John hadn't touched a drop. They started having their Bible study the second day John was there, while he was still hung over.

Ern had been there for a week and had taken the couch when Billy and John had taken his car keys at the same liquor store where John had lost his. Ern was recently out of prison for petty theft and hadn't been in long enough to find Jesus. Billy looked at him now intently.

"I don't know Billy." Ern didn't look Hispanic, but Billy always thought he sounded like he had some kind of Spanish accent. He had tried asking him about it, but Ern had simply refused to talk about his past. "I guess I understand, but I don't know if I believe it."

John spoke up, "I didn't believe it at first either. But just keep reading the Bible, and it starts to make sense." John was such a good-natured guy, thought Billy. Billy said, "Here's the deal, guys. We talked yesterday about when sin entered the world through the first man. Ever since the wrath of God for sin has been aimed right at the earth. You saw in the flood. You saw it in the way God disciplined his people. And you see it here."

"See, that's what I don't like," interrupted Ern, "What have I done to deserve that? What does Adam got to do with me? I don't see how it's fair that God would punish me for what he did." Ern was getting upset.

"That's the thing, Ern. You're punished for your own sins. You sinned because Adam let in sin, but you are not being punished for what he did, only for what you've done. Have you ever done anything wrong?"

"Not really…" Ern got quiet. John sat and

remembered his own similar conversation with Billy. "I really ain't done nothing. Not like those other guys in prison."

"But," said Billy, "This isn't about those other guys. This is about you. Don't compare yourself to someone else. The Bible says that God is our comparison."

"Oh, yeah," John got excited, "Romans 3. We all have sinned and fall short of the glory of God."

"What's that even mean?" protested Ern.

"It means that God has a standard for us, and we don't meet it."

"Well, what is the standard?" Ern was literally whining.

"Perfection," answered Billy.

"Impossible!" Exclaimed Ern.

"That's what I said!" Chimed in John.

"You're right about that, so…what does it say here in John 3?"

They read it again and talked about Jesus Christ on the cross. John and Billy could see that God was finally beginning to melt the icy heart of their new friend. They finished the Bible study, and the two of them prayed for Ern, that God would continue to reveal himself to him and that he would save him. After that, Billy sat back on the couch while John finished off the last piece of pizza. They all agreed that this frozen pizza tasted like cardboard but that with enough BBQ sauce, it could be swallowed.

"Boys, I wanted to tell you that I'm leaving for a while."

"Where are you going? Even Ern looked disappointed.

"I've been praying a lot about it, and I think I need to go find my boy and try one more time to get back into his life."

"I would think he'd want to give you a chance," said John encouragingly. "I know if my dad was still alive and wanted to know me, I'd jump at the chance, even though he was a jerk. Every boy loves his dad. Mother is good to me, sort of, too good, really, but I feel like I'd be a lot better if my dad hadn't taken off. I know she drove him crazy, but still, I wish he was around."

"I still love my dad," said Ern. "I know he's disappointed in me, but he's cool with me. I just don't want to go back home until I've done something good."

"Well, I know you are going to make something of yourself, but I would bet another one of these cardboard pizzas that your dad would like you to come home to him no matter what you're doing," said Billy. "I wouldn't care what my boy was up to if only he would give me the time of day."

"Didn't you say he was a writer?" asked John.

"Last I heard, a ghostwriter," answered Billy.

"He writes ghost stories?" Ern was interested in all things paranormal. He swore all the time that the state penitentiary is haunted.

John provided the correction. "No, Ern, a ghostwriter is someone who writes a book anonymously in someone else's name."

Ern dwelled on this for a moment. "Doesn't he want the credit for his books?"

"I don't know," said Billy. "I guess he just wants to write and doesn't care who gets the credit."

"Well, I hope he gets paid," said Ern, who had a strong sense of justice for an ex-con.

"I'm sure he does," answered Billy.

Ern said, "Tell him that he should write something in his own name."

"I surely will if he'll let me tell him anything at all."

"When are you leaving?" Asked John.

"I'll head out tomorrow. You think you boys can

hold down the fort while I'm gone, keep each other accountable?" The men looked at each other. Each of them was hopeful but wary about Billy being gone. Neither of them felt ready for that, but both would do whatever Billy asked. Billy knew that, so he didn't ask much, only that they stay sober and work a job. As he looked at the two men, he silently prayed and asked God to keep them sober, and bless them, and help them stay focused on Him. He remembered what it was like to be an angry drunk. He also prayed that God would let him see his son soon and that he would send someone to work on his heart, no, that God would send a whole army of Christians to work on his heart and pray for him. Billy didn't know that God was already on that and that it would be the family of his old friend and mentor who God would send to do the job if the job could be done. His son was a hard one, but then so was Billy.

Zach sat down at the kitchen table in his house. One or two of the guys were probably there, but they would be sleeping right about now at 10:00 A.M. They were swing shifters and night owls and probably had not been in bed all that long. Zach had his laptop open next to a yellow pad of notes taken from his brainstorm session and the stack of papers Hazel Grace had practically thrown at him at the cafe.

He looked at the sermon from Wilbur Lee Tucker and read the first part one more time.

Sermon.

Pastor Wilbur Lee Tucker

1 CORINTHIANS 9:22 BY ALL MEANS

God has a plan for every single life that is born into this world. We were born to serve him and to fulfill His plan for our life. If we fail to seek God's will, we are missing the real meaning and purpose of life. Without God, there is something missing, an emptiness or void in our life. We can try to fill that void with material things, but they cannot satisfy. The only thing that can fill that emptiness is Jesus Christ.

Zach tried not to get cynical too quickly. Zach had heard all about the void in his life from his sainted mother. He made himself continue reading.

They say that life is what happens while we are busy making other plans. Sometimes life seems so haphazard, doesn't it? But I assure you that God has a plan! He fills us with His love so we can be like Jesus; always looking out for broken lives, broken homes and using God's love to help those all around us. If we can share our life with those that are broken, they too can find hope for eternity. I want to show you through my experiences how God is always there and always has a plan. His love, mercy and grace made something beautiful out of my life.

"Here comes the part I can use," said Zach to no one. He had a habit of talking to himself when he was writing. If he was writing in a public place, he whispered.

I was the youngest of 5 children. Our mother died when I was 4 years old. While my brothers and sisters were scattered to different homes of our mom's family, I stayed with my dad. During the day, he would often leave me with the bootlegger that lived next door. The man would give me a quarter and send me away. One day while making my way to the store, I got ran over by a car. I got up and ran home.

(Note from H.G.) He doesn't expand on "I got hit by a car" and he never told us about it. I assume he had no one to tell or help him at the time so he just got up and ran home. Since he mentions it here, I think he attributes it to God taking care of him when no one else would. His childhood was incredibly difficult. His dad was an alcoholic. His sister's Lilly and Willow tried to help take care of him, but they were all split up and sent to different family members and couldn't see him often.

Zach wondered if he would be allowed to write

about the neglect and an alcoholic dad. He made a note to check with Hazel Grace.

My grandmother would pick me up and take me to church every time the doors were open for service. At an early age, I learned to pray. I learned to trust in God. I remember kneeling at the altar and praying sincerely, in confidence. When I was 7 years old, I was at my grandmother's for a week during the summer. I had a bad toothache, and she asked the pastor to come and pray for me. The tooth quit hurting instantly. I never forgot that experience. I felt the call to preach at that time. However, I thought it was the last thing I ever wanted to do.

At 8 years old, I worked in a gas station – fixing flats, pumping gas and whatever else needed to be done. I never met a stranger; they were all my friends. Many of them would give me a Christmas gift. I wasn't content until I gave them something back. God does have a plan!

In my teens, I was like everyone else. I went astray, did my own thing; whatever you might call it. I sinned against God, doing what I knew was wrong.

"Ok, here's plenty to get started." Zach began to type, slowly at first, but then furiously.

"Wilbur, get over here." Wilbur, at five years old, was scrappy and always game for a fight. His older brothers, Colt and Jack Tucker loved to pit him against the neighbor kids, most of

whom were older than Wilbur. That was alright with Wilbur Lee. He loved to fight. Though he was small, he was ferocious. His brothers picked on him a good deal. Sometimes such treatment can cause a boy to retreat into himself and become fearful. That was not Wilbur's nature. He would always find ways to get even with them, even if it cost him a beating.

Today, he was squared off against an older boy, Wayne Tillman. Wayne was seven, but Wilbur did not worry about Wayne. Had it been Wayne's brother, Shawn, who was twelve, it might have been a fight, but Wayne was the other kind of boy. Timid. He was not small and should have been a match for Wilbur, but he didn't have that same stuff that Wilbur had. Whenever his daddy got drunk, which was daily, he picked at all the boys. If Wilbur had heard him say it once, he heard it a thousand times, "It ain't the dawg in the fight, it's the fight in the dawg that counts." Wilbur didn't know how to hate anybody, so he didn't hate his daddy, although maybe he should have.

Wilbur's mother had died the year before, and Wilbur, at five years old now, already could not quite remember her face. There was not one single picture of her in the house because his daddy, drunk and grieving, couldn't bear to look at them. Wilbur would find some pictures years later, but for now, they may as well have been thrown away. This made him cry when he was alone. He missed her so much. No one could tell if Warren Tucker drank much more now that he'd lost his wife. To Wilbur, Daddy always *drank. However, his sisters said their parents were happy at one time. Wilbur was too young to understand or even think about such things. What he thought about now was Wayne Tillman's face that he was about to punch.*

Jack stood in between them and said, "Ok boys. I want you to have a good clean fight. No hittin' in the bad place, and no bitin. Everthang else is ok. Fight!'

With the speed and ferocity of a demon, Wilbur was into the gut of Wayne Tillman. Wayne, who was fighting Wilbur because it was the only way to avoid fighting Jack, was trying his best to block the blows, but he was failing and went to the ground in a ball. Wilbur, the opportunist, flew on top of him and pinned down his arms to get an open target.

"Hit em," cheered Jack!

"Break his teeth," encouraged Colt. But there was something in the look on Wayne's face that took all the fight out of Wilbur. He felt…pity. Even though he was only five, and he loved fighting, Wilbur Lee had a compassionate heart. Wayne did not want to be fighting. Wilbur could see that. His fist froze in the air. Wayne, head turned, and eyes shut to what he was expecting, dared to open one eye to see why he had not been hit. Wilbur was looking confused, and then kindly.

"You better hit him, Wilbur, or I'm gonna hit you" warned the nine-year-old Jack, who was beginning to approach. Wilbur just sat there atop Wayne Tillman and waited as Jack

approached, hollering the whole time for Wilbur to "finish him off!" A few more seconds went by as Jack got closer…closer…closer…

And then in less than one second all the fight swooped back into Wilbur Lee and he was off Wayne Tillman and on his brother Jack. Jack had been surprised, so he got the worst of the first few seconds of the round. But he soon got control of the situation, and with one mighty blow, Jack, four years Wilbur's senior, knocked the lights out of Wilbur. If you were Wayne Tillman, you'd have seen a bloody Jack Tucker standing over a sleeping Wilbur Lee.

Zach was always amazed at himself and at how easy it was to write for other people, while it was so impossible to write for himself. Writer's block was a funny thing. But this made him think that it had nothing to do with not having the skill to write, or with not being able to come up with ideas. He feared the worst, and a psychologist would say he was correct: Writer's block was a function of fear and pride. Zach was at least self-aware enough to know that when he sat down to write, the first thing that popped into his mind was the words of whatever critic might read it. Then he thought of his creative writing professors in school, and then the boys who had picked on him as a kid, and then the teacher in grade school who had belittled him, and then his mother, and lastly, his damned father.

But writing for someone else, that was easy, especially if his name was nowhere on the book. It was plain fun. What it would take to finish something that he was going to stamp his identity on, he had no idea, but he knew that was a dragon he would one day have to face if he was going to be a real writer, which remained to be seen.

Zach took a break. He was hungry and thought of going out to pick something up to eat. He decided he was craving Thai food, and then he checked his bank balance and decided he was craving one taco from Taco Bell. He needed to find a part-time job. The landscaping company did snow ploughing in the winter, but so far, global warming, if you believe in that sort of thing, had done its work, and there hadn't been a flake yet this year. He supposed they'd all burn alive by the time he was seventy, or not, depending on who you believe.

He'd start looking for work tomorrow. Meanwhile, he needed to make progress before meeting the Jacksons next week. Tacos could wait. He put in his earbuds. One of the roommates was watching some Japanese cartoon with subtitles. *Kids today*, thought Zach, as he turned on the noise app and heard the ambient sounds of *"Alpine Winds"* drowning out the world.

Zach's truck was running on fumes as he pulled into the Collinsville neighborhood where he was to meet the Jackson's and Connie Tucker. He was looking at the "gas" light that had come on and calculating how far it had been since he passed a gas station. He didn't quite have the cash to fill the tank, but he could at least get himself back to Tulsa. He would probably make it, but he wished he'd have stopped on the way and just risked being late. Was the engine starting to skip a little? Now he was imagining things.

The houses were modest but in good shape. It looked like a standard 80s model brick neighborhood, or maybe early 90s. Zach noticed that nearly all the yards were immaculate. This would be the typical outer suburb, though he wasn't sure if he could consider Collinsville a suburb of Tulsa. It did seem like the boundaries of the larger city were beginning to encroach on the Oklahoma countryside between the two. This neighborhood was probably made up of old folks who had forgone the flight to Florida or Arizona for the winter and young families who found the small but nice homes affordable. Hazel Grace's family lived next door to her grandparents on the outer rim of the development on Meadowlark

Lane and backed up to miles of farm and ranch land, which made for a pretty view. The land itself was in the family, so it served as an extended backyard for Hazel and Jillian to grow up playing and aunts and uncles before that.

When Zach pulled up into the driveway, he noticed that Hazel Grace and her father were out front adjusting some Christmas lights. Thanksgiving had been the Thursday before, and the Jacksons had a family tradition of decorating for Christmas on the same weekend. Zach scolded himself for feeling nervous. "This isn't a date, Zach." He tried to decide if her dad was trying to look intimidating or he just was intimidating. He decided it was the latter, but still, *it's not a date.*

For her part, Hazel Grace was trying to play cool. Did she have to invite him for dinner? Sure, she had to. Didn't Zach need to meet Connie and the family and see the home of his subject? She was trying to figure out what to do with her nerves as Zach got out of his truck. She decided to play the businesslike professional. After all, she had hired him. She was the boss. At the same time, she was taken with the sight of him in her driveway. Trucks in the driveway had been boyfriend territory in the past. She was reminded for the second time that he looked more like a cowboy than a writer. She also noticed that he had had the good graces or the good sense not to wear any Texas Longhorn attire. Instead, it was a simple, clean, and pressed button-up, sleeves rolled part way to reveal the results of half a year of manhandling a weed whacker. And his jeans. Well, Hazel Grace had to admit that they fit just fine over a simple pair of brown boots. He could have had a jacket—both Hazel Grace and her father were in sweaters, though it was not as cool as it could have been for this time of the year between Thanksgiving and Christmas.

"Hey there!" Hazel Grace walked toward him with her dad right beside her. "Zachary Stone, Ghostwriter, meet, Russell Jackson, Esq., Attorney at Law."

The two men shook hands and locked eyes. It took less than a second for each man to realize the other was a kindred spirit. Hazel Grace didn't know how she could tell that her father approved of her employee, but she knew he would be using his highly trained legal eye to size him up. Why was she so relieved to see her dad approve? She did not want to admit the answer just now.

"Welcome to our home, son. We're glad to have you, although I can tell by looking at you that the rumor has to be a lie," said Russell, with mock seriousness.

"What do you mean, sir?"

"If you were really a Longhorn, I wouldn't like you at all." Hazel Grace was enjoying this, and she looked to see how Zach would respond to that one.

After the briefest pause, she heard him say, with a smile in his tone, "Well, remind me never to hire you to defend me then." The three of them burst out laughing, and the night was off to a good start.

"Let's get inside. I think your mom and grandma just about have everything ready," said Russell. The three of them headed for the door.

As the front door opened, Zach was greeted by a warm blast of air and the smell of heaven. Apparently, chicken and dumplings were a Connie Tucker specialty, which had been passed down to Sarah and was being passed to Hazel Grace, who was only just beginning to take an interest in cooking.

"It smells wonderful," Zach said, looking around the room. It was not an overly large home, but it looked to Zach that the owner could have afforded a large home, choosing instead to make the smaller home as comfortable as possible. Zach had worked on more than one construction site as a teenager, and he could tell that the open floor plan was a later alteration. It wasn't that it wasn't seamless because it was. It was only that he knew houses built in the eighties, as he rightly guessed about the whole neighborhood, would have been more cut up. The place was immaculate and beautifully decorated, if not a little bit crowded with the important keepsakes of a long habitation.

"You must be Zachary," said Sarah, her warmth and charm was a natural accompaniment to the words.

"How are you doing? Thank you for having me. It smells incredible in here." Zach was aware that he had already commented on the smell, but Sarah graciously accepted the compliment on behalf of the two cooks.

"You will have to tell my mother." Her mother was drying her hands to come over just then.

"How do you do," said Connie. "We heard an awful lot about you, and we have been dying to talk your ear off about our favorite subject."

Zach could see that Connie Tucker was still mourning but also cheerful. If he had known his Bible, he might have come up with the phrase, 'Sorrowful, yet always rejoicing.'

"I can't wait to hear about him. I can tell he was a great man by how much everybody loved him." Zach scolded himself on the inside. More than once, the thought had come to him that Wilbur must have some skeletons in some closet somewhere. He wondered more than a few times if he would be the one to uncover them. In the very beginning of the process, he hoped he would. Why? He didn't know. It was not something that this family would appreciate, but Zach just found it exceedingly difficult to believe in the goodness of humanity. Now, though, seeing this warm and loving family, he hoped that Wilbur was just what they thought he was.

"He wasn't perfect," said Connie, "but he was a great man in our eyes. Do you like chicken and dumplings?"

"I do." Actually, Zach had never had chicken and dumplings. He ate Asian dumplings and those he liked. He also liked chicken, so technically, he wasn't lying. He decided to come clean a moment later. "Actually, what I mean is, I've never had them, but I can tell from the smell that I will like them." What was it about this family that made him want to be totally honest?

Sarah said dinner was ready, and they took their seats around the table, Dad at the head, Hazel Grace and Sarah on either side of him, Zach next to Hazel Grace, Grandma Connie at the other head, and there was still an empty seat next to Mom.

"Jillian!" Yelled Sarah. From somewhere in the back of the house emerged a tall, strawberry blonde teenager, decked out in OU hoodie, leggings, and a beanie.

"Sorry. Trying to finish up some cheer choreography before the game."

"Jillian, this is Mr. Stone. He is writing a book about Grandpa," said Sarah.

"Oh, cool! I heard about that." The way Jillian looked at Zach as she held out her hand for a shake made Zach feel like he needed to stand up to greet the girl, which he did.

"It's good to meet you, Jillian." The thought that came to Zach's mind was, *I feel sorry for Russell! She's only a teenager and already striking like her sister.*

The food looked delicious. Zach had come hungry and was ready to start filling his plate. There were the chicken and dumplings and some green beans that looked like there was some bacon in them. *Brilliant*, thought Zach, who, as a rule, thought there weren't many things that didn't go with bacon.

Dad reached for the two women at his side, which signaled prayer. Hazel Grace held out her hand for Zach's, and he, in turn, reached for Grandma, who was politely waiting for him to offer.

Russell prayed a prayer of thankfulness to God for supplying the meal and for the women who cooked it. He asked God to bless their evening with their guest. Zach was taken with the fact that Russell was not reciting some scripted dinner prayer such as he'd always heard. Russell was praying as though he knew the person he prayed to. But then, with one eye open toward Zach, Russell asked God to help the poor players from Texas not to get too hurt when OU beats up on them later.

"Russell!" Gasped Grandma, in a mock scold. She clearly adored her son in law who was now the senior patriarch of the clan.

"Amen," said Jillian, with approval!

Zach liked them already. The women heaped his plate full of dumplings, green beans, and some sort of cheesy potato concoction.

Russell said, "How's the book coming, Zach?"

"So far, so good." He meant it. It was coming along well. To Connie, he said, "Your husband is an easy subject and seems to have been a colorful character."

"That he was," said Grandma wistfully.

"You must really miss him." Hazel Grace thought Zach seemed surprisingly compassionate. Her mother noticed the look in her eye as she considered him.

"I do. I forget every day that he isn't here," said Grandma.

"I think I know what you mean. My mom passed away more than five years ago, and I still forget," agreed Zach.

Jillian said, "You forget?" Jillian, even at her young age, knew better than to be insensitive, but she was truly intrigued.

"Yeah. Don't you sometimes have something happen that makes you think something like, 'I should tell Grandpa about that'"?

"I guess so," said Jillian.

"That's what I mean. I had a prof at UT…"

"Hey now!" Russell faked an outrage at the mention of tonight's opponent.

Laughing, Zach continued, "I mean at a school that shall remain nameless, who said something about the conscious mind and the subconscious mind. I know my mom is gone. But in a moment when something happens, it is my subconscious mind, trained by all those years of having her around, that kicks in first. Once my conscious mind catches up, I know better." Then to Connie, "I can't imagine what it must be like after spending fifty or sixty years with a person in your daily life."

"It's just like you said. I know he's with the Lord and having the time of his life, but part of me forgets," said Grandma.

Hazel Grace added, "That sounds a lot like Scripture."

"I was thinking the same thing," said Sarah.

"How so?" Asked Jillian.

Hazel Grace answered, "Didn't Paul say that we had to put our mind on certain things if we wanted to remember them?"

Mom added, "Yes, he said to 'be transformed by the renewing of your mind.' That's in Romans."

"He also said, 'whatever is good, true, just, praiseworthy,' something like that, to think on those things," added Hazel Grace.

"Philippians 4:8," said Grandma. One of Grandpa's favorite verses.

Hazel Grace noted that Zach was not squirming, and she wondered if it took any effort. She decided to spare him and change the subject.

"I heard Alex Miller is coming off the injured list tonight," she said excitedly.

"Don't remind me," said Zach, who seemed to appreciate the shift.

"What's a matter," replied Hazel Grace, "Are you thinking the Horns aren't up to the task?"

The fact was, Zach did not think the Longhorns would beat OU, especially with their star running back returning to the field. That guy was impossible to stop. "Well…I'm not saying I hope he gets injured again, but…"

"Oh, Zach," said Connie playfully. "I know you don't mean that!" Hazel Grace could tell that Grandma liked the ghostwriter. If she hadn't, she certainly would not have pretended to.

"Nah, I'm just kidding." Hazel Grace wasn't so sure.

They ate, and they talked about football, and then they got around to sharing stories about Wilbur. Zach ran out to his truck for a legal pad, apologizing but not wanting to forget any of it. After dinner, everyone helped clean up, and then Sarah said, "Kick off is in two minutes. Why don't you go on in there and turn on the game? We'll get dessert ready. While the two older women got busy cutting up a cobbler, the other three Jacksons and Zach sat down in the living room area to watch a game that was closer than the Sooners in the room had wanted to see, but at the finish, they breathed easy thanks to a last-minute field goal. Zach went home afterward, strangely happy, despite the loss.

The next day Hazel Grace was in the kitchen

making cookies with her mom, grandma, aunts and cousins. She smiled as she remembered years past. She could not remember a Christmas when these ladies did not spend a whole day together in this very kitchen, baking and gossiping the day away. They would make at least twelve different kinds; chocolate chip, of course, sugar, peanut butter, peanut butter chocolate chip, no-bake, snickerdoodles, and various other kinds, plus candy. The sugar cookies were cut into the shapes of Christmas trees, Christmas ornaments, snowmen, Santa Claus, and reindeer. Most of these would be given to the neighbors as gifts, but just as many would be eaten by the family.

Sarah carefully iced a sugary Santa Claus, and when she was done, she looked up, "Zach is handsome."

Hazel Grace did not know exactly why this made her blush. "Yeah, I guess so." Grandma did not look up, pretending attentiveness to her Kitchen Aide.

Mom continued. "You seem to like him a lot."

Hazel Grace said, "He's easy to get along with."

"I wish he were a Christian," added mom.

"I do too," said Hazel Grace. I've been praying for him. I wish everybody was a Christian. Mom looked sideways at her daughter and decided to be direct.

"Hazel Grace, I feel concerned for you. I know

your values, and I know you would never be with an unbeliever."

"I wouldn't," Hazel Grace knew she was getting defensive. Mom chose not to notice this.

"I love you, dear, and I can see that your heart is already in. Please listen to your momma. You do not want to be unequally yoked."

Hazel Grace and her family had talked about these ten thousand times. It was an easy Bible verse to agree with unless you really liked a boy. The fact was, Hazel Grace had seen more than one young college friend who loved Jesus but then began dating a boy who did not love Jesus. It never ended well. Never. At least never that she had seen. But still, couldn't God use her to lead Zach?

"I know what you're thinking," said her mom. "Dating evangelism will never work."

"Oh, I know, mom. Who said he was even interested in me that way?"

"Oh, he's interested," said mom, "this much I know." Hazel Grace expected that her mom was right about that, but she also could not bear to believe it. She agreed with everything her mom was saying, and she silently prayed that God would take away any feelings she had for him. She even forced herself to pray that God would take away feelings that Zach had for *her*. That made her sad.

Later that night, Hazel Grace was at her grandmother's house. They were sitting in the living room with Grandpa's old dog, Dodge. Grandma had promised to teach Hazel Grace how to knit.

"Put your left hand here, and then wrap the yarn around from the bottom to the top, just like that." Hazel Grace was getting it. She had noticed that her Grandma was conspicuously quiet when her mom was giving her the 'talkin to' about the ghostwriter. She knew her grandparents had always tried to stay out of her parents' business when they were parenting. But Hazel Grace valued her grandmother immensely and knew that she never missed a thing.

"Grandma, I assume you agree with mom."

Her Grandma did not need to ask for clarification. "Mostly."

"Mostly?" Hazel Grace paused her knitting. Grandma did not pause her knitting. Unlike her mother, her grandmother seemed to be capable of her best thinking when she was otherwise engaged.

"I certainly do agree with her in principle."

"In *principle*?"

"I agree that you should not be unequally yoked.

I agree that to marry someone who is not a believer will lead to misery."

"But…"

"But I have known of an occasion where, in the process of getting to know someone, they have come to know the Lord, and what was not a possibility became a possibility."

"Really? How well did you know these people?"

"As well as you can know someone," answered Grandma, mysteriously.

"Mom and Dad!" Hazel Grace was incredulous.

"No," said Grandma mischievously.

Hazel Grace was truly puzzled. She knew her Grandma well enough to know this would be a bombshell. Still, she was shocked to hear the next words, which came a little too casually.

"Your Grandpa fell head over heels in love with me, and *then* with Jesus."

"What!" Hazel Grace simply did not know how to take this news. "I thought Grandpa got saved when he was seven."

"I think he did, but you wouldn't have known it. He told me he was a believer when we started dating after his cousin introduced us. I had heard all about Wilbur

Tucker. He was wild. He hadn't been raised right, and he used to raise all kinds of trouble."

Hazel Grace suddenly looked at the clock. "It's eight, Grandma. Strawberry or chocolate?" Hazel Grace had tried to be over there every night that she was able for ice cream at 8 o'clock. Everybody knew that Wilbur and Connie ate ice cream every single night. Hazel Grace was getting used to it and was happy to stand in for Grandpa.

"Strawberry, dear." Grandma knew that Hazel Grace was being thoughtful, and she very much appreciated it. The fact was that Grandma would be just fine skipping it, but it touched her that her granddaughter would think of her in that way.

Hazel Grace got down two large bowls and filled them. Grandma would usually have strawberry, plain, but Hazel Grace could not resist the vanilla with hot fudge…one of her grandpa's favorites.

Once they were settled at the kitchen table, Hazel Grace pressed for details. "So, you dated him, even though he wasn't a strong believer."

"He was a passionate man at twenty-two, and he had set his sights on me. You know that your Grandpa only ever walked a straight line from where he was to where he thought he needed to be."

"So, he went after you."

"That's an understatement, dear. I can honestly say that your Grandpa could not take his eyes off me when he would be with me. It took a powerful lot of willpower to hold his gaze. Being *seen* by him was a revelation."

"What do you mean," asked Hazel Grace?

"I mean that I had been taught not to think of myself. My mother taught me to be helpful to others, to consider others as more important than myself. As one of eighteen children, you don't really know where everybody ends, and you begin. My own father adored us but was rarely able to produce my name without naming a slew of others." Grandma only ever recalled her childhood with fondness, but Hazel knew it must have been difficult. Being raised with 18 siblings was more than she could wrap her mind around.

Connie continued. "But when Grandpa was staring at me, he wasn't playing games. He just couldn't look away. He always said he wanted to be able to think about my face when he wasn't with me."

"That is incredibly sweet," said Hazel Grace, whose heart was melting as fast as her ice cream.

"Some girls might not have liked being stared at like that, but I didn't mind. I asked him the first time we met if he loved the Lord. He said he was a Christian. I said, 'I didn't ask that. I asked if you love the Lord.' He said he loved *me*. I said he didn't know me. He said he knew me well enough. He also said he'd go to church with me every time the doors opened. I don't know if he knew what he was saying. My family went to church Sunday morning, Sunday night, Wednesday night, and for any revival or other event the church was putting on. We practically *were* that little church."

"So, I'm assuming he got serious about the Lord, and then you married him?" Grandma looked sheepish. "No?"

"No, he didn't really start to follow Jesus until after we were married, but it wasn't long."

"I really don't know what to think about that, Grandma."

"I know what you're thinking. I don't know how to say that; I just knew your Grandpa had it in him to love the Lord. What does the Lord tell you about your Zach?"

"Well, first, he is far from *my* Zach. I don't even know if he would be interested." Hazel had to admit that she hoped he was, but there was a very rational part of her that hoped he was not.

"He's interested. A grandmother knows.

Whether he is interested in Jesus, only God knows," said Grandma.

"I have no reason to suspect he is, but maybe if I told him I would date him only if he would go to church and become a Christian…" Hazel Grace knew better than that. Grandma looked at her, but words were unnecessary.

"I know," admitted Hazel, defeated.

"Honey, you know you can trust God. Let's pray about it," and they did.

The following day, Hazel Grace was having trouble keeping her mind on anything but her ghostwriter. Her grandma seemed to be encouraging it, but she was also right. If this was God's plan, He'd work it out some way that Hazel Grace couldn't imagine. She was also determined that she would not encourage him unless it was clear he had become a believer. She felt slightly guilty that she didn't just want him to be saved for the sake of being saved. But the fact was, she really, really liked him.

Lord, I know my motives are a little off, but I do pray that you will save Zach Stone. Even if it is not your plan to put us together, I pray that you will touch his heart that he could be born again. I pray even now, wherever he is and whatever he's doing, that you will move on his heart. That he'll begin to find himself believing in you. If it is not your will for us to be together, please take away my feelings for him. Amen.

She was not able to bring herself this time to ask God to take away any feelings that Zach might have for her. She thought God could do that if He wanted to. He didn't need her permission.

Chapter 7

Wilbur was in the kitchen looking for something to put on his bread for a sandwich. He found some mustard and spread it on the bread with a knife that was on the table. He missed his brothers and sisters. He wondered why Jack and Colt got to be together, but he had to stay alone. He was glad he was still with his daddy. Wilbur was vaguely aware that his dad ought to be sober like some other dads, and he was aware from seeing other kids that he did not have a normal life. But he was happy enough.

If he hadn't been so incredibly good-natured, he'd have realized that a great injustice was being done. His brothers and sisters were scattered over three different relatives, and it didn't seem like any of them were having an easy time of it. The fact was that all of them were struggling in some way. It was Wilbur's good fortune to be only hungry and neglected. His father, when he was not too hungover to go to work on some construction site, would leave him with old Gideon Green down the street. Who knows what made Wilbur's father think that that old bootlegger was going to watch him? Mr. Green would give Wilbur a quarter for the store and tell him not to come back until the end of the day.

For a quarter in those days, a boy could get quite a lot.

Candy and soda was Wilbur's routine choice. Wilbur was thinking about this when his father came into the room, pulling on his suspenders. Warren Tucker was not a mean person, but he had not been a great husband, and he drank his conscience away. Wilbur watched him curiously. He loved his father, just as most boys do. When people at his grandmother's church made comments about him, none too nice, Wilbur accepted them without emotion. He never heard anyone say anything that was not true. It would not have occurred to him to be offended or embarrassed. His dad pulled half a long sandwich from the fridge, pulled off a third of it, and tossed it to the boy. Wilbur ate the stale bread and bologna with relish.

Warren finished and said, "Come on, boy," as he escaped the messy kitchen through a screen door without a screen. Wilbur followed him and shut the big door behind him without locking it. Wilbur jogged a little to keep up with his father, who was late for his job and was at his side when he knocked on the door of Mr. Green's house. The bootlegger was in the back of the house and didn't hear the door right away. Warren said, "Stay here and keep knocking. I gotta get going."

"Ok, daddy." Wilbur sat serenely, watching both cars and walkers going by. His curiosity was passive. He just took it all in, noticing everything. A lady walked by hurriedly, pushing a stroller, but she was carrying the baby. Wilbur wondered why. A milk truck drove by, and the man driving looked right at him.

Wilbur locked eyes on the man, and the man nodded to him before he turned his head back to the road.

Just then, the door behind him swung open. Mr. Green said, "How long you been there, boy? You can't come in today. I have company." This was not unusual. Mr. Green often entertained a woman that Wilbur knew to be the waitress at the diner. "Here, go get some candy, and come back this afternoon. Don't get in no trouble, and if you do, I don't want to hear about it. Be back by the time your daddy gets home."

Wilbur nodded and started the four blocks toward the store. It was not a long way, but it was nearly all the way across the only town Wilbur had ever been since he'd been old enough to remember.

The phone vibrated next to Zach for the third time, and he pulled out his earbuds. The coffee shop came into focus, and Zach looked at the number. It was the college kid. Zach knew why he was calling, and he knew he wouldn't answer just now. He had to get some money somehow. He wasn't just late on his rent. He also owed the last three months of his student loan. If he could finish this book, that would help a lot, but even then, he'd need a plan. The job in New York was looking better and better all the time. Why did he think he was some kind of writer? He was a hack. If this book he was writing was his own, he knew he'd be staring at the screen with this old friend, writer's block.

He got up to go use the bathroom in the coffee shop, and on the community board, he saw a notice that the university was looking for test subjects for a hundred bucks for some psychology experiment. He tore off a tab with a phone number. He also saw the business card of his employer, hoping for snow removal. That would be good for Zach. He could get some work if there was enough snow. But so far, there had not even been a flurry.

He settled back down, won a major battle with himself not to check the news, email, or do anything but just write.

Wilbur walked out of the store thirty minutes later, soda pop and candy in hand. He'd go on home to his house now, which is what he usually did unless one of the other boys was out playing. There was one busy intersection in the little town, and if you hit it just right, the drivers coming around the bend from the west would be blinded in the morning sun. Today a Ford rounded the corner, saw the boy too late, and skidded sideways into Wilbur, sending him five feet in the air. The driver, a salesman from Tulsa, jumped out of the car in a flash, shaking with shock, his mind racing and dwelling already on what his life would be like now that he had killed a boy.

Wilbur should not have been able to get up, but get up he

did. He stood up, locked eyes with the trauma victim that was the driver. If you could have asked the driver what he saw in the eyes of the boy, he could have told you he saw himself being thoroughly seen by the eyes. If Wilbur had opened his mouth and preached the Sermon on the Mount, the man would not have been surprised. But he was surprised that the boy, who should have been dead or at least broken, suddenly turned and ran.

"Wait a minute, boy! You need to see the doctor!" As he watched him disappear into a hedge, he wondered if the whole thing had actually happened.

The fact was that Wilbur was just fine. When he got to his house, he laid down. It seemed like the right thing to do in such a circumstance. He knew better than to go tell Mr. Green. Hadn't he told him to stay out of trouble and stay away? He spent the day in his house, playing alone until the old clock told him it was time to go wait for his daddy at the bootlegger's.

Zach thanked the man and took the package from Hazel Grace inside. He opened the box and found a Bible. It looked expensive. It was dark brown leather and well built. Zach tended to appreciate books in all forms. There was a note that said, "You said you didn't have one, so I picked this up for you, in case you need it for the book." Zach assumed correctly that there was more to it than the stated purpose of research for the book. He thought back to their last conversation. They had met up again at Talley's in Tulsa. Hazel Grace had brought some notes from her grandma to fill in some gaps in the story.

"You really think we should put the study questions in the back?" asked Hazel Grace.

"I do. Like I said, I think they will break up the flow too much if you put them in between each chapter, and I don't necessarily think that every chapter is going to have huge life lessons in it."

"I wouldn't be so sure," answered Hazel Grace. "My Grandpa was a walking life lesson."

"Maybe so, but I still think they should go in the back. Are you going to come up with the questions?" asked Zach.

"I can come up with some, but can you also be thinking about it?" Hazel Grace was fishing now. What exactly did this man know about God?

"Yeah, but...I seriously know nothing. I don't even own a Bible." Zach was not making this easy for Hazel Grace. *Come on, man! Give me something!*

"What do you have against God?" She asked.

"I don't have anything against God. I'm fine with

God."

"Do you consider him your Savior?" Things were getting personal.

"I guess so. Didn't Jesus pretty much die for the world? The one verse I know is that he "so loved the world, that he gave his only Son," Zach said.

"Yeah, but then it says that "whoever *believes* in him would have eternal life." Hazel Grace knew she was taking a big risk. He said he basically believed that Jesus died for him. She should call it good and consider him eligible, but she knew better than that. She pressed harder.

"Zach, it matters that you know him personally."

"How? I've never met him," said Zach, although not defensively.

"God wants to know you. He wants you to know that he died for your particular sins."

Zach said, "That's a tall order. Why would he want to do that?"

"Because he loves you, Zach. Because he's your *Father*." Hazel Grace noticed an immediate change in Zach's demeanor. They'd been having a philosophical conversation up until now. They'd been speaking of theories. But Zach suddenly got tears in his eyes, although he attempted to hide it.

"I think that's enough for now, Hazel Grace." Zach did not want to fight with her, but he was done with this conversation. He really didn't know why he was being emotional. It was embarrassing. He guessed it was being raised by a single mom. He really hated himself when this happened. "I've got to get to a thing. I'd better get going."

"Okay," said Hazel, gently, "Want to get together again in a few weeks?" she asked, as he packed up his notes.

"For sure, I'll text you." Zach couldn't leave the place fast enough, but he managed a smile and tried to make himself sound casual. "Sorry, I have to run like this. I'll make sure next time that I have more time."

"No problem." Hazel watched him leave and wondered what just happened. What did she say? *He loves you…because he's your Father. Yeah, that was definitely it. I know he hates his dad.* Hazel sat and chided herself for saying the wrong thing and making a mess of their time together. Then she prayed that God would give her the right words next time. Words that will help Zach heal from the inside out and seek the love of Jesus Christ.

Zach sat in his truck out in front of his house. He had made enough from the psychology experiments at the university to cover two more weeks' rent, so he still had a bed. When he'd gotten in his truck at the cafe, he turned up the radio as loud as he could stand. For some reason, he knew that his hope lay in avoiding whatever thoughts were knocking at his conscious mind. He knew he'd gotten embarrassingly emotional, but to know the reason why would be too much and would make him want to drink. He already wanted to drink so that he could avoid thinking. He got out of his truck and went inside.

It was four days later when he had gotten the Bible. That was sweet. He knew enough about Christianity to know that Christians were obligated to proselytize. He didn't mind in this case. The fact was, he really liked Hazel Grace and had to work to avoid the fact. There seemed to be lots of things he was avoiding. It felt like he was running away from someone or something who was chasing him. He looked at the Bible. Was God chasing him? He considered opening the Book, but instead, he put it in his desk drawer.

The other fact was that Hazel Grace had gone to a lot of trouble to pick out that Bible for Zach. She spent an inordinate amount of time considering him and what kind of binding suited him best. She would be in serious contemplation and then catch herself, telling herself to stop being silly. In the end, she spent more on the Bible than was necessarily appropriate.

*"Let me just get cleaned up, Daniel. I'll meet you there."
Wilbur needed a bath and started heading for home.*

*"All right, but don't be late. All the good stuff will be
gone," warned Daniel. Daniel and Wilbur worked together as
apprentice welders, and Wilbur was as filthy as he could be. The
weather was hotter than usual this time of year, and Wilbur
thought he must have lost ten pounds in sweat. He'd be doing okay
if he could manage not to drink his bath water.*

*He came into the house and put down his lunchbox by the
sink, filling a large glass with water. He drank it down in one
breath and refilled it twice. When his belly stuck out from the effort,
he began to fill instead the pots on the stove. His bathtub was in
his kitchen. He'd inherited the small house that he lived in with
this father two years ago when the drink and old age finally took
him. The clock on the wall said he only had thirty-five minutes to
scrub down, get dressed, and get outside to meet Daniel. Daniel was
from the next town over, and he had invited Wilbur to his family's
church for a potluck supper.*

*Thirty-eight minutes later, Wilbur was in Daniel's new
F-100, and twenty-three minutes after that, they were standing on
the front sidewalk of the Olive Street Church of The Nazarene in*

Hominy, Oklahoma. Two-thirds of the members of church were related. Heck, two-thirds of the town was related. Wilbur knew Daniel was part of the majority bloodline and looking around at all the folks filing into the church basement, he could see the resemblance.

Daniel was true to his word, and the spoils would go to the swift. They didn't want to be very first in line, but they wanted to be close to the front. A man, a second cousin of Daniel and a deacon in the church, said grace, and then the church, well-practiced in the exercise, formed into two lines as the chaos of the crowd came to neat order. The older folks were ushered to the front of the line, the children to the very back. The children in this church were taught a strict respect for their elders. Wilbur assessed that as a single young grown-up, he belonged someplace toward the back, but as a visitor, he was moved forward between the elderly folk and the married folk. A battalion of church ladies posted sentry over the tables, watching for empty pans, bowls, and pots so that they could replace them with full ones.

So it was that Wilbur managed to secure three fried chicken legs, mashed potatoes, fried okra, three colors of fruit salads, and a pile of baked beans. The paper plate was soggy and about to give way when he sat it down at the folding table just in time. Daniel was not too far behind but had had to settle for meatloaf, the chicken being a popular item for which there was more demand than supply.

Across from Wilbur was a venerable old woman that everyone called "Grandma Butcher." She was a beautiful lady. You could just tell by looking at her that she was love and kindness, heart and soul. She only had potatoes and some jello on her plate. She looked across at Wilbur and said something. "Ma'am?" asked Wilbur. She spoke again, and Wilbur started to get embarrassed. He could not make out her words.

"She said you didn't get dessert." Wilbur turned toward the voice. In every life, there is at least one defining moment. Something happens, and you know right then that you are changed. You can't go back. You know something that you didn't know. For some, it's something bad. The day they were damaged. You would think, with the hard and lonesome life that Wilbur Lee Tucker had had up to age twenty-two, that he'd have already had his moment. But you would be wrong. His moment was now.

"Connie Butcher, meet my good friend, Wilbur Lee Tucker." The moment was not ruined by the arrival of Daniel, hardly noticed, to the table. Did Wilbur answer right away? Or did he float through space for a thousand years in the revelation of her face? He would never know because it felt like he was transported. His lifelong obsession with staring at her began in earnest in the first moment he saw her. Her brown eyes had the effect of looking like she was wearing makeup, though she was not. They were intense, deep, kind, gentle, trustworthy, and increasingly, bashful. But something in her made her unwilling to look away.

She simply didn't know what to think about him. Right away, he made her smile, the first of a billion times he would have this effect on her. His face looked such that he seemed incapable of a frown. When he could finally speak, he said, "I'm very happy to make your acquaintance."

"Connie is my cousin," came a voice from somewhere off to the side. Daniel snapped his fingers in the ear of his wiry friend, attempting to bring him back from the third heaven.

Connie added, "It's very nice to meet you."

"Connie is one of eighteen children," added Daniel.

"Eighteen! I can't even count that high," said Wilbur.

The rest of the night was as close as Wilbur had ever been to pure heaven. The power that was shooting in and out of his heart the whole night kept him feeling like he was elevated two feet off his chair. They talked, and after a short time, although Wilbur would never know exactly how long, it was as though they had known each other for a thousand lifetimes. This is what some would call finding your soul mate. Not everyone finds that. In fact, most people don't find it, but those who do would know exactly what they were both feeling that night. To be honest, for Connie, it wasn't love at first sight as it was for Wilbur. But by the end of the night, she knew she had met the man she was going to marry. How he had grown on her so quickly, she couldn't say, but her heart was his, and that was that.

They talked and laughed and fell in love. They had ice

cream together, their first time of a million to come, and they fell all the way. When the night finally came to an end, Wilbur asked, "Pretty Connie, where can I find you again?"

"At church. We're here whenever the doors are open."

"I love church." He wasn't lying. If he had said it that morning, it would have been a lie. But he just had his second religious experience in a church dining hall. The first one had come when he was seven. Back in those days, dentistry being the primitive art that it was, Wilbur got a mighty powerful toothache. His grandmother, who did her best to stay in the boy's life and take him to church whenever she could, called up the preacher. The preacher knew Wilbur. The boy was, in fact, a vigorous participant whenever his grandmother brought him along. After hearing the boy pray earnestly at the altar of the little church, he consented to baptize him. But this day, grandmother wanted the preacher to come and heal Wilbur's toothache.

What she did not know was that the preacher, faithful as he was to preach the Word of God, did not have a great faith in his own ability to heal the sick. Having tried on several occasions without success, he had begun to develop a rather unbiblical theological position that God didn't do that anymore, that healing was just for the apostles until the Bible was written. This would have been complete nonsense to Wilbur's grandmother, who had seen mighty things from the Lord in her 65 years.

The pastor came into the house where the boy was curled

up on the floor, and he laid his hand on Wilbur's face. "Oh Lord, we believe that you healed people through your Son, Jesus Christ. If this boy has committed some sin and has incurred your wrath, Lord, have mercy upon him!"

"Yes, Lord!" Grandmother added. That thought had not yet occurred to grandmother that Wilbur had sinned his way to a toothache, even if the sin was too much candy, but she was warming up quickly to the revelation.

"But forgive him, Lord, and I pray that you would heal him in Jesus' mighty name!" The pastor turned to Grandmother to begin his routine explanation of why, sometimes in a fallen world, people don't get healed.

Right then, a universe of pain in the tooth of Wilbur Lee Tucker simply vanished. The boy sat up, slapped his own cheek once or twice to make sure he wasn't imagining things and looked with wonder at the preacher.

For his part, the preacher was having trouble believing what he was seeing. This would be the beginning of a healing ministry for the man that would last until the day he died. Today, he was finding faith again, although Grandmother and Wilbur knew none of this. Grandmother seemed to take for granted that this was the obvious outcome, and Wilbur felt something even more powerful than the healing.

It would take him some years to work it out, but he was called to preach that day. The calling came with terror. It was the last thing he wanted, but even at seven years old, somehow, he knew he would preach. By ten years old, he'd forgotten the fact, and by his teens, you might be forgiven for thinking he'd gone and disqualified himself. By the time he met the love of his life at twenty-two, he had not given it a thought in years. He remembered all of this as he walked the seven miles home that night.

Daniel had given up waiting for him and had gone back to town. Wilbur wasn't about to leave while Connie was still there. Now that he was walking home, he wondered what he would need to do in order to get her father's blessing. He had glimpsed the sight of a man looking at them disapprovingly. That must have been him. One thing was for certain, Wilbur had a new interest in church.

Hazel Grace clicked off the document. She really liked this boy. She should just admit it. She *liked* him. She picked up her phone and texted: *just finished your last installment. I love it. How do you suddenly know so much about theology?*

He texted back within seconds. *Research. Do you want to meet up next week?* Zach texted.

Sure. Her heart was racing. What was there to talk about regarding the book? It must be that he just wants to get together because...he likes her. Just then, she freaked out a little and texted again. *Wait, I can't. I'll get back to you. Maybe the week after that. Keep the pages coming.*

And then, to keep it businesslike, *I hope you're going to go back and get the typos.* She had only noticed one or two, but she needed something to put some distance back in. She probably should have emailed rather than text.

Zach was confused. The fact was, he was falling for her pretty hard. But the other fact, one that he was struggling to admit, was that this is what he always did. He was thinking about her constantly now, but he was just approaching the age where scientists and auto insurance adjusters say that young men get their frontal lobes fully developed and can start to be trusted a little. He did not want to continue being a hopeless romantic, and he did not want to fall in love with the beautiful young woman with an even more beautiful heart, only to crush her, which he surely would, when he lost interest. It was true that he could not imagine losing interest in Hazel Grace, but he just knew himself. He hated himself for what he was capable of. He never liked to hurt anyone, but he always hurt women. He texted back, *OK, sounds good. I'll go back and check for the typos at the end. Let me know when you want to meet up...If you want to. We don't have to. We can just email.*

Hazel Grace was panicking now. Maybe he isn't into her at all. Well, wouldn't that be a good thing? It took every ounce of fortitude she possessed to refrain from texting back and setting up a date for this week. Not a date, but a *meeting*. In the end, she managed to leave it alone.

For his part, Zach had already had his two-afternoon beers. When his buddies called and suggested a nightclub, he didn't hesitate. Maybe he just needed to meet some stranger. He had never been able to pick up women in a bar, handsome as he was. Fear of rejection always either prevented him from trying or coming on at first meeting like a friend. He hoped tonight might be different.

Chad, Kevin, and Jamal drove together and met Zach at the club. It was typical; line outside, bouncers letting in pretty girls first, and Zach and his friends waiting. Kevin was an operator, and he came with a plan. He strolled casually and confidently to the front of the line and said something to the giant at the door as he put something in his meaty hand. Kevin waved his posse forward as the giant unhooked the barrier rope, letting them in without so much as looking at them. *I need to be like Kevin,* thought Zach as he watched him go to work.

Zach had not gotten to the bar to order before Kevin and Jamal were standing in the midst of a group of five girls. Chad had disappeared somewhere, and Zach decided to grab the one open barstool. On his left was the back of a woman who was engaged in conversation with the man to her other side. On his right was another man, around his age, and looking about as pathetic as Zach figured he looked.

It took some time to get the attention of the bartender. It gave him time to plan the drink he was going to order. He wanted to get something hip and cool, so he planned to ask for a martini. Maybe he should ask for it to be shaken, not stirred, and then he'd have the James Bond effect when he decided to start approaching women. The bartender that suddenly presented herself was confident and movie-star beautiful. "What can I get you?"

"Um. Miller Lite." So much for James Bond.

"Coming right up. Want me to start you a tab?" she asked seductively.

"Yeah, sure." Zach didn't want a tab. But was he going to say no? He nursed his beer. To get drunk or not to get drunk, that was the question. Getting ready that night, he was certain that tonight was going to be different. Tonight, he would throw caution to the wind and talk to people. Zach could win the heart of a woman that he was given plenty of time with, someone from his study group, or a workplace, or club on campus. He could ease in that way. He could take his time and make certain at every step of the way that he had the next green light. Truthfully, he rarely failed in this.

But this was a totally different kind of thing, picking up women that he didn't know and didn't know him. He had never been able to pull it off, and quite often, he would go the whole night without attempting to start a conversation. Zach wanted to be in love. It was one of his favorite things. He knew that he was weird in that way. A good psychiatrist would have a field day with that one. He also knew that a bar was no place to start a relationship. It was probably the fact Zach took romance so seriously that caused him to be so bad at picking up women.

The seat on his right opened when the woman and man got up to go to the dance floor together. *There's one guy who pulled it off.* The seat next to him was immediately taken by a sweaty Kevin, taking a break to get his first drink of the night. Kevin realized Zach was next to him, "Dude! What are you doing? Get out there!"

"I will," said Zach, "Just let me get a couple of beers in me."

Kevin knew better. "You started the night with a couple of beers in you. You always do this. Come on, man, this is your night."

Zach looked at his friend and asked him for the

hundredth time the question he always asked, "How do you do it?" Did Zach think he was going to get a new answer? He got the same scary answer that Kevin always gave to this simple question.

"I'm going to tell you this one last time. Forget what you've heard. It's not about what you look like. You're twice as good looking as me," which was true, "It's not about any smooth pickup lines or anything like that. The simple secret is this. I don't care if I get rejected."

"Do you get rejected?"

"Rarely. But even if I did, it doesn't mean anything. You are too worried about what people think of you. You spend all your time trying to get people to like you, and they usually do, but why?" Zach thought the conversation was taking a different direction than he expected. "Forget about it," said Kevin.

"I don't see how that is a bad thing," Zach protested.

"I'm not saying it's a bad thing...well...yeah, I am saying it's a bad thing." Zach was utterly confused. Again, why were they talking about this now?

Zach said, "What does that have to do with this moment? Why wouldn't I want these girls to like me?"

"It's not that you want these girls to like you. *I*

want these girls to like me, but you *need* them to like you. And that's your problem."

Just then, the beautiful bartender interrupted, "You want another beer don't you," she suggested, even more seductively than the last time.

"Yes, thank you," said Zach. When he looked back at Kevin, Zach said, "What?"

"This is what I'm talking about, man."

"What?" Zach was getting defensive.

"You don't want a beer," said the sage.

"Yes, I do."

"No, you don't. You only said yes, because you don't want to disappoint that hot bartender, who is way out of your league anyway." *Ouch.* "That's sick, man. Do you see how sick that is? You don't even know her. She does not care about you, only your tips."

Zach was starting to wake up a bit to what Kevin was saying. "Did you major in psych or something?"

"Nope, I just know stuff," said Kevin, matter-of-factly.

"Ok, let's just assume you're right. What am I supposed to do? Just get drunk?"

"No, man. You can't get drunk enough to fix that. Just think. You're here to have a good time and maybe meet a girl, or two, or ten. You're not trying to find a wife here. Just go up and say, 'Hi.' Watch me." He turned around and noticed a nice-looking girl walking by, twenty-ish, sober. He grabbed her arm, but not too tightly. She turned to him.

"Hi," he said.

"Hi." She seemed somewhere between neutral and pleased to be talking with him.

Kevin continued, "How are you tonight? Are you having fun?"

"I am." She was willing to play along.

"Did you see the game earlier today?" The whole town was buzzing over the OSU, OU game. Kevin made a guess that this girl was tied to one of the schools.

"Yeah, that was crazy!"

"I know! What's your name?" asked Kevin.

"Lainie."

"It was good to meet you, Lainie. Are you going to dance tonight?"

"Yeah, for sure." She was playing with her hair, and all the signs were there that she was warming up to Kevin. Even Zach could tell. Kevin was acting like he owned the place.

"Cool. Maybe I'll see you out there. Have fun

tonight." What was he doing? Zach couldn't believe that he didn't go out right now and dance with her, or ask for her number, or anything.

"I know what you are thinking," said Kevin when he turned back to Zach.

"What am I thinking?"

"You're wondering why I let her go when she was obviously warming up to me," said Kevin, knowingly.

"Well, yes, that is what I was thinking. Seems like a dumb move. That girl was pretty."

"She was, and I liked her. But I'm here to have a good time and meet lots of girls. I'm not trying to find a wife. I was hoping she would reject me, so you could see that it's no big deal. But why do you think she didn't?"

"I suppose you're going to tell me it is because you didn't care." Zach understood. Kevin seemed confident, Zach realized, because he knew there were lots of fish in the sea, and rejection, contrary to what your nervous system might be telling you, will not kill you. "Ok," said Zach. "I'll give it a try."

"That's my boy!" Kevin was pumped and started looking around the room. "Ok, hero, look over there." Kevin was pointing to an attractive woman standing and laughing talking to her friends. "Go up and talk to her.

You can do it."

Zach felt surprisingly brave as he started to move across the room. It seemed like an awfully long way over there, and he walked with confidence, talking to himself. *Ok, Zach, you can do this. All you must do is walk up and talk to her. Who cares if she rejects you? There are lots of beautiful women here. It's fine if she acts like you are beneath her. If she looks at you like you are pathetic, it's not going to bother you. You can just move on. She probably has a boyfriend. He's probably here somewhere. But that's fine. No big deal. He might want to fight you, but you've been in fights before. He might be a big guy. I don't really want to be in a fight with a big guy tonight. Maybe she doesn't have a boyfriend. Maybe she doesn't want one. Maybe she just got out of a bad relationship and has sworn she is going to humiliate the next chump that tries to talk to her, which will be me. I'm walking into a disaster.*

It is not possible to understand the rate at which these thoughts were bombarding Zach from every corner of his mind.

She is really pretty. I wonder what it would be like to be married to her. That would be nice. It would be nice to not be lonely. If that girl loved me, I could maybe finish my novel. I hope I like her family. Zach, what are you thinking? You don't even know her, and she's probably going to reject you, and you will die alone and rejected someday. Come on, man! Get it together. You are only ten feet away from her. Come on! Think of something, quick!

Every step closer increased his heart rate. Soon he was seven feet from her, six feet, five feet. Now she was looking at him. Four feet, now she was looking at her friend. Was she alarmed? Three feet. Now she had turned her back to him. Was this on purpose? *It's probably on purpose. Her friend is looking at me. Did she just say, "here he comes?" Is that a good thing or a bad thing?* Two feet, one foot, two feet, three feet, four feet, five, six, seven, EIGHT FEET! And just like that, Zach had passed her by and went into the bathroom.

As he looked at himself in the mirror. He said out loud to the image. "What the hell are you doing here?"

"What?" said a tattooed-up guy coming out of the stall.

"No, sorry, I was talking to someone else."

Later, at 2 AM and back home again, Zach Stone, in a weird mood and still a little buzzed, decided to email Hazel Grace.

Chapter 8

Zach Stone had always been in love with love. When he was five years old, he married seven different girls in his kindergarten class on the playground, though not on the same day. He would not be able to count the number of girlfriends he'd had, and he almost always was the one who broke it off. He'd even been engaged twice and nearly a third time.

He knew he was a mess, and he told himself every time he had to crush someone's heart that he would never do it again. And then he would do it again. The latest stretch of singleness had been a real point of growth and maturing. But the failure at the bar set him back, and he regressed to a former version of himself. As he was emailing Hazel Grace, he deliberately avoided thinking about what he was doing. He was being driven by emptiness and loneliness. The truth was that he did like her. He was even convinced he *loved* her. He didn't because he really did not know how to love someone. But his heart and hormones didn't know that. It was convinced, again, that this time was different.

Dear Hazel Grace,

Forgive me for emailing you. Zach even knew this was the cowardly way to go about it. Could he not just talk to her?

I was thinking about you tonight, and I wanted to tell you that I have developed feelings for you.

"Come on, Zach, aren't you a writer? You can do better than that." He hit the backspace and tried again.

I wanted you to know that I think about you all the time. I know I'm working for you, but I can't deny what's going on in my heart. You already mean a lot to me, and I don't even know you that well. I might even love you.

"No, you don't," said a voice. But Zach pushed it aside. Sure, he did. And that was the sad thing. He really believed it, at least part of him did. But then again, there was the more recent part, the wiser part of his mind that was saying, "You know you should not do this. You know that this will not end well if you do it like this."

When I went to your house and hung out with your family, I couldn't help but imagine being a part of it. You have opened my eyes to so many things. I even find myself wondering about God.

This was a new low. Zach stared at what he had written so far. He stared long and hard. The truth was that he was not wondering much about God. He had problems, but his mom's God was not the one to fix it.

Even his dad had supposedly turned his life around with God. If Billy Stone's God was real, Zach wanted nothing to do with him.

But even if he didn't believe in his dad's God, his mom's God, or even Hazel Grace Jackson's God, *something* was telling him that he needed to discard this email and sleep off this sentimental attack he was having. He did like Hazel Grace a lot. That is exactly why he needed to stop himself right now and go to sleep. Isn't this the kind of thing he always did? It's exactly that. Had it ever worked out? Zach was confused. He should just send it and see what happens.

He got a very real blast of chemicals at the prospect. He craved it. He craved the sensation of sending that email with all its possibilities. He stared at the screen for what seemed like hours but was only minutes. He reached for the touch screen and pushed…the "discard draft" link. After that, Zach got drunker than he had been since college.

Billy hung up his cell phone and tossed it on the motel queen bed next to him. The boys were fine. John was getting ready to tell his mom that he resented her and forgave her for making his life a nightmare. This would be his greatest challenge, right up there with getting sober. She had been calling him every day and berating him for not coming back home to her. He had avoided telling her that he wasn't going to go home, ever. He just kept saying he needed a little more time, and then he would be back. Billy silently prayed for John's courage to hold up. He knew that parents were often the first place to start with coming clean and giving forgiveness. Billy had never gone to AA, but he had naturally followed some of the steps when his own time had come.

As Billy scrolled through the channels on the TV, he wasn't really paying attention to them. He stopped on the Weather Channel, and his mind went back twenty years to an angry drunk on a construction job and the remarkable man of God who changed his life.

It was an oil refinery in Louisiana. As a young man, Billy hated oil refinery work. It was hot, dirty, and plain hard. Billy had a mouth to make a sailor blush, and his constant complaining and defensive posturing made all the other guys hate him. That was fine with Billy because he hated them too. The only thing good about the job was that it kept him away from home. He and his wife had married young, and they had two kids. They drove him to drink almost every night. He was a mean drunk, and he'd never said it out loud, but he hated the woman for trapping him into the prison of family life. He had had no intention of marrying her, but her father forced the closest thing to a shotgun wedding that you can imagine. Billy never saw the gun, but it was always implied. If he hadn't done right by his princess, that son-of-bitch would have killed Billy for sure.

The first baby was a boy. For about two minutes, Billy got a kick out of having a son, but the crying, the diapers, and postpartum wife were not worth it. And, having no self-understanding, Billy could not have told you the extent to which he resented the constant needs and financial burden. His one salvation was that as a welder, he had to travel for work. The fact was, they would have done just fine if Billy hadn't drunk up half of everything he made. His wife never relented telling him what a worthless bum he was. Her mother often came to stay, and she may have been the only person on the planet that Billy hated more than his wife.

And that was saying a lot because, frankly, Billy hated everything and everybody. He hated his dead parents, both of them. He hated his abusive grandmother, who took him in just so she could have a slave to order around. He hated the world and whatever god that made it. His constant and favorite pastime was to imagine ways to die. Here he was now in Louisiana on another crap job, with a bunch of hillbillies who didn't know a damn thing about their jobs. And there was one guy who really made his blood boil. Wilbur Lee Tucker.

Most of the other men were antagonistic toward Billy. Not Wilbur. In fact, Wilbur was worse than all of them because he was nice. What made Billy so mad was not so much that Wilbur was nice but that he was happy. Who the hell had a right to be happy in the scorching heat of the refinery? It always threw Billy off that he couldn't drive this Okie away from him with his complaining. He knew Wilbur was a Christian because he never stopped singing songs about Jesus and saying, "Praise the Lord anyhow," and things like that.

One day Billy was in the foulest mood he'd been in since he'd gotten there. Wilbur was minding his business, working on some piece of welding and singing his infernal songs. Billy had had enough. Something took over his mind, and all he could think about was doing harm to this man. Wilbur was the opposite of everything Billy thought about the world. The world was bad, and Billy was bad. The problem with Wilbur was that he was good. Billy could not have known that Billy's true object of hatred was God. The fact was that, while Billy claimed to be an atheist, he had a deep conviction that there was a God and that someone ought to do something about the son-of-bitch. Billy did believe in God, and his belief was shown through a deep and powerful hatred for him and for all things good. Nothing had a right to be good in this god-forsaken world, and no person had a right to be happy. Nothing mattered.

Billy knew someday he would do something truly evil to show God how he felt about the world that he made and the life he had given Billy. He did not care what happened to him. Any given day, if he died, he died. The thing that came over him today was to hurt the singing preacher. That damn idiot drove him insane and made him want to rip his own ears off. Today was the day. He picked up a pipe and walked up behind the man. The rest of the crew had always made it a point to be nowhere near the young man, so they didn't have to hear his bitching and moaning. This meant that they were all alone. What Billy would do after he knocked Wilbur in the head, he would decide later, but he was compelled as though full of demons, which, looking back, he was.

As he crept up behind Wilbur, the preacher stopped singing and turned to Billy. The two men faced each other, one with a crazy and evil look in his eye and the other with the eyes of Christ looking on a lost child. Wilbur saw the look, and he saw the lead pipe and worked out what was happening. He prayed in his mind to God to help him, to give him courage to obey Jesus' words to turn the other cheek, no matter what happens, and for this poor soul in front of him. "What can I do for you, young man?"

Billy processed the words. A voice in his head said, "He's mocking you! Strike him down where he stands!" But something made him hesitate. Still holding the pipe, he said, "You can shut your damn mouth! I'm sick and tired of your fake attitude like everything is great in the world, and like we don't have this shitty job to do and those snotty-nosed brats to feed and the nagging wife waiting at home to take every last cent we make on this damn job in this hell hole of a state! And you, you make me sick with your singing, your praising, and your kindness, as if there were some reason to be kind to these assholes. I hate you, and I hate your God, and I want you to SHUT UP! SHUT UP! SHUT UP!" There were tears in his eyes, and Billy didn't even know why he was crying. He just felt so hopeless and lost. The desire to kill Wilbur had strangely passed.

Wilbur walked to him and put his hand on the arm that still held the pipe, and said, "Let's take a break, Billy. It's lunchtime anyway." The men walked over to where they had their lunches, and they unpacked them, sitting down in the shade to rest and eat. They ate in silence for twenty minutes, and then Wilbur asked, "Why don't you tell me everything?"

Strangely enough, Billy did not ask for clarification. He just started talking. Wilbur never said a word but just listened. Ordinarily, Wilbur would have been sharing the gospel at this point. He would always say, "You don't know when somebody will be breathing their last breath, so you can't wait." But this time, a voice in his heart told him to wait. So, he listened to the boy. The fact was that Billy was much younger than Wilbur, and Wilbur came off older and wiser than he was. Billy came off younger than he was because of his hot head. When lunchtime was over, the men got back to work.

As the days went by, Billy continued to cuss and complain, but not quite as much. He continued to hate everyone, but not Wilbur. If he had a chance, though he didn't want to show it, he always tried to work near where Wilbur was. He was beginning to like the singing. The other guys on the crew would make requests all day. Wilbur did have a good singing voice. "I'll fly away!" someone would say, and Wilbur would start in, "*Some glad morning when this life is o'er…*" and five other men would join in, "*I'll fly away!*"

One day, Billy woke up in one of his moods. He

had begun to tone down the complaining a bit when he was around Wilbur, but not today. Today was special. He'd gotten a letter from his damned mother-in-law that morning telling him he was worthless and that he needed to quit drinking up his money and send it home because his boy was growing fast, and for a five-year-old, he ate like a grown man. This put him in a foul mood because he knew it was true. He walked by Wilbur, cussing and complaining the whole way. Wilbur just looked at him and said, "Well, praise the Lord anyhow." It was all Billy could do not to curse him.

That was probably the hottest day of the summer, which didn't help his mood. He was cussing out the beam he was working on at the moment when he felt a cool gust of wind on his neck. It felt good. He didn't have to look back, and he wasn't in the mood to acknowledge that he knew Wilbur had been the one to put the fan on him. He did not look at him, but he did tone down the swearing.

Anyone who has ever listened to an industrial fan will know that sometimes you can hear things. You start thinking you hear a song, or maybe that you can hear people talking. Well, what happened to Billy that day was not the tricks of the physics of sound that you normally hear in a fan. It was a voice, clear as anything coming into focus from the white noise. It said, "I have never given up on you, and I never will." Billy stopped what he was doing. He turned to look across the yard to where Wilbur was working intently. It could not have been him.

Billy turned back to his work, and then he heard it again. "I have never given up on you, and I never will…I have never given up on you, and I never will…I have never given up on you…" As the fan blew in steady rhythm, the voice kept coming. That's all it said, over and over again. Billy must have heard it a million times in the last three hours of their shift. At the end of the day, he was reluctant to leave the fan. He walked back to the motel where he was staying, and the voice came again. "I have never given up on you, and I never will."

The next morning, everyone noticed the change in Billy. He seemed to be the one most surprised. Billy kept watching himself, still unable to believe what had happened the day before. Things that would usually set him off somehow did not bother him today. There were men he really hated, but somehow, he did not hate them today. He got busy with his work and hardly raised his head before lunchtime.

"Hey Billy. How's it goin' today?" asked Wilbur as they unwrapped their sandwiches. Billy looked at his one friend in the world for a long moment.

"Wilbur, did you put that fan on me yesterday?"

"You know I did," said Wilbur, with the first bites of his lunched packed in his right cheek.

"What if I told you I heard a voice in the sound of the fan?"

"I might say the heat was getting to you, depending on what the voice said."

Billy continued, "That's just it. What if I told you that I heard a voice, repeatedly saying, 'I have never given up on you, and I never will?' And what if I told you that the voice followed me all the way home, and what if I told you that in my room last night, I prayed to God and told him I wanted him to save me and make me into a different person?"

Wilbur got excited and loud and said, "And what if I told you that all day yesterday, I was praying that God would show you how much he loves you and that he has not given up on you!"

There was a pause, and then Billy said, "I would say that this is all impossible, but not as impossible as the difference I feel today in my heart. Wilbur, I don't feel like I hate anybody today. I don't feel like I want to kill anybody. I don't feel like I hate my wife or even my mother-in-law. I have an overwhelming desire to go home and see my babies."

"Hallelujah! Son, you've been washed in the blood of Jesus! I know what we should do. Does your room have a bathtub?" asked Wilbur.

"Yeah."

"I'm coming over, and you're gettin' baptized in the name of the Father and the Son and Holy Ghost who was talking to you all day yesterday!"

"All right," said Billy. If Wilbur said this was the next thing, it was the next thing.

"Billy, I've been praying that God would give you a heart to love your own children. In the Bible, it says, 'And he shall turn the heart of the fathers to the children, and the heart of the children to their fathers, lest I come and smite the earth with a curse.'"

"Man, I can't wait to get home to them and be a better man!" The two men talked through the lunch hour, and that night, Wilbur was as good as his word. He came over and preached to Billy about new life in Christ and how Billy was a new creation, and then they filled up the bathtub and did the deed.

Billy was truly different; anybody could see that. There were two more days on this job, and then he could go home and make things right. He grinned every time he felt himself missing his family. God had truly done a miracle. He loved to imagine what they'd think when they saw the new Billy.

The next day a letter came from his wife. She was done. She was taking the kids, and she was not telling him where they were going. She didn't want anything to do with him, and he better not try to find her.

Sitting in his motel room so many years later, it still made his heart ache. This, his greatest test of faith, had come on only the second full day of his new life. Before he went to sleep, he got on his well-worn knees next to his bed and prayed for his son, begging that at long last, God would allow him to do what he'd wanted to do since the first night of his salvation.

Zach and Hazel Grace were at a branch of the Tulsa Public Library system in Collinsville, and they had checked out a private room to go through details for the book. They were going on an hour and a half, and they had not yet spoken of the book or of Wilbur Lee Tucker. They assumed they'd get around to it, but the truth was that neither of them wanted to stop talking. Hazel Grace had had the good fortune of being the daughter of parents with the desire and the means to travel. She had even studied abroad in Germany.

Zach had not been to all the places that Hazel Grace had, but Germany was the one place he had been. In college, he had gone with some friends to Germany, primarily Bavaria, and had a wonderful time on a shoestring budget. Millions of people have been charmed by this ancient world in Europe, but Zach had a favorite spot when he was there. "Did you ever go to Dinkelsbuhl?" Hazel Grace's face lit up as they said in unison, "the storybook village!"

"I loved that place! What I like about Europe is how old it is. Being from America, especially in the midwest, you just can't imagine looking at a building that has been standing for seven hundred years! It brings me a lot of comfort at looking at something so…"

"Stable?" Zach knew exactly what she meant. His life had been anything but stable, so he craved things and people that were old. At the same time, he was full of instability that kept him in constant change as he searched and searched for who or what might fill him up and settle his soul. He had not found it yet, but he could easily be convinced that this girl was his salvation.

"I've asked dozens of people who have traveled to Europe, and you are the first person who even knows about Dinkelsbuhl, let alone who has been there," said Hazel Grace.

"Same for me. Wow. My most vivid memory of that place is of going into a bakery. They had the most beautiful pastries. My mouth watered at something like a cream-filled, cream-covered donut. It looked so good that I had to get it. I paid my food budget for the whole day to buy it," said Zach.

"Did it taste like shaving cream?"

"You tried it too?" Zach could not believe it.

"Not there, but I thought in general that Germans have never heard of sugar," said Hazel Grace.

Hazel Grace was having a wonderful time. She was aware that they had not talked about the book, and she was aware that she was in dangerous territory, but she was determined not to consider it until later. For now, she was having a good time. She decided to shift gears, and she took a risk.

"It seems like you have a big problem with your dad?" This was not a casual statement. Once, when Hazel Grace was dating a kid from her high school, she remembered her father saying that some of the things that concerned him about the boy had to do with the fact that he had a bad relationship with his own father. She could tell that her dad was compassionate towards the boy but that he was even more concerned that she might get too close to him. He had said, "I've noticed that he has that rebellious streak and doesn't trust authority. I've seen where that kind of thing can go." It seemed kind of cold, but dads don't mind being cold to protect their daughters. This was on her mind when she brought it up with Zach.

His face darkened, but he didn't seem offended at the question. On the contrary, he seemed to be glad to ascend to a more intimate topic with this girl. "That's a bit of an understatement. I know you aren't supposed to hate anyone, but if he comes to mind, I hear my own voice saying, "I hate that guy." I'll generally do almost anything to avoid thoughts of him."

"Oh, I'm sorry, we don't have to…"

"No, it's fine. I want to talk to you about it," said Zach. "Frankly, I have very few memories. I was five when he stopped coming home. Before that, I only remember him as loud, angry, and distant. He seemed to hate my sister and me. I do remember once, I guess he was drunk, and he was sitting in his chair, drinking and watching the news. The Twin Towers were smoking, and he was raging at the TV. I remember that he looked at me and said the world was coming to an end and "there ain't nobody who cares." Zach said this last part in his best white trash impression. "He grabbed me by the shirt and said, 'Boy, don't expect this life to be anything but shitty,' and then he burped in my face. It took me a little while to get used to the taste of beer because whenever I smelled it, I just smelled that burp and got mad. I got used to it by age twelve. I made myself. I don't know why I did, but I did. I still hate him, though."

Hazel Grace was overwhelmed with compassion. "And that is the last thing you remember?"

"Yeah, after that, we moved. My mom said that my dad didn't want to come with us, said he didn't care about her or his kids. She said he was mean to her and that we were way better off without him."

"You never heard from him again?"

"Not until my mom died. Then he started sending me letters," said Zach with obvious bitterness.

"What did they say?"

"I don't know. I never opened them. I returned them. He tried calling me too. Still does."

Hazel Grace asked, "Don't you want to hear what he has to say? Maybe he wants to make things right."

"I'm sure he does, but, Hazel, he's an awful person. You should have heard the stories that my mom and grandmother told me about him. Whenever I did anything remotely wrong, they'd say, 'You're going to be just like your father if you keep that up.' It became my number one obsession to be different than my dad. No, I don't want anything to do with him."

"Don't you think it could help you? You seem angry still. Do you think it affects you? Like you have some unresolved issues?" Hazel was being bold, but something compelled her to say it. Zach was getting agitated.

"I don't have any unresolved issues," said Zach, a little elevated for a library conversation. "I'm fine, and life just is what it is. Shitty! Most men are toxic, just like my mother said, and I'm just trying not to be one of them, like him!"

"Ok, I don't mean anything." Hazel Grace could see that this wasn't the time for this. Her heart broke for him, though. She was torn between the feelings she was developing for him, the devotion to her values and her God, and the compassion that had always characterized her. Zach changed the subject.

"Hey," looking at his phone, "It's been two hours, and we haven't talked about the book."

"I was just thinking that," said Hazel Grace. "Why don't we plan to meet next week? I'll read what you have over this week, and then we can get together again."

"That works...I've enjoyed this." The way Zach

was looking at her now set off alarms in Hazel Grace. They were not unwelcomed alarms.

"Me too."

Zach looked at her for a moment longer than was necessary, and she knew he was working something out. Would he say what he was thinking? Did she want him to? She did, but she didn't. Whether good or bad, he put her out of her turmoil for the moment when he said, "I'm going to stay here and write a while."

This snapped her out of the spell, and she said, "Great, ok, yeah. I gotta get going, so, like I said, I'll read what you have, and we can set up a time next week. Text me or something."

"Ok, I'll have more for you when you're done."

"Great. Ok, I'll see you soon. Bye." Hazel Grace left the room, and Zach wondered how he had been able to stop himself from saying what he so desperately wanted to say. The fact was that he was maturing, even a year ago, things would have been different. It wasn't that he didn't have strong feelings for her because he did. But he just knew that Hazel Grace was different, and the absolute best part of him knew that this was not something to screw up. He simply didn't trust himself not to make the same mistake he always made. Maybe he would in the end. Probably he would in the end, but he would put it off as long as possible.

In her car, Hazel Grace got herself together. Why could she not just forget about Zach? Obviously, she couldn't forget about him while they were working on the book, but why couldn't she just keep it business? Nothing was right about this. Well, something was right. She loved him. Crap! She loved him! She might as well admit it. But she could not act on it. She wanted him to act on it, but she knew it would be a catastrophe. Unless, of course, God saved him. But she knew better than to think that she was the bait for God. No, girls that think that way are just kidding themselves. Hadn't she seen her friends go down that path to misery? She would not make that mistake.

But there was something even more important— Zach's soul. The question was, would it be more of a witness for her, a good Christian girl, to forsake her values for this boy and date him against biblical wisdom? Would that show him the love of Christ and change his heart toward God? No. She had to be honest, and the pain her honesty caused ripped her heart out. She thought of what her Grandpa would have said. He would have said that a greater witness would be to reject him despite her strong feelings for him, that if anything could show him the power of God, it would be her conviction to the truth and obedience to God. "But won't that just make him madder at God?" she said out loud in her car.

The answer came to her heart clear as anything, "Trust me."

Wilbur and Connie were married, and though Wilbur went with her enormous family to church three times a week, he did not immediately follow God. But this was the godliest family he could have joined, and before long, their faith began to have a significant impact on Wilbur.

Wilbur was an incredibly hard worker. Since he was eight years old, he'd held a job. His first job was as a gas station attendant, pumping gas, changing flats, and doing whatever needed to be done. Now, at twenty-two, he became certified as a welder and began working on construction sites all over the country. Faith continued to creep up on him at this time, and he found himself believing all of it. He believed the gospel, the whole rest of the Bible, the glossary, and the maps! Wilbur was all in.

Soon after he had given himself to God, he was at work joining in the singing with another Christian on the job. The man asked Wilbur, "Are you a Christian?"

Wilbur was happy that there must have been something in his character or his demeanor that made the man ask. Maybe it was just that he could tell Wilbur was singing the hymns from his heart. Maybe the man could see the love of God in him. "I am a Christian! What made you ask?"

"I can tell by the kind of cigarettes you smoke," said the man, genuinely.

This was perplexing to Wilbur. Whatever logic had led the man to that conclusion, the man did not share. That night, Wilbur thought it over in his bed. Could he see Jesus walking down the street, healing the leper with one hand, and smoking a Winston with the other? No. He prayed that night and was delivered from addiction to smoking once and for all time. In the same way, he gave up alcohol and cussing. He was a new man. God even delivered him from an anger problem that was so common to younger men, especially when they have an absent father.

Zach had to stop there. He had not intended to think about himself, but he couldn't help but consider his own anger issues. Wilbur's dad had basically been around, but not really. Zach's dad had totally abandoned him. It was probably a similar feeling. Zach would have liked to be free from anger. He would have liked to be free from the craving for the attention of women and from the compulsion to drink. Wilbur seemed to find freedom in finding God. Zach could not even imagine himself turning to God.

He knew his own father had supposedly turned

his life around. His sister seemed to have made amends with their dad and had urged Zach to as well. He knew Billy Stone wanted to see him. He'd tried to contact Zach many times, but Zach felt so much hatred for the man. His hatred for Billy was something that he needed. He didn't know why. Zach even suspected that deep down, if he gave up his hatred for his father, he'd have to give up his favorite excuses *not* to make it in life. He wasn't ready to bring this thought to consciousness, but it was dogging him and getting closer every day. He also did not want to consider why he did not want to change his life, and yet he was so miserable. He shook off whatever thoughts were floating upward in his mind and got back to the manuscript.

Wilbur was a new man. He was so glad to be a part of God's plan, and he looked forward to the ways God would want to use him. He had called his wife from the job when God got a hold of him and told her that he wanted God to use him. Use him he did. When Wilbur was welding, Wilbur was "witnessing." He loved to tell others about Jesus and how he had helped him kick smoking, cussing, drinking and fighting. Some men seemed hungry to hear what he had to say, others asked why they would want to quit all that stuff. Wilbur learned in this way that a man has to be ready if God is going to work on him. Wilbur knew that some of his work was getting men ready, and some of it was "harvesting."

One day, Wilbur was contemplating the fact that, while he enjoyed his job, hard as it was, what he really loved was ministering to the men. He began to wonder if this was a call to ministry. As this thought became stronger, Wilbur knew that it was not something to be taken lightly. He needed to go to Bible College if he was to become a pastor. This was a big step and would cost him both time and money. He knew that if God wanted it, then he'd make a way.

By now, Wilbur, who was a sponge for all things in Scripture, knew the story of Gideon in the Bible. When an angel showed up to call Gideon to serve the Lord, Gideon wanted some proof. Now, Wilbur thought that if an angel showed up to tell him to go to seminary school, then he would not need more proof than that. But, minus the angel, Wilbur was intrigued by Gideon's method. Gideon had asked that if he was really called, then when he put out a lamb fleece overnight. God would make it wet while the ground was dry. This God did. Gideon was impressed but needed to double-check to make sure. He asked God that the next night, it could go the other way. Sure enough, when Gideon checked the next night, the ground was completely soaked with the morning dew, but the fleece was dry. One day Wilbur described his own plan to his brother-in-law, Bill.

"Bill, you ever read about Gideon?"

"Of course, I have," said Bill.

Wilbur gave him the details, then said, "I've got a plan.

I been thinking more and more that God would have me go to seminary school in Colorado Springs. But I don't know. I borrowed this thimble from Connie's momma, and I plan to put it out on the car tonight."

"I see what you're sayin'. If the thimble has water in it and the car is dry, you'll know God wants you to go." Bill was quick on the uptake, although he had his doubts. This seemed like the kind of thing that was perfectly natural for Bible characters, but ordinary good ole boys like him and Wilbur Lee are not Bible characters.

"I can see you are skeptical," said Wilbur with understanding. That night he left out the thimble. In the morning, he went outside early. It was chilly outside, but the ground was dry. Bill had questioned if the wind might blow the thimble off the car, but Wilbur had faith that if this was something God wanted, then that thimble would be there. Sure enough, the thimble was there. As Wilbur approached the vehicle, a 1968 Plymouth Fury, his heart began to race. He didn't know if he was surprised, but the thimble was full to the top with water. He briefly wondered if Bill had come in the night and filled it, but he dismissed the thought.

"Ok, Lord. I know you won't be surprised if we do this one more night. I probably don't even have to tell you that I'd be obliged if you could turn it around tonight. I really do want to go to Bible College and be a pastor, but I need to know I'm not crazy and just making stuff up. Please don't see this as me doubting you,

Lord. I would never doubt you or your plan. But when it comes to hearing you, I doubt my own ability. So, although I don't have to say it, I will. Please Lord, let the thimble be empty and dry as a bone while the Plymouth is covered in water. I'll do whatever you say after that."

Wilbur knew this was risky. If it didn't work tonight, he'd be left with the predicament that the first night, the thimble was full. Maybe God would be irritated that Wilbur didn't trust him the first time. If the plan didn't work tonight, Wilbur would still not quite know what to do. Of course, if the thimble was empty on a wet car, he would not doubt God, and he would do what he had to do to become a preacher.

By the end of the following day, Wilbur was putting plans in place to move to Colorado Springs to start seminary school. The thimble was empty, and the car was soaked.

Zach was making good progress now, but he was thinking more and more about those missing pages because he was going to need them. He had reminded Hazel Grace, who promised to look for them, but had not yet produced them. Zach was beginning to have a downright compulsion to see those pages. If you asked him why he couldn't have told you. It was as if something was moving him from the inside.

He also just really wanted to see her. Shouldn't

he call her and ask her about those pages? Didn't he need to get some more stories about Wilbur for the book? He texted her. He did want those pages, but seeing her was the real motive, and he didn't hide that fact from himself. *Can we get together tomorrow? I need those missing pages, but I also want to hear more stories about your Grandpa for the book.*

He waited five minutes before he heard the text message come in. *Sure. I can meet you, but tomorrow I have promised to babysit my cousin. We're going to the zoo.*

Dang. Zach could only meet that next day because he had plans for the rest of the week. He was trying to think of a way to get out of them when his phone vibrated again. *You could come with us…:)*

Zach didn't want to hesitate, but he did hesitate just a little, playing it cool, before he texted back. *Sure. I haven't been to the Tulsa Zoo since I was a kid.*

Hazel wrote back, *would that work? Do you think we could talk about the book while we walk around?*

Oh yeah, the book. *Sure. If I need to stop and take a note, I can just record it into my phone. So, yeah…what time?*

It opens at 10, so we'll probably be there at 10.

Ok, meet me at the monkeys at 10:15.

Ok, see you there. :)

At 10:15 the next day, Zach was waiting when Hazel Grace and a girl who looked to be about four years old came walking up among a large crowd that was already gathered. It was a perfect day, and many in Tulsa had the same idea of a day at the zoo. The animals were active and doing their best to entertain.

"Hey!" Hazel Grace was holding hands with her cousin, who was using Hazel's hand to jump over the cracks in the sidewalk.

"Good morning," said Zach. "Who's this?"

Hazel Grace said, "This is Lucy Marie. Lucy, can you say 'hey'?"

Lucy looked up at Zach and paused for a moment. Shyness overtook her, and she covered her face with the arm of Hazel Grace whose hand she now held with both hands.

"Are you being shy?" Hazel Grace smiled at Zach as he crouched on his knee.

"Hey Lucy. My name is Zach. I like your shoes." This lit the girl up. Her shoes happened to be one of her favorite subjects. They had lights that came on with each step. She still did not speak, but she did begin stomping up and down to put on a light show. "Oh wow! I bet you're fast."

At that, Lucy let her aunt's hand go, and she took off running, making a circle around a nearby park bench and returning to her aunts' side, still holding her hand, but no longer in front of her face.

"What is on your shirt?" Asked Zach.

Lucy answered with her first audible words, "a monkey."

"Do you like monkeys?" Asked Zach, and the little girl nodded her head in affirmation as she looked past Zach and at the enclosed habitat behind them. That was their cue to make their way over. The chimps were putting on a show when they got to the glass, and Hazel Grace had to lift Lucy up to see above a group of children who were all wearing the same T-shirt from the same daycare on a field trip. Zach could see young daycare workers keeping order, along with mom chaperones pushing younger siblings in strollers, and there were even two dads. Zach imagined that one of them was taking the day off, but the other looked like he knew what he was doing and was probably a stay-at-home dad.

"You're good with kids. You're a natural. She's usually even shyer than that," said Hazel Grace when Zach had finally found a parting of the sea of children.

"Huh. I guess so. I'm never around kids, but I really like them." He was being sincere. Zach liked any kid he met. Hazel decided this was more evidence that Zach was just a genuinely good person.

They spent an hour seeing the apes and then the snakes. Lucy didn't care for the snakes, so they hurried through and on to the exotic birds. To say it was loud was an understatement, and inside the indoor sanctuary, it was humid for the birds of the rainforest. Zach was interested to see the plants in the room, as it was one of the few places in Oklahoma to see the fruit trees of the tropics.

After they left that room, Zach said, "should we grab some lunch?" There was a cafeteria near the entrance and a few snack bars sprinkled throughout the complex. He got out the map to begin the trek to the cafeteria.

"Sure, I've got it covered." Hazel removed the backpack she'd been wearing all day and retrieved a lunch bag. She had brought cold fried chicken, potato salad, chips, cookies, and fruit punch.

"Oh wow! I was planning to buy you guys lunch," said Zach with sincerity.

"Well, now you don't have to. The food here is expensive," said Hazel Grace.

They found a table that a family was just beginning to vacate, and they tried not to be too annoying as they hovered over them, guarding the precious real estate. When the family had moved on, they slipped into their place. Hazel was busy setting up the table, while Zach and Lucy, good friends by this point, played some kind of patty cake game. Lucy was trying in vain to teach it to Zach and getting frustrated.

When she had lunch all set up, Hazel Grace produced some hand sanitizer, and the child obediently presented her hands for treatment. Zach accepted some of it as well, and he was grateful that the stuff was unscented. He didn't want the smell of fried chicken to be ruined by flowery perfume.

Zach was about to take his first bite when Lucy asked, "Can I pray?"

"Sure, you can, honey," said Hazel Grace, who avoided looking at Zach.

Hazel Grace and Zach both made "praying hands" in front of their faces and bowed their heads. When no prayer came, Zach opened one eye to see that Lucy looked put out as she held both of her hands out to the adults. She wanted them all to hold hands for the prayer. Hazel Grace noticed this too and involuntarily looked at Zac with concern and surprise on her face. She couldn't help smiling.

The adults took Lucy's hands and then, somewhat awkwardly, reached for each other's. It would not be an overstatement to say that for each of them, the moment was electric. They could have both been kidding themselves up to this moment about what they were doing. They had not talked about the book yet today, but they still had time. But now, everything had shifted. This just became a date.

"Amen," said Lucy, as she finished the memorized child's prayer.

"Amen," repeated the adults.

They enjoyed their food and each other. Lucy was not that kid who demanded the attention wherever she was. She was content to eat her chicken and let the grownups talk. After a while, as they were cleaning up the table, the child asked, "Are you married?" Hazel Grace blushed, and Zach said, "What do you mean, Lucy? I thought I was going to marry you!"

"Gross! You're an old man! You should marry Aunt Gracie."

They laughed awkwardly at this, and Hazel Grace was glad that Zach had been quick on his feet.

"That kid is precocious!" Said Zach as they were beginning to move on to the lions and the zebras.

"No kidding! She's hilarious. I try not to have a favorite, but of all my cousins, she'd be close to the top if I did."

"I can see why." The three of them continued to

walk. Lucy scurried from enclosure to enclosure, talking to the animals that were looking at her, and they all seemed to be doing just that. Zach and Hazel Grace were able to talk and continued to learn about each other. The more they learned, the more the connection and attraction became obvious.

"We have time for about one more area, and then I gotta get this one home for a nap," said Hazel Grace.

"I gotta get *this* one home for a nap too," said Zach, pointing to himself with both thumbs. "How about the elephants?"

"Yeah! The elephants!" Lucy makes a trunk with her arm and trumpeted her best elephant call.

"You think we should do that?" Asked Hazel Grace.

"Yes!" Lucy seemed to know the way as she first took off running into the crowd, remarkably, in the right direction.

Hazel looked panicked, "I got this," said Zach, as he took off after her. Hazel Grace quickened her pace and caught up with them because a peacock had apparently been allowed to roam freely in the area and was having a moment with Zach and Lucy.

All together again, the three of them made their way to the elephants. There was a giant who was feeding himself on one side of the enclosure, which had been expertly made to look like some part of Africa. It was hypnotic to watch the big male reach out with his trunk and grab a batch of hay before putting it into his mouth.

Hazel Grace said, "It looks like the trunk is a separate animal."

"I was thinking the very same thing," said Zach, surprised.

From the opposite side of the enclosure, there was a higher-pitched trumpet blast, and the crowd around let out a collective "awwww." A baby had come out of the indoor part of the habitat and was running for his father. At least, Zach guessed that the big male was his father. Behind him was his mother, who Zach would have been impressed with had he not already seen the male. The baby nuzzled up to his father, and his mother joined in the action. Zach noticed that Hazel Grace was tearing up. She caught him looking and began to laugh through the tears as he grinned at her.

"Don't make fun!" She said as she wiped her eyes.

"I know, it's precious." Zach was thinking what a sweetheart Hazel Grace really was, as the three of them, Zach, Hazel Grace, and Lucy, stood together watching the elephants love each other. There was a playground in eyeshot, and Lucy bolted for it. Zach and Hazel Grace resigned themselves to follow and found a park bench to sit on together. Lucy made three friends, all boys, and they began to chase one another in some kind of climbing tag game.

They sat watching her long enough to begin to be self-conscious about how closely they were sitting to one another. Hazel, seeking to break the tension, said, "What kind of music do you like?"

"Mostly country."

"What CD is in your truck right now?" Asked Hazel Grace.

"Well, my *playlist* on my iPhone is cued up to Willie Nelson's greatest hits."

"Oh, you're old country." She understood and thought it made sense.

"Yeah, I can't stand anything after 1993," said Zach. "But primarily, it's Johnny Cash, Merle, and I like Alabama. Other days, I'm in more of a hard rock mood."

"Like what?" She asked.

"Like Zeppelin, AC/DC, Guns n Roses."

"Oookay…" she looked at him sideways. She didn't really have a problem with any of it but just wanted to tease him anyway.

"What? What do you like?" He asked in mock defensiveness.

"New country; Carrie Underwood, Kelsea Ballerini, Kane Brown."

"Never heard them, at least the last two." Zach pretended like he was just kidding her, but he really had not heard of Kelsea Ballerini or Kane Brown.

"I'm sure you've heard them, but from what you said, you probably didn't like them. I also like Christian music."

"O come on," said Zach. "I can completely understand that you have faith and believe in all that stuff, but you cannot tell me you think Christian music is good."

Hazel Grace was truly mystified at this? "What do you mean? Have you even heard any of it?" She said. "Even Justin Bieber and Chance, The Rapper have a song out called "Holy." It's more mainstream than you think." She added.

"I'm not buying it! I can tell a Christian pop song in three notes!" Said Zach arrogantly.

"What do you mean? How!?"

"Because there is always something fake about it."

"What!"

"Yeah, I have a theory. Wanna hear it?" Zach asked.

"Do tell!" Said Hazel Grace, leaning away and folding her arms.

"My theory is that when most people write a pop song, they are singing about something they are really into, and they really believe, like love, or the pain that goes with a breakup. But I feel like Christian music is someone mimicking a love song and making it about God. They are trying to sing love songs to Jesus, but they don't really believe themselves." Zach had a self-satisfied look on his face.

"Huh…" Hazel was thoughtful. "Wow," she said finally, "that's true!" Hazel looked a little troubled, then a thought came to her, "Wait a minute! Wait, wait, wait." Hazel Grace had been scanning her internal file system to disprove what Zach was saying, and when she got to the S's, she hit on what she was looking for. "Here! Exhibit A!"

"Spoken like the true daughter of a lawyer," said Zach, good-naturedly, "Show me whatchu got."

"Skillet."

"Never heard of them," said Zach without missing a beat as Hazel Grace retrieved her phone from her back pocket.

"Play "Whispers in the Dark," said Hazel Grace into her phone. After a moment, the music began to play, but the crowd around them was too loud.

"Hang on," said Zach, and he dug through his pockets until he found the tangled-up earbuds. He untangled them two-thirds of the way and began listening. After a minute, he said, loudly, "That's not so bad, actually."

Hazel Grace reached up and took his wrist, pulling his hand and his left earbud to her right ear. This brought them closer in proximity, and she did not let his hand go, though she could have released it and held only the earbud.

Zach was no longer listening to the song but rather his heartbeat, strangely loud, pulsing in his ear. This was just nice. He had the feeling that he could sit like this all day if it were possible.

Hazel Grace was in the same moment, with the same breathlessness. What was she doing?! She resolved to wait until later to answer such a silly question. It may have been twenty minutes that they sat like that, listening to three or four songs. For his part, Zach was ignoring a cramp in his neck. It was a small price to pay for what was happening between them. There was a powerful energy field between their two faces. Zach felt like his mouth was a magnet pulling towards the opposite pole. Hazel Grace felt the same, and Zach did not have a doubt in his mind that this was true. They were going to kiss, right there in front of all the animals and the crowds of people.

This was how their relationship would start except for one thing; Lucy had become tired, and when her three new friends were called away, she came over and crawled up into Zach's lap and fell asleep.

Chapter 9

Billy had been sitting in his truck for a half-hour, wondering if his son, who was in that house, was awake yet. It was 10 AM. He had had breakfast already at a diner, where he frequented to the point that he was on a first-name basis with the staff and regulars. They had all wished him well that morning when he left to put his plan into action. Now he was about ready, and his nerves were getting the best of him.

He prayed for a bit, adding ten minutes to the five million hours that he had already spent praying for his boy in the last twenty years. His spirit calmed down, and he became focused. He climbed down from the pickup, shut and locked the door, and began walking toward the house, not fast, but not slow. His lips were moving as he continued his prayers.

The little house was nice. The flowerbeds were tidy, and the paint looked fresh. It could have been inhabited by a little old lady who had owned it for decades. He took a deep breath and knocked on the door. The man who answered was not his son. He had shorts, long socks, a shirt that said Atari, and a hoodie hanging open. He had some sort of headset and not quite on his ears. This was Steve, who shared the attic. He was a jolly and portly fellow with a mangy beard that hadn't seen a razor since his mother's third wedding last year.

"Can I help you?" asked Steve politely.

"I'd like to see Zach," said Billy earnestly.

The man didn't look like a salesman. He seemed to know Zach, so Steve said, "Come on in, I'll get him for you."

For a large unathletic-looking guy, Steve surprised Billy when he bounded up the stairs two at a time. He almost looked like a dancer. This caused Billy to grin, despite his nerves. He was glad the boy didn't ask him his name. He thought it would be better to surprise his son this time. He knew that what he was doing was somewhat disrespectful. The boy had said he didn't want to see him. Billy had offered dozens of times. If Zach threw him out this time, he'd let him be, but he had to try just once to face him. He needed to be eye to eye to apologize and ask forgiveness. He needed his son to see his face. He wanted to let him know that he loved him.

In a few minutes, a pair of socks emerged on the top of the stairs. Socks gave way to sweatpants, which gave way to a T-shirt filled with the manly form of his little boy. A lot can go through a person's mind in one second, and Billy had time to be amazed that his little boy was so old-looking. He felt full of pride at the handsome man in front of him, who was now stalled on the third step from the bottom.

For his part, Zach could not have been more stunned. His very first impulse was to run back upstairs. His second impulse was to charge the old man, but something in the posture and expression of Billy Stone made him hesitate and choose option three, stunned silence.

"Hello boy," said Billy in a tone that was both kind and settled.

Zach slowly covered the last three steps and stood on level ground with his father. He did this because he didn't want to. Everything in him told him to stay above the man. In truth, Zach was a little taller than his dad. Zach was a fury of thoughts and feelings. He always thought that if he saw Billy, he would see a mean-looking villain. He imagined a washed-up drunk who yelled. He had heard from his sister that his father didn't drink anymore, but he refused to see him cleaned up in his mind. But the reality before him was unsettling. Zach was not able to say what he always thought he'd say. He was not able to do what he always wanted to do, which was kick the man's ass. What did he feel like? He kept searching his emotional memories, and he had to go back farther than he ever liked to. The fact was, he felt a twisted pride in this man, this son-of-a-bitch, which was the most confusing thing Zach had ever experienced.

"W-what the hell?" was all Zach could manage. He looked into the man's eyes and said a novel's worth with only his look.

Billy understood. He was patient. "What do you want to say, son?"

The kindness in his voice unnerved Zach, and he exploded. "What the hell are you doing here? Who told you could come to my house!"

"I'm sorry, son."

"Stop calling me 'son'! Who said you could call me that?" Zach was out of control. Steve came halfway down the stairs, "Is everything OK?"

"It's fine!" said Zach, lying. Then to his father, "Get out!"

"Ok, son…Zach. I'll go, but I had to see you, just once. I had to let you know…"

"Shut up! Get out, you old man!"

"I'm going. But I love you, and I wanted to say I'm sorry for not being there."

"You son-of-bitch! You have no right!" Zach moved toward his father. He felt the only way to keep from embracing the man would be to kill him, which he might do.

"All right, Zach. I'm going. But I'm asking one thing, that you could forgive me. You have a right to hate me, but it's no good for you. I love you, and I want to make things right."

Zach lunged forward and pushed his dad, who let him. Zach muscled past him and opened the door. "Get out or I will throw you out."

Billy looked at his son, risking a few extra seconds to memorize all the details of the face of this boy who his heart ached for. This gave Zach a minute longer to load up the next verbal assault.

"You asshole. I'll never forgive you for what you did to us, leaving us like that, for what you did to mom. She never got over it."

Billy knew that Zach thought his mom was an angel. He knew that Zach did not know that his mother had lied to him all those years about Billy. Zach did not know how Billy begged to come home to them. He did not know that his hatred for the man had been masterfully crafted by his mother. Zach never saw the letters that came, hundreds of them, letters for Zach.

And now that she was dead and not here to answer for it, Billy was not the kind of man to bring it up. No matter what she had done to sever the relationship between the kids and their dad, it did not change the fact that she did it because Billy had hurt her deeply all the years before his conversion. He deserved what he'd gotten. He did not deserve the love of his boy, but he needed it, wanted it, and knew that it was the very thing, short of being saved, that his boy needed above all else.

"Zach, I know I was a bad man. You need to know that I'm sorry for it, and I regret it. I have regretted it every day of my life for twenty years. I'm sorry. You and your sister did not deserve that. I can see that there is no way for me to make it up to you, and I will accept that. I will not try to see you again, but if you *ever* feel like you want to have any kind of relationship, or if you ever need me for anything at all. Call me. I will stop whatever I'm doing, wherever I am, to come to you. I pray for you every day…"

This was too much for Zach. He could not stand and hold on to the warring emotions and thoughts going on. "Just go." He went on autopilot. He'd feel later. For now, he had to get this man out of his house without assaulting him.

Billy looked into the eyes of his son and willed

him to accept his love and affection. After a last look, he turned and walked out, not looking back until he was in his truck.

Zach sat on the couch, weak from having every circuit blown. He did not know if he would recover. Right here in this moment, what needed to happen was a cathartic release. He needed to weep and wail. He didn't. He took great pains to hold on to feelings of hatred. He imagined his dying mother and her pain. It was Billy's fault. He had killed her. Whatever part of Zach was beginning to doubt that fact was overruled and repressed. He did not cry. He did not rage. He called Hazel Grace and left a message. Then, at 10:30 in the morning, he got drunk and stayed drunk for the rest of the day.

Zach had insisted on seeing her. It was the day after Billy had come to his house and two weeks after their date to the zoo with Lucy. Zach was still somewhat hung over. But he had showered and shaved and now was sitting in front of her at the same cafe where they had first met. Hazel Grace could tell this meeting was not about the book. She had been growing more and more fond of him, so she wasn't sure what this sense of dread was that she was feeling. Zach was staring at his coffee and didn't seem to be finding the words.

"Hazel Grace…". He hesitated. "I really don't think I can keep going without telling you that I have feelings for you. What I mean is…I'm quite sure I love you."

Hazel Grace knew that she must have gone white because she felt suddenly like she might pass out.

Zach said, "I never noticed you had freckles."

"You can't see them unless I'm about to faint." Hazel Grace was a mix of emotions. On the one hand, this was not unwelcomed or unexpected. She did like Zach a lot. She even loved him. But on the other hand, how could she love him, and how could he love her. They still barely knew each other. There was something about this that was not right. It was too intense. Why suddenly come on so strong? Oh, but she did want this.

Zach, for however inept he was at picking up girls in bars, was master at reading this kind of situation. He saw in her eyes that he had an "in." This created a confidence and knocked away the awkwardness that he'd begun with. This was the thing that possessed him in these situations. He was madly in love and could see that it was reciprocated. Everything in him wanted to be with this woman. He truly, with all his heart and soul, believed that they should be together forever. He genuinely believed that he could slay any dragon, climb any mountain, or swim any ocean.

This thing that possessed him blinded him to a simple fact. The fact was that Hazel Grace was in an extremely precarious situation here. Her heart was getting ready to plunge into an abyss of a romance with this broken boy. It was powerful. It is not that there weren't voices screaming in her head from way far away that something was off. But for the moment, she was desperate to ignore them. Here she was with her toes over the edge of a cliff. She never wanted anything so much as to jump, to fall to whatever was at the bottom calling to her. She said, "Zach, what makes you think that you are in love with me? You barely know me."

Zach had the capacity to fall in love with a stranger. She did not know what she was dealing with here. A Zach, fresh off the storm of the confrontation with his hated father, and then the total denial of feelings, is a force of nature. He would have this woman. In his mind, the only thing that could end his pain was for her to say, "Yes." He wanted it like a starving man before a feast. He was all charm and intensity now, and caution was blowing in the wind somewhere far away from here.

"Hazel Grace, when you know, you know. I love you. I know that I can't live without you. I never stop thinking about you."

"Zach, I…I don't know what to say. I do like you. Maybe I love you. I want to be with you, but…"

"But what?" he asked.

"But something just…"

"Hazel! I *worship* you!" The look in his eyes had a desperation that, along with his words, snapped her out of the spell she was under. Did she want Zach to worship her? She knew that he couldn't have meant it seriously, but the words reminded her of what mattered most to her.

"Zach, if you worship me, it will never work."

Zach was thoroughly unable to understand. "What are you saying? I know you want this. I can tell that you feel the same about me as I do about you."

"Yeah, Zach, I do. But…there is something more important than feelings."

"What, Hazel? What's more important than love?" he protested.

"God is!" Why had she been trying not to say that? Hazel suspected that it would crush him but that if he knew she was rejecting him because of God, then he might never want to know Him.

She thought back to the conversation she had recently with her mother. She asked her, "Won't it drive him away from God if I reject him because of God?" But Sarah was wise and confirmed what Hazel Grace had already worked out. She responded, "Sweetheart, it is a harder but better witness for you to give him up because of your faith, then to let him see that you will compromise for a romance. If you absolutely love Zach, and I can see that you do, then the only way for you to witness to him, would be to hold to your faith and values. Pray that God would use you doing the right thing to turn his heart."

"I'm afraid it'll do the opposite," said Hazel Grace, defeated.

"It probably will in the short run, but you have to trust God with that."

Her grandma, who was with them that day, added, "What did your Grandpa always say, honey?"

"I don't know." She said, frustrated. Her grandpa said a lot of wise things, and Hazel could not call up the right one.

"If you don't stand firm in your faith, you will not stand at all!"

Now at this moment with Zach, the words came flooding back. As she silently prayed for God's help, she

.elt His strength. This was the right thing, but it was torture. The truth was that if Zach had not been so out of his mind, she would have had a more difficult time of it, but something was dark about the way he was coming after her. She felt…compassion, and trepidation.

She put her hands around his and said, "Zach, I cannot be with a nonbeliever. I feel my heart breaking at the idea of us not being together, but I love you too much to go and compromise on what is true. Feelings are not the most important thing, and sometimes they can wreck us." Hazel Grace knew that this reserve of spiritual power was limited and that if she did not make a hasty exit, she would give in. Everything in her wanted to stay with Zach and comfort him, but the absolute best part of her compelled her to leave.

"I'm going now, Zach. Let's talk later." She began to gather up her things and put on her jacket. Zach stood up, stunned and speechless.

They walked outside. When they reached Hazel Grace's car, he said, "Why? Please…" Zach was stupefied. He had rarely experienced this. He had never turned this treatment on a woman who could resist it. His obsession when it came on him was powerful. Hazel Grace couldn't believe that she had been able to withstand it. He hugged her, and she let him.

It was nearly enough to break her. Her face was so close to his she could feel his breath. She was holding hers and praying. It was yet another feat of spiritual significance that she broke away from him. She got into her car after nearly fainting and drove away with what little reserves of strength she had left. If she had looked back, she'd have seen him rush to his truck. He had an impulse to follow her, but he didn't. Instead, he wept. In the glove box was a bottle of bourbon. He took a large swig before starting the truck.

By the time he got to the liquor store for a refill, he could barely drive. As he stumbled out of his truck, leaving the door open, the voice of an old man said, "Whoa there, son. Let me help you."

Before Zach could focus on the familiar face making those words, the world went dark.

Billy had not been trying to follow Zach. It was sheer fate, or more accurately, God, that Billy happened to be going to Tally's Cafe for lunch at the same time Zach got into his truck. When he saw him take out the bottle, he decided to follow his son. Now he was helping Steve to get Zach up the stairs to his room. When they were back downstairs, Steve said, "I'll make sure to let him know you were here and you helped him."

"I would ask you not to do that, Steve," said Billy.

"Ok, but why?" Having a great relationship with his own father, Steve was truly puzzled. Billy did not say that Zach would be embarrassed and upset and that it would make things worse between them.

"I just would appreciate it if you didn't."

"What if he asks how he got here?" asked Steve.

"That's a good point. I'll buy you lunch if you'll go back to the diner to help me bring his truck back. I've got the keys right here."

Steve was such a good-natured guy, and he was truly delighted both at the prospect of a free lunch and getting to spend some more time with this cool old man. They went back to the liquor store and the truck, and then back to the diner where they spent a good hour talking about Steve's life and becoming buddies. After they were done, they exchanged numbers, and Steve drove Zach's truck home.

Billy had been going to leave that week, but he decided to hang around Tulsa a little longer.

A month had gone by since Hazel had last seen Zach. She had not even heard from him and hadn't gotten any new installments of the book either. She suspected he wasn't working on it. As messy as things had gotten it would have been way worse if she had given in to him. Though it came to mind a lot, she couldn't say she regretted her decision, and she was thankful for the grace of God to resist. But she did miss him a lot! She knew he was a good man, and if things were different, she could be happy with him. She had nearly broken down and contacted him a dozen times.

The office manager at the firm was back from taking care of her daughter and grandbaby, but her dad kept her on. There was plenty of work to do, and this gave her some time to figure out what was next. She'd probably try to get a teaching job in the fall. Graduate school could wait a while, and she wasn't quite sure what to study anyway. Today she was having lunch with her father.

"Thanks for giving up the billable hours for a lunch date," said Hazel Grace, grinning.

"Oh, I'm billing you. I'll take it out of your check," said Russell, deadpan.

"Are you going to make me pay for lunch too?"

"We'll see. How are you doing?" Russell knew

that his daughter was struggling. He was not worried about her. She had a wisdom and a maturity that would keep her as stable as anyone could be, but he knew she was in a good deal of pain, and he hated it.

"I'm ok." She lied.

"I know you did a hard thing. It was right."

"Thanks for saying that, Dad." Hazel Grace meant it. There had been so much second-guessing that she needed her father's encouragement. "I'm sure you didn't like him anyway."

"That's not true," protested her dad, "I liked him a lot. I was tempted to go meet with him."

"No way! I'm glad you didn't," said Hazel Grace. "I figured he didn't pass the 'good relationship with his father test' and was hopeless to win your approval."

"True. But after getting to know him, I had compassion for him, and I can see he has a lot of potential and is a good man despite those issues." Russell was warming up for something he wanted to say. "How would you feel about going on a blind date?"

"Dad!" Hazel Grace was horrified. At this moment, the suggestion made her admit that she still had strong feelings for the ghostwriter.

"I know, honey, but I've prayed a lot about it. I do think you'll like this young lawyer."

Hazel Grace looked at her dad for a good long time. *What the heck*…if her dad thought this could be good, maybe she should try it. "Ok…there is nothing I want less to do, but why not?"

The restaurant was too nice. Everything was brand new but was supposed to look old and established. The waitress was a little out of place; pierced, tattooed, friendly, and efficient. They drank their ice waters from nice glasses with short stems, and Hazel Grace was buttering some bread. The bread was good, but cold, as though it had only just come from the refrigerator, but the butter was soft and warm. It was going awkwardly.

Lawyer Shawn was a junior associate in a Tulsa law firm where his father was a partner. He was beautiful. Hazel Grace noticed, however, that the expression in his eyes did not vary much. He was built like a gymnast who also ran distance races. His chin, perfect; nose, also perfect. So why was she not into him? It wasn't just that she was still thinking about Zach Stone. Although she was, he did not seem real. How could someone so beautiful also be so unattractive? Under the surface of his face, there was something going on. His eyes told her that he was not consciously aware of it. She didn't like him. He was nice, but she was already thinking of how to get out of there without giving him her number.

"Your father says you are a teacher," said the lawyer, politely.

"Not quite. I have a teaching degree."

"What subject?"

"Elementary Education," she said, "with an emphasis in English." This was hard. "Did you major in pre-law in undergrad?" She was trying.

"Yes."

There was a pause. When Hazel Grace realized there was nothing else coming, she said, "Oh, cool." She began to butter another piece of bread that she really didn't want. Mercifully, the waitress came back. Hazel Grace asked her about her tattoos. This had the effect of killing some of the time, but also of delaying getting their order in, so as far as time killers, it was a net neutral. They struggled to make small talk. The worst part was that lawyer Shawn did not seem to realize there was anything awkward. Hazel Grace was dying. She would need to coach her dad on how to pick a blind date for her. She suspected he knew she wouldn't like him and that it was secretly fine with Russell.

When the date was finally over, the lawyer did not ask for her number. Despite herself, Hazel Grace was offended, but this she was laughing about by the time she was buckling the seatbelt of her car. *Hazel Grace, you are a mess.* As she drove home, she wondered what Zach was doing.

Zach had been sober all day. His plan was to make serious progress on *Wilbur*, as he liked to call it, but he was staring at a screen and daydreaming. He had written a few lines that he knew he would probably rewrite, but now he was totally stuck. It wasn't that he had writer's block. He didn't. He knew exactly what he wanted to write next. But there was no motivation to write. There was no motivation to shower, or eat, or even drink. Zach went back to bed.

He woke up two hours later and laid in his bed, thinking. He had made such an ass out of himself when he'd last seen Hazel Grace. He had not communicated with her since. That was six weeks ago. His plan was to finish the book, deliver it, and move on with life. He was stuck on phase one of the plan, and it should have been the easiest part. Delivering the book wouldn't be too hard, except it would be the end of the "relationship" with Hazel Grace, not that he held out any hope of anything with her. Moving on with life would be the hardest part. He had avoided thinking of it up to now.

What would he do? He'd gotten no more inquiries to ghostwriting since he'd started the project, and he wasn't in any frame of mind to write his own book. Maybe he should rearrange things. Maybe he should move phase three in front of phase one.

Zach stayed in bed and thought about it. Then he fell asleep again. When he awoke, he texted his friend Brad in New York. The job was still his if he wanted it. As it turned out, the decision was made for him by the college kid. Zach was two months late on rent and had to be out by the end of the week. The kid had another guy waiting to take Zach's half of the attic bedroom, so Zach had to go. Zach had no hard feelings and thought the college kid would be rich someday.

That evening Steve entered through the front door and found Zach on the couch, still oddly sober and watching a movie. Steve looked a little bit guilty, and Zach asked, "What've you been up to, Steve?" The fact was that it was unusual for Steve to leave the house. He was a programmer, a gamer, and his social life was online.

Steve paused a moment too long and said, "I was at a Bible study."

Zach was genuinely surprised at this. "Seriously? Why?"

"I've just been interested in God lately,"

answered Steve.

"Ok." Zach couldn't tell if Steve was wanting to talk more about it or if he was trying to change the subject. "Are you going to church or something?"

"Not exactly," said Steve, vaguely.

Steve was not forthcoming, so Zach didn't pry any further, although he could tell there was something that Steve wasn't telling him. If he had known the truth, he would have been perplexed and furious. Steve had been out with Billy. It was a weekly thing that Steve and Billy would get coffee and talk about the Bible. Steve didn't think Zach would like it, but he did want to try to find a way to help Billy reconcile with Zach.

"Zach, I've been thinking about your dad." Zach went on alert. "What happened that you hate him so much?"

Zach looked at Steve long and hard. Did they really know each other well enough to go there? Zach felt oddly tempted to open up to the stranger he'd been living with for two years, but he didn't. He wasn't in the mood to get drunk, and if he had to access this part of his brain, he would have to get drunk. "Steve," he said, "Sometimes it is better not to look under the hood. If the car is running fine, why jinx it?"

Steve knowingly said, "Is the car running fine? I

heard you got kicked out."

"The car is more than fine. I've taken a great job in New York." What he did not say is, *I've allowed my hopes and dreams to be crushed. I'm giving up the two things I want most in life, to be a writer and to be with a girl in Collinsville.*

"That's great." Steve's voice did not sound like he thought it was great. For one, he liked his roommate. The other thing was that he had begun to pray that Zach and Billy could reconcile and have a relationship, and this seemed less likely with Zach across the country. But the very worst part for Steve, is that he knew Billy would not stay in Tulsa if Zach left. *Oh well,* he thought. *It is what it is.* Steve would be fine. God had a hold of him, and he would start going to church. He also had a loving family and solid relationship with his own dad.

Steve could see it was not the time to press Zach on Billy. Instead, he said, "Well dude, you've been a decent roommate, even if you did quit paying rent."

Smiling, "Thanks man. You too."

One week later, Zach was in New York. After dropping off his two suitcases full of everything he owned at Brad's house, he sold his truck for way too little. This gave him some cash to get to the first big city paycheck. Walking down Broadway through the hustle and bustle, Zach did an admirable job of kidding himself.

This was going to be great. He did not miss Hazel Grace, and he did not care that he was publishing other authors and that he was done with writing. Something in him did feel genuinely positive about this new phase of life he was entering. That something was false optimism, and it lasted only twenty-four hours.

Chapter 10

Zach was staying on Brad's couch until he could get his own place, which would be no problem in a month. Brad was back in his room, getting ready for the night. Brad went to clubs at least five nights a week. Zach wasn't sure, but he had a strong suspicion that Brad ran on illegal drugs. He was a machine, and even for a young man, his pace was not natural. Zach went out with him when he'd first arrived a week ago, but since then, he hadn't had the desire to join in again. Tonight, Brad was pressing pretty hard. "Come on, man. I'm meeting those twins from personnel, and they are bringing some friends. Even I can't handle all of them."

"Man, I really need to finish this book, so I can close a chapter of my life."

"You need to finish a chapter so you can finish a chapter?" Brad cracked himself up.

"Yeah," said Zach, "Something like that, only it's about ten chapters I need to finish."

"Well, you can do that tomorrow."

"Dude, you know I don't have anything to wear

to the fancy clubs you go to." It was true. Zach still dressed like he was unemployed and from the country.

"I told you, man, just wear something of mine." Brad and Zach were nearly the exact same size. Zach was an inch taller than Brad, but Brad had weirdly long legs and a short torso. This meant that Zach and Brad wore the same inseam.

"Nah, I'm going to stay here and pound out some words."

Brad looked at him hard, then gave up, but not before writing down an address for Zach. "If you change your mind, meet us here." He handed him the slip of paper which read, "Club 23," and the address. Zach looked at it and tossed it on the couch.

"I will. Have a good time."

"Don't wait up for me." Brad grabbed up his keys, phone, and wallet and exited the apartment.

"Looks like it's just you and me," said Zach to his old frenemy, his laptop. This old friend had gotten him through his last year of college, two years of grad school, and had ghostwritten a half a dozen books, but it had utterly abandoned Zach when it came to his own attempts to write novels. Zach had a teacher at U of I who said he should try handwriting his books. Zach tried it but didn't like it. If he was going to write, it would be on this machine. But now, he couldn't even seem to finish *Wilbur*. He had all the information he needed. He had the story. He just couldn't get the motivation to start typing. He knew all he had to do was start.

He couldn't remember who said it, but somebody successful said just write two crappy pages a day. It was good advice and had helped him in the past. But something was stopping him. What was it? Zach didn't know it, but the reason, buried so deep in him that Sigmund Freud wouldn't be able to find it, was that he did not want to finish *Wilbur*. If he finished, that was the end of his association with Wilbur Lee's lovely granddaughter. But this was not information that was accessible to his conscious mind at this time.

He stared at the screen. He checked his email. Work stuff. He stared at the screen some more. He checked the news. The world was falling to pieces, *still*. He stared at the screen. He checked Facebook. That was as depressing as always. He scrolled through pictures of Hazel Grace and her family, but there was not much new there. Hazel Grace did not seem to curate her life for public consumption the way most people did. He went back to the doc and stared at the screen. He stared, and stared, and stared.

Then he looked next to him on the couch. Where

was that slip of paper? A quick exploration of the couch cushions yielded results. Thirty minutes later, he was in the subway, washed, and looking like a city boy in Brad's best club outfit.

"Billy, I do not want you to leave!" Steve knew he had no chance to stop Billy. With Zach gone to New York, Billy needed to get back home.

"I know, man, but you need to come to see me in Springfield. You need to meet John and Ern. They're good men, like you, just starting out in their faith but serious about it. Steve had carried Billy's bag outside for him and was putting it in the passenger side of the truck.

"I will," promised Steve. "I've got some time off in a couple of months. Plus, with my job, I can work from anywhere." The two men had just finished an all-you-can-eat pancake challenge at a diner next to Billy's motel.

Billy's stomach was impressively flat, usually, but this morning it was full of pancakes and bacon, and he patted it gingerly. "I'll be lucky if I can stay awake with this food in me. I won't need to stop for lunch, and maybe not even dinner!" The men laughed.

"Well, you know I'm a hugger," said Steve, just before embracing his mentor.

"Ha, ha, that's ok, son." Billy hugged him right back. "You take care of yourself. Call me anytime and come see me." He got into his truck and turned the key. Steve shut him in and backed away. Billy had taken him to a church on Sunday and he already had a coffee date set up with one of the pastors. As Billy drove away, he thought, *that boy will be just fine. He's a good dude.* And he prayed for Steve as he headed down the road.

Seven or eight hours later, worn out and still not hungry, Billy pulled up to the house in Springfield, IL. There were three cars there. He had been looking forward to seeing John and Ern, and he wondered who else was there. He got out of his truck, and the door slamming caused the head of John to poke through the curtain and then disappear, reappearing on the body charging out the front door to meet him, kicking up the dirt of the gravel driveway all the way to the old man.

"Billy!" He hugged him, and Billy could feel the impact on the pancakes not fully digested. Two more bodies came out the door behind him. The first was Ern, more reserved than John. Billy was glad to see the man still here and still sober. When he had left, he wasn't totally confident that Ern was ready.

"Ern! How's life been treating you?"

"Good, Billy. John's been keeping it real." Ern looked peaceful and happy. Billy could see that the two men had bonded beautifully in his absence.

"And who's this?" Billy moved toward the third man out the door.

John made the introductions, "Billy, meet Joe Thomas." Joe was a fifty-something black man, and Billy liked and trusted him on sight. This was no small thing, as Billy knew people.

"Joe Thomas, it is good to meet you."

"Good to meet you too," said the man, looking straight into Billy's eyes.

"Joe's been sober for a week." John and Ern had been doing well. They studied the Bible together, they prayed together, and then, a couple of weeks ago, they decided to continue Billy's liquor store ministry without him. For the first week, they only sat in the parking lot and prayed. They tried speaking to a woman who they knew must have been drunk, but she misread the situation and screamed for help. They were forced to leave the premises by the management, and they never found out if she got back into her car.

They changed liquor stores, and finally, a week ago, they had their chance when Joe rode up swerving on his bicycle. The rest was history, and now Joe was a roommate, as long as it was ok with Billy. It was ok with Billy. The men went inside and force-fed their mentor as they all caught up. They were sad for their friend when they heard that he had not had success with his boy, but they finished the night by praying for Zach Stone before they all retired for the night.

It had been a week since Zach joined Brad at the club. They had gone out every night since. Two things had changed. The first thing was that Zach was now in his own city clothes, having received his first paycheck, more generous than he had expected. The second change was that Zach had managed to master the art of talking to women. In fact, he was doing more than talking. He simply could not believe it had taken him this long to learn how easy it was. His old friend Kevin had been right. As soon as you don't care about rejection, you stop getting rejected.

Zach did not care about rejection. In fact, Zach did not care about anything. He drank all the time, but it wasn't that he was drunk all the time. He wasn't. He was simply on another planet. New York Zach was determined about two things. First, he was going to be someone different. He was not going to be the failed writer. He was not a writer. He was a businessman, a publisher, a networker. He was fearless, and he didn't care what anybody thought about it.

The second thing was that he was not going to think. He was only going to act. If he was hungry, he'd eat. If he was thirsty, he'd drink. Why didn't he want to think? He didn't know why, but he liked the results. The reality is that thinking was too painful. Giving up writing was hard, but then living life around writers was torture, or at least it would have been torture if he would let himself think. But Zach, the writer, had to stay dead, and the only way for him to stay dead was for Zach, the publisher, and party animal, to feed his appetites on autopilot.

Zach and Brad did not just go to clubs. They also went to parties. These parties were full of glamorous people and easy women for the new Zach. By the second night of this routine, Zach did not even try to learn the names of the women that he was going to take home. Names were not important. His name was not important, so why should theirs be? Along with running from his writing dreams, Zach could not have admitted that he was also running from Hazel Grace. The life he was living was not only designed to keep him from stopping to think, but it was also designed to make him the opposite of the man who fell in love with the Christian country girl, and the man who the Christian country girl both fell in love with and rejected. This was much better. No feelings, no pain.

Two more months went by in a blur. When he did stop to think about that, he could not decide if it flew by or if it seemed like he'd been in New York for a lifetime. If his old life did come back to haunt him, it felt to him like it had happened to another person or in a movie he had seen about some loser. Occasionally, when he was a certain level of drunk, it would all come back to him, and then he wanted to murder his old self. This he did, in his mind, many times. At first, he just simply imagined himself killing the fatherless bumpkin, wannabe author, the Okie. He stabbed him, shot him, hung him, and threw him off a bridge, off a cliff, off a building. He ran him over with a car. But the bastard wouldn't stay dead.

The next tactic was to ignore him. To drink, to party, to have sex with strangers. This eventually did work. He fed into his new personality by doing the opposite of whatever the Okie would have done. If the Okie would have been nice, Zach, who now went only by "Zachary," would be rude. If the Okie would learn a girl's name, New York Zachary didn't want to know it and called every girl he met by the same name "Sally." The girls at the clubs and parties he frequented, for some reason, didn't mind. Occasionally one would really seem to like him. He made sure never to see them again.

Across the country, Hazel Grace Jackson was trying to move on as well. She was not one to kid herself, so when she went on a couple of dates with a young teacher from a school where she was subbing, and she found herself thinking of Zach, she decided to let the man down easy and wait awhile before dating anyone else. This did not mean she wasn't moving on, but she was not moving on by denying reality or ignoring what was inside her. She knew that the experience with Zach had left her a little messed up. She knew it would take some time but that God would get her through it, and she also knew that it would not be fair of her to keep trying to forget him by going out with other guys who wouldn't have a chance until she was over him. So, she stopped dating. "I think it sounds wise," said her mom. "You'll know when the time is right."

"Yeah, I know." Hazel Grace picked at her biscuit, which was still a favorite comfort food. Normally she would want six of them but eat two. Today, she didn't have much of an appetite. It was a warmer than average March day and she was killing time before a 10:30 am tee-time with her dad, who had been taking advantage of the golf lessons Hazel Grace and Jillian had gotten him for Christmas. He bet her a cheeseburger at the clubhouse that he could beat her this time.

She was so glad to have the family that she had. They were the most solid thing she knew of in this world, and she found herself thanking God for the millionth time for putting her in such a family.

"Have you heard from Zach?" Hazel Grace knew that her mom had two motives for the question. The first was her genuine concern for her daughter's heart. She did not want to see her end up with the boy, and she was secretly glad that he was out of the state and unreachable. But the first motive conflicted some with the second because the second motive was that she also wanted to see the book finished and did not want Hazel Grace to be taken advantage of. Her daughter had paid the advance in good faith, and it wasn't right that the book had not been completed.

"No."

"Have you tried calling him?" Asked her mother.

"No."

"Don't you think you should? I mean a deal's a deal," said Mom.

"I know, but I'm not ready to talk to him, and from what I can tell, he is not the same person right now." Hazel Grace had been a little surprised by the changes she'd seen on Facebook, and that hadn't shown the half of it.

"Do you want dad to call him? He can lawyer him and make him finish."

"No! I mean, I've thought of that. Maybe down the road, but, no, I don't want dad to get involved." She knew Russell would call Zach in a heartbeat if she wanted him to. She truly had no idea what to do. She just knew, at least she thought she knew, what *not* to do. She would continue to wait and trust God.

For the next month or so, Hazel continued with life. She was applying for graduate schools. She was surprised at how many times her mind drifted into the possibility of school in New York. She always put it out of her mind, but why couldn't she forget the boy? She wasn't just sitting around. She was volunteering at church, substitute teaching at five schools, golfing with her dad, shopping with her sister, hanging out with friends and family, all the good stuff of life. She read books, saw plays in Tulsa, and cooked and knitted with her grandma and aunts. She had a full life. But still, Zach.

One perfect spring day, after a long walk around her neighborhood, smelling flowers, enjoying breezes, and listening to birds, she was in a certain mood. All the conditions were perfect, and when she got back to her phone, she dialed a number she had wanted to dial for a long time but had so far refrained. It was a Tulsa area code, but the phone on the other end was in New York. Somehow on the walk, she had made the decision that God would just have to use her love for Zach to save him. She knew she was rationalizing, but in this moment, she just didn't care. She would throw caution to the wind. She called Zach's number. It was disconnected. Zach had gotten a New York number, and he had not given it to her. Well, that was that.

Zach, or Zachary, was at the home of one of the more successful authors published by their firm. He noticed that he hated all the successful authors, no matter how pleasant they were. He didn't wonder why he felt that way, but he didn't try to stop the feelings either. Zachary avoided all feelings except that one. That one seemed safe. He was on the upstairs balcony with a group gathered around the author, who was holding court when he saw *her*. It was the second time he'd laid eyes on her. The first time was at another party, and she was on the arm of a well-known billionaire. Zach thought he'd seen her on a magazine cover, and he was right. She was that supermodel, Katya Radaslovav, whose face everyone knew without knowing they knew it.

The billionaire was missing tonight. Zachary was not aware that the billionaire was married and that Katya was not attached to him permanently. Zachary approached her. He was not the same Zach Stone from Tulsa who couldn't talk to women in bars. He had changed. He had become a man who knows there are lots of fish in the sea. He had willed himself with iron force to see women as faces only. They were all the same, he thought. Though it was partially true of the girls he ran around with, it was primarily a lie that he had force-fed himself. But this woman was testing his ideology in this regard. She was perfect. She was tall, but not as tall as him, elegant as though she were from another planet where they had mastered DNA and genetics and only produced perfect specimens. Zachary thought he was looking at a goddess, a statue in an expensive art gallery. She was putting a cigarette to her lips but was not bothering to look for a light, knowing it would be there.

Zachary was the first to her side with a lighter, and he pretended not to notice the first and second runners up who were already moving along in their disappointment. It took every ounce of will for Zach to maintain "Zachary." He kept his cool. She said in a charming accent, "You are Zachary Stone."

"Umm, yes. Who are you? I know your face, but not your name." Zachary knew he was taking a risk. He should have known her name, but she seemed un-phased.

"My name is Katya." She took in a deep draft of smoke and blew it to the side, never taking her eyes off Zachary.

"It is a pleasure to meet you. Are you having fun here?" Zachary was beginning to waver. He simply could not seem to get his cool persona up and running on all eight cylinders.

This woman was miles out of his league, or so he thought, until she said, "Where do you live?" Zachary felt a wave of relief that he had moved off Brad's couch into his own apartment three days prior.

"I live in the East Village," said Zachary, trying

to appear more confident than he was.

"Let's go there," said the woman, and that was how their relationship started. Zachary always wondered and never found out why this happened. He had done nothing to win her. He had not been especially smooth. In fact, there was no reason she should have gone home with him that he could think of. But just like that, she was living with him.

Katya Radaslovav had emigrated from Romania three years prior, full of potential, a blank canvas. She had been contracted immediately by the first modeling agency she had wandered into, who used her and abused her. The man who owned the agency was not good to her, and she learned early on that she would have to compromise to get along in New York. But when he suggested that she let him pimp her out for money, she walked out. She had learned about men, and she had learned her own powers. She continued her modeling career at a more reputable agency and soon was a top performer in the business.

Now she was making plenty of money, but her secret was that she sent nearly all of it home. The fact was that she had a younger sister back in Romania who was not able to secure the permission to come to America and would never be able to make the kind of money that Katya made. Katya paid all her expenses. That was why she used men to pay her own. She was in her prime and had a long list of potential patrons. Zachary could not understand what made her pick him. Even if he realized that she was using him, he knew that she could have her pick of the richest men in town. But there were some things he did not know. First, Katya had had her fill of powerful men. They were not kind. What she saw in Zachary through the act he was putting on was kindness and potential. In fact, she could have loved him, but that was not an option for her.

Her first goal in the relationship was to survive. She didn't mind if they had fun, which they did. But she was never going to let this man or any other truly know her. Zachary Stone didn't really care. It would sometimes trouble him that this woman would seem so distant, so unknowable, but since it suited his purposes of not thinking about anything real, he went with it. Katya seemed to enjoy her new hobby, which was to further build this man into the New York mover and shaker type. She took him shopping, sometimes using some of her own precious money, but usually using his, and completed his transformation. Zachary Stone was truly a part in a show of some kind.

They also drank a lot, and Katya did a lot of

drugs. They went out every night and became popular fixtures at the biggest parties. Katya opened a whole new social world to Zachary, plunging him further and further into his made-up life. Though Zachary made what he had considered a boatload of money, he now began to see it as paltry, compared to the circles to which he was now admitted. He tried not to think of the debt he was racking up on credit cards. Any fourth grader with a calculator could see that he would be bankrupt within the year.

The closer he came to awareness of this fact, the more he began to fear the consequences. Chief among them was that he had no illusions that his girlfriend would stay with him if he ran out of money. He knew he was in an arrangement, and he had vowed to himself not to think much about it. He was mostly having fun, but it was requiring more and more work to ignore some of the realities, and it was taking a lot of booze and distraction to hold back the creeping self-hatred that always returned to ruin his fun. He had tried to find some sense of identity and esteem from his new life and this goddess who gave him the time of day. Sure, she was using him, but he rationalized, she could use anyone, and she had chosen him, right? Or did that just mean he was chump? No, he didn't think so, mostly because he was having a good time playing this role.

As time went by, Katya suddenly and strangely began to get nasty. She was ruder and ruder to Zachary. Zachary was becoming more and more dependent upon her. He had arrived at the point in the relationship when he normally should have been walking away from her, but her power over him was like black magic. He was starting to even hate her, but he could not stomach the thought of losing her either. On top of that, his body was starting to give way, and his job performance was suffering. This pace had him on a collision course with disaster, and it was only a matter of time before a crash. He knew it. He saw it coming. He was helpless to do anything about it.

It was worse than that. He didn't want to stop it. Zachary…Zach Stone had become somewhat nihilistic. The fact was that for a long time now, he had given up on real life. This attempt to bury his true self in this new persona, this mask, was just the latest. The more he realized this wasn't the answer, the more he didn't care if he lived or died.

Mercifully, before he was bankrupt, and before he was fired, and before his body gave out, and before he did something worse to himself than he was already doing, something happened. Katya, who deep down still had some love in her heart, kept alive by love for her baby sister in Romania, developed a conscience concerning him. She'd been increasingly rude because she was determined not to fall in love, but now there was a sliver of humanity, a tiny crack in her own false persona. For whatever reason, one day she woke up next to the boy she had been living on for six months, and she felt compassion for him. He was truly kind to her. She had been careful not to love him, and she did not intend to love him, but she found she had no stomach to see him hurt. In a few moments, she decided. She got up, she got dressed, she packed her things, and she left. Zachary, exhausted and hung over, never stirred once from his sleep.

Chapter 11

Hazel Grace had not tried to find Zach's new number. She also had avoided getting on social media because she knew that was a way to find him. Though she had never called him in the last year, she had desperately wanted to. It would not have been hard to get in touch with him. She knew the firm he worked for. She still had his email address. She was friends with him on two different media platforms. It was nine months since she'd seen him, but her feelings had grown for him. Had they really? Or was she just in love with an idea? Had she made him up at this point to be something that he never had been? No, she thought, it was that she knew what he really was, what he was capable of being. It did not seem like that was what he was becoming. She knew she must forget him and move on.

Hazel Grace had been on three dates with yet another man from church. This time was a little different, though. She liked him. He was tall, handsome, and he seemed to love the Lord. She enjoyed being with him. He was a structural engineer in Tulsa, something about concrete, and he couldn't be any more different than Zach. This was a thought for which she scolded herself every time it popped into her head, especially when she was with him. His name was Jason.

Her parents like him, but by now, they had learned not to get attached to any of these guys. Still, this one seemed a little different, and Hazel Grace seemed to be trying to make it work. Only Grandma seemed to know that it was hopeless. This she kept to herself until Sarah asked her mother directly.

"Hazel has a broken heart. You can't get into a relationship with a broken heart," said Grandma as she kneaded her bread. They were in her kitchen.

"Mom, haven't you ever heard of a rebound? Sometimes those work out."

"Hazel Grace is a different sort of person. She's too honest and too kindhearted to use a man. I may be wrong, but until she gets over that ghostwriter, you won't see a love connection." Both women had mixed feelings about Zach. Despite themselves, the whole family liked him. No one thought it would be good for Hazel Grace to be with him, but there was no ill will towards him, even from Russell. After all, hadn't Hazel Grace broken his heart first? Still, they didn't like to see her hurting.

Hazel Grace sat on the couch watching the game

with Jason at his house. Like her, he was a hardcore OU fan. This should have been another point of connection between them, but it only made her think of Zach. He would have been rooting for West Virginia in this game simply because they were playing OU. She smiled as she thought of it.

"What are you smiling at, cutie?" *Oh no*, thought Hazel. She felt she was betraying him in his own house.

"Oh, I'm just having fun with you," she lied.

"I'm having fun too. Do you want me to make some more popcorn?"

"Sure. I would eat some." Hazel watched Jason going into the kitchen. He really was perfect. She did like him a lot. Didn't she? He came back five minutes later with a full bowl.

"No butter?" Asked Hazel, incredulous.

"Nah, I'm training," answered Jason.

"For what?" Hazel was curious.

"Nothing in particular. I just think it's a good idea to be prepared to be useful." He said this with a matter-of-fact tone in which he said everything. And then, "Come on, ref, gimme a freakin break!"

"That was quite a turn," said Hazel Grace.

"Huh? Oh, yeah, sorry, I meant to tell you that I

really get into sports. Now that football season is back on, you'll see my true colors."

"I get it. I can be the same way." Hazel tried to focus on the game. Being an OU football fan herself, she should have enjoyed this connection. Her mind began to wander. Soon, she was lost in her imagination and drifting through the pages of *Wilbur*.

"What are you thinking about?" asked Jason. He was not at all suspicious, but Hazel Grace felt guilty. She had reread Zach's account of Wilbur and Connie falling in love, and she was thinking about what a romantic heart he had. Now that she was brought to earth, the thought gave her some pain.

"Oh, nothing. I must stop at the store on the way home. I was just thinking of what I need to get." She lied again.

"Oh, you want me to go with you?" offered Jason.

"No, that's ok. I'm pretty tired, and I think I want to get going." Hazel Grace knew that she should stay a while if she was really trying to like this guy. She had planned to let him kiss her tonight, but now she was praying that he would not try. He was a gentleman, and he did not try.

She promised to see him again in three days and

left. She decided to stop at the store so she wouldn't have been lying. She didn't have anything to get, but she grabbed some ice cream and thought she could go see Grandma. When she got home, she could see that her Grandma's light was out, so she went in her house and ate the ice cream alone. When she was finished, she sat at the table for thirty minutes, and then opened her mother's laptop and logged in to her email account.

Dear Zach…

Zach was in a weird spot. Katya had left a week ago. She finally did send him a text after she'd been gone two days. It simply said, "Zach, I've left. I don't want to be with you anymore. Thanks for everything. God bless you."

God bless you? What the hell? Zach would never know if there was any real meaning behind the words for Katya. God was certainly not someone who had ever come up before in their relationship. But it had the effect of making him think about Hazel Grace. Here he just got left by the woman he was cohabitating with, and he was thinking about Hazel Grace? He drove that out of his mind. He called Brad.

He had hardly seen Brad throughout the whole blur of time he'd been with Katya, except for when they were at the office. Though Zachary had disgracefully abandoned his former circle, he had now fallen back into his life, pre-Katya. This meant that he was still partying, still living fast, but not spending the kind of money he was spending before. This was fast-paced but manageable.

One other thing had changed. He didn't really have a desire to pick up girls. He thought of Katya some, but he thought of Hazel Grace even more. That's why, a week after Katya left, Zach sat in front of his laptop in turmoil. He read the email again.

Dear Zach,

I hope this email finds you well. I hope that you are enjoying your life in New York. I don't know why I am writing you, but it's late, and I'm thinking about you. I probably won't send this. I hope I won't, but if you're reading this, I must have. I've wanted to contact you a thousand times. Once I even tried to call you, but your number had been disconnected. I am dating someone. It is not serious, but it should be. The reason it is not is because I think I love you, and I think I made a mistake not being with you when you told me you loved me. I thought it was the right thing, but the fact is that I regret it. I don't know what would have happened, but I'd like to find out. You probably have forgotten all about me, but I just wanted you to know that I have not forgotten about you. I don't know what I'm trying to say, but I do know that I would be happy if you still loved me. I would come to NY and see you. But if you don't feel the same, that's totally fine. I would understand.

With Love,

Hazel Grace

Zach was stunned. For the last week, his real self, the Okie from Tulsa, the failed writer, had been dogging his steps. This email was a major blow to his project to change his life and become someone new. Here was a crossroads. What did he want? He wanted to get on a plane and go fulfill a long-denied desire. So why didn't he? He read and reread the email. He went to the kitchen and poured a gin. "Zachary" did not drink beer.

He drank the glass down and poured another, and then one more. He sat down to respond to the woman that he loved with his whole being.

Dear Hazel Grace,

Thanks for the email. It's nice to hear from you. But I don't want you to contact me ever again. I'm sorry I did not finish the book. I'll send you back your money in the next couple of weeks when I get paid again.

Take care,

Zachary Stone

That was that. Once he sent her the money back, he could move the hell on. Now, how could he numb the pain? He downed the last glass of gin, grabbed his keys, wallet, phone and jacket, texting Brad on the way out the door.

What have I done? Hazel Grace was just stirring when she remembered her email from the night before. She groped around the nightstand for her phone and opened her email. Her heart skipped a beat, and she sat up and threw the phone down on the bed. *I need to pray.* Then out loud, she said, "Lord, maybe that was a dumb thing I did last night, but I did it. But now, Father, I want to say that if this is not your will, let him reject me, but if it is," she prayed, breathlessly, "If it is, Lord, please make it work. Please save him. Please, just…I just pray that your will would be done and that I could accept it. I'm sorry if I did something stupid last night, and I'm sorry for anything else stupid that I might do."

She bravely picked up the phone and read the email.

Billy had been home for several months. He was delighted to see John, Ern, and Joe all growing in the faith. The men had gotten involved with a small local church where Billy attended and was good friends with the pastor. John, gifted for business when he wasn't drinking or squashed under the thumb of his mother, had taken the first steps to start a nonprofit ministry organization to help people quit drinking and using substances while teaching them about Jesus. He had explained it to Billy when he first returned from Tulsa.

"It's like AA, but the "higher power" is always Jesus. Also, I think the twelve steps are powerful, but there is something that doesn't sit right with me about the idea that you have to always for the rest of your life identify as an alcoholic. That doesn't seem biblical to me."

Billy had had the same thoughts. He'd seen many set free with help from AA, but his own experience was that when Jesus washed him clean, he washed him clean. It wasn't that Billy could no longer be tempted, but he found it more helpful to focus on believing what God said about him now: he is a new creation in Christ. It is no longer Billy that lived, but Christ lived in him and through him.

"I agree with you, John. I do love the prayer they

pray, though," said Billy.

"Me too, and I'm keeping it. 'Lord, give me the strength to change what I can, to accept what I can't, and the wisdom to know the difference.' At least, that's basically how it goes," said John. He was excited, and Billy was too. The three men, John, Ern, and Joe, were planning to start small and do just what they had been doing, but they hoped to expand it.

So many well-meaning people start nonprofits with big dreams and go too big right out of the gate. Billy had advised them to think of it like Jesus said to think about life, from the perspective of stewardship. "You remember when Jesus said God was like a man who had some servants, and he gave them each a certain amount of money to do business with? Each man was expected to make the very most of what he'd been given, and then the master would give them more to manage."

"I think I see what you're saying," John had said, "But how do I know where to start and when to expand?"

"You'll know," promised Billy. "Just walk along with him and don't go gettin ahead of him."

"When am I going to get my first talents to manage?" asked John rhetorically.

"John, you've already gotten them, and you have

been passing the tests."

"When?" John was genuinely confused.

"When you first heard about Jesus after you came to my house. He saved you, didn't he?" asked Billy.

"Well, sure, but that was all him," protested John.

"Right, and the fact that you believe that is a great sign. But it is equally true that you had to do your part. You had to use your will to accept him. Then, you had to use your will to quit drinking."

John was getting up tight. "That was all him too, Billy!"

"True, absolutely true. And you should thank him for it. You should pray that he keeps leading you that way, but you gotta hold on to the paradox."

"You mean how the Bible teaches that God saves who he wants, and we have free will?" John was aware that the Bible taught these things equally. Trying to figure it out made him feel like he was drinking again. "I feel too dumb to understand that one."

"No, John, the fact is it can only be understood spiritually, and then it can only be accepted," Billy said. "Back to stewardship then. You received an invitation, and you "managed it" or "stewarded it" well by accepting. You were commanded by God to lay down the drink, and you obeyed. You managed well. Then you were given the opportunity to help Ern and Joe while at the same time facing the test of maintaining your new faith and sobriety even though I was leaving the house for a while. That was a talent, a mina, and you managed it well. Now, it would seem that God is saying to take another step, to manage another talent. So many people try to do something for God without being able to do the very basics of taking care of their own self, their own souls. You're doing great, by God's grace, and you just have to keep walking in the same way."

"How will I know if I've arrived where I'm supposed to be?" Asked John sincerely.

"John, if you are walking with Christ, you don't even need a grand vision. Wherever you are is where you are supposed to be. Period," said Billy.

"What about you, Billy? Where are you supposed to be? Do you want to help us?" This question was a good one, thought Billy.

"Now that you ask, I think I need to come to terms with the fact that I am probably supposed to be in New York City." Though John knew that Billy's son was in New York, he had trouble imagining Billy Stone as a New Yorker.

"How long will you go for?" Asked John.

"As long as it takes, I guess. I'm going to pray about it, though. It didn't go so well for him and me in Tulsa. I want to make sure I'm not the one trying to run ahead of God."

Later that night, Billy went to bed praying for his boy and asking God for direction. The next morning, he packed up his truck, prayed with and said goodbye to the men in his house, and turned his old pickup truck eastward. He had no idea how, but he felt full of faith that God was up to something this time. He was not giving up on Zach. That was settled. He'd go where Zach was as long as there was breath in him. He would not give up, just like God never gave up on him.

Nine hours later, the country station he was listening to in the truck played a song that took him back in time to another worksite. It wasn't the song itself but the era of that song and others like it that gave him a powerful feeling of being transported to that happy time of his honeymoon with God. It was a happy time, but it was also brutally difficult in other ways. He returned home to find his wife and children were gone, and he had realized his wife was lying to the kids and keeping them from him. He had gone to see his friend and mentor, Wilbur, a practice that he would keep up for the rest of Wilbur's life.

"Wilbur, it just isn't fair," said Billy in their first meeting after Billy's conversion.

"I know it, Billy," said Wilbur, "but you can trust God. Just pray and keep holding to Jesus. He has a plan!" Wilbur was compassionate, but he was confident that God was up to something good in this situation.

"But why now? Why did God do this?" Billy was facing an important moment, and Wilbur, always a shepherd after God's own heart, was sensitive to it.

"Billy," he said gently, "You have to start with the whole truth. God is not the one that did this. Your wife made a choice, and before that, you made the choices you made that led to this." Billy had his powerful hand on the shoulder of his friend to steady his body and his soul.

"I know, Wilbur, but I just thought that now that I follow God, he would…"

"Take care of you?" Interrupted Wilbur.

"Yes."

"Billy, he is taking care of you. You could have been going through this without him, but you are going through it with him. He is going through it with you. You are not alone. Even if you didn't have me, you wouldn't be alone." Wilbur was preaching now. He loved his new friend, and he prayed for God to give him the right

236

words as he spoke. "Do you think Jesus was close to God?"

"Of course," said Billy, "He was his Son."

"That's right, and yet Jesus didn't have an easy life, but it was the one God had marked out for him, and you and I have to walk out our life with God too. It won't always be easy. Jesus told his disciples as much. He said, 'In this world, you will have trouble." Wilbur let it sink in.

Billy thought about that for a minute. New as he was in the faith, he had not been tempted to think that he'd be rid of all his trouble this side of heaven.

Wilbur continued, "But then the next thing Jesus said was, 'take heart, I have overcome the world.' Billy, I don't know how God is going to work it out, and I don't know when, but I know he has a plan in all this. He always has a plan."

Billy had been encouraged, and he went away and trusted God. He never gave up trying to convince his wife to let him come back. He never married again, even after the divorce was final because he always considered himself to be married. He wanted to go to her in the hospital, but she had refused to allow him. The hatred for him in her heart never went away, even on her deathbed. It was truly tragic. Billy thanked God that he had been able to reconcile with his precious daughter shortly after that, and he prayed once again for his boy that this would be the time that God would bring them together.

As his thoughts drifted in and out memories, he saw an exit for the last rest stop before New York City, and he pulled over. By tomorrow he'd be a New Yorker, for how long, only God knew, and he would trust him like he had been trusting him for years.

Chapter 12

It wasn't that Hazel Grace didn't still have love in her heart for Zach, but mercifully, she was over him, fairly. She had moved on. Mostly. The week before, she had realized that there was a whole day when Zach had not entered her mind. This was progress, and Hazel Grace wished for more such days. As for the book, she had pretty much given up on it. Off and on, she had considered writing it herself but had thus far made no progress towards that end. One afternoon, she was talking to her mother about it.

"Don't you want to try to get your money back?" Hazel Grace could see that this bothered Sarah a lot.

"No. I'd rather just chalk it up to an expensive lesson learned," said Hazel Grace.

Jillian, who was nearby, chimed in, "Yes, a life lesson that everyone must go through so that for the rest of their days they won't hire a ghostwriter to write about their deceased grandfather, only to fall in love with the writer, but be unable to be with him because he's not a

Christian. It's one of those pitfalls everyone falls into at some point and has to learn about the hard way. Now you are wise!" Jillian had an advanced sense of humor for a girl her age.

Despite herself, Hazel Grace laughed. Their mother gave "the look" to Jillian, who pretended not to notice. The truth was that Jillian did feel compassion for her sister and had enough social awareness to know that her humor would be appreciated and wouldn't be hurtful. She also had liked the ghostwriter and had rooted for him all along.

"I think I'm going to go over to Grandma's after lunch and help her clean out Grandpa's office," said Hazel Grace.

"Oh good," said mom. "I was afraid she wouldn't have the heart."

"No, she said it was time and that she wanted to donate a lot of his things. I'll probably stay and eat with her."

"Ok, dear. Let me know if you decide not to. I'll make enough for you either way," said mom.

Later that day, Hazel Grace was in her grandfather's office. It was virtually unchanged, though it had been more than a year since he passed away. Grandma had gotten her started but made the excuse that she was tired and needed to lay down. Hazel Grace thought that she had been doing a great job going through stuff but knew that it must be taking an emotional toll on her. She kept working and thought she might be able to take care of a lot of it before her grandma woke up. She had the dog, Dodge, to help, but he was mostly moral support.

"What do you think, Dodge? Keep or throw away? Dodge didn't answer, but Hazel Grace kept up the game. "Donate? OK. Someone will love these." Hazel Grace held up a massive pile of neckties. Wilbur had apparently kept every tie he ever owned. "They might come back in style," he would always say. Plus, most were gifts and he just couldn't bear to get rid of them.

She found some John Deere suspenders, a bronze statue of a cowboy on a bucking bronco, an incredibly old silver dollar, five broken watches, his father Warren's dog tags from the army, a few photographs of his siblings, a box of western dime novels, and another box full of papers. She was sorely tempted to put off going through it, having already started to become decision fatigued, but she forced herself. *One more hour, Hazel Grace, then you can have a break.* Old mortgage papers, a welding certification, a union newsletter, and some sermon notes, were the first items she came across. The next thing she saw made her heart skip a beat. It was an envelope, and written on it were the words, "Wilbur, that's exactly how I remember it. Thanks, old friend, for the reminder of how faithful Jesus is to us. God bless you!" There were two pages inside numbered eighteen and nineteen, and it looked like it went with the sermon. Mystery solved!

Now she had the missing pages, and it made her think of Zach. Should she send them to him? She did not deliberate long but fired up her Grandpa's printer and made a copy. That afternoon she took a chance and mailed the originals to Zach's old Tulsa address, not having his new one and being afraid to ask him for it. She prayed that his old roommates would know where to forward his mail. If he didn't get it, she wouldn't worry about it. If he did, well…who knows?

Miraculously, two weeks later, Zach did receive the forwarded letter with the missing pages. While this was mildly intriguing to him, he quickly stashed them out of his sight, not wanting even to read them at this point. He couldn't bring himself to throw them away, but he was not ready to think about Hazel Grace or his promise to send her money back to her. He did need to send it, but he still didn't quite have it, having gone terribly into debt during his former experiment to change his life.

Now he wondered if he had dreamed it all. Was Katya for real? Did that part of his life really happen? It must have, but he already felt far removed from it.

Later that same week, Zach had to attend a party for work. This wasn't something he felt like doing. He had been going out less and less lately. The void in him that he had tried to fill with his New York lifestyle change and reinvention of himself had just about worn off. Now he was completely rudderless but still managed to get up and go to work in the morning. Was he back to his old self? Well, he was drinking beer again. What that meant, he had no idea.

When he arrived at the party, there were the usual people he knew from office. Brad was there but had moved himself more to the peripheral of Zach's life in the time with Katya and the jet set. Zach walked into the den of the house and noticed a senior colleague in the corner nursing her drink. Zach walked up to her and started a conversation. "Hey, Jennifer. How are you on this fine New York evening?"

"Just wonderful." She said this with a flat tone and an even flatter expression.

Zach respected the older woman and usually enjoyed her no-nonsense approach to the business. He asked, "Do you enjoy these parties?"

"Yes…no. Not really. Strangely enough, I think my husband has a better time at them." Zach looked across the room where she was pointing and saw Tom, Jennifer's second husband, an upper-middle manager at some investment bank. Zach had noticed before that Tom was always the life of the party. "How about you?" She asked him.

"Oh, yeah, I'm having a great time," he lied.

"You don't have to bullshit me, Stone. I know we're the same," she said.

"Yeah. What do you mean?" Zach was genuinely curious.

"I mean that, like me, you gave up your dream of being a writer to come to these damn parties and publish other writers."

"That's not true." Zach sounded more defensive than he had intended to.

"Isn't it?"

Zach looked at her a long time and then said, "You wanted to be a writer?"

"Hell, yes I did, but I didn't have the stomach for rejection."

"Did you ever write anything?" He asked.

"Three novels. I still think they are the great

American novel, but nobody else did."

"And you don't regret quitting to be an editor?" Asked Zach, hopefully.

"I didn't say that. If you would have asked me even five years ago, I'd have said I didn't regret it, and I'd have meant it, though I was delusional," she said.

"So, you regret it."

"Yes." Zach became quiet. Jennifer looked at him with wisdom in her expression and said, "It's not too late, Zach." She was a kindhearted woman, and she suddenly had the feeling that to save Zach from her fate would be like saving her own soul. It was as though it was penance for her own "sin" of denying herself at his age.

Zach thanked her and decided to move on. He did not like the feelings he was having as they spoke. Who was Jennifer anyway? He hardly knew her. He moved around the room, greeting acquaintances and being introduced to promising young authors. He noticed through an open door a den area where a crowd had gathered. Curious, he wandered in to find one of their more famous novelists pontificating on being a writer. He was quite spellbinding and held the crowd in rapt attention. Something about it gave Zach a repulsion, and he made a quick exit. Why he wondered, did he have such a reaction to the author? He had managed to work with authors every day since coming to New York, but now, he could hardly stand the sight of one of them. The more successful they were, the more he had to get away from them and get them out of his mind.

He needed to leave this party and take in a club somewhere. He needed to go drink and put on his "who cares about rejection" attitude and pick up a girl. He needed to put back on his persona and run from his feelings, or things would get ugly. These thoughts were beginning to bubble to the surface despite himself when he turned a corner and found another senior publisher coming out of a bathroom.

"Hey Zachary." The man was fifty, successful, and by all accounts happy. He married his college sweetheart and they had raised two happy children who had only just recently left the nest for good. Zach had heard someone congratulating him earlier in the year for a college graduation and an empty nest.

"Hey Rob." Like most people, Zach liked Rob. He was about to pass him by on his way to the front door when he stopped. "Rob!"

"Yeah?" Rob had taken a couple of steps and was now turning back.

"Did you ever want to be an author?"

"You mean like everyone else at the firm?" Asked Rob.

"I guess so." Zach already assumed the answer, but he was surprised when he was wrong.

"No. Never." Said Rob, as though he answered the question often.

"No bullshit?" Asked Zach.

"No bullshit. I never wanted to write. My great love is reading, and I found that I love the business side even more.

Zach looked at him as though he was seeing an alien. He assumed everyone at the company was just like him. "Do you think you may want to write when you retire?"

"Retire? I'm not ever going to retire. Anything that makes me retire would also leave me unable to write."

"You mean you'd have to be brain dead?" Zach went ahead and stated the obvious.

"Yeah. Why would I stop doing what I love? Plus, I'm Jewish. We don't retire. It's the secret of our happy life. You Christians think work is a chore you must do until you can get a weekend, a vacation, or a retirement village. We understand that work is part of what gives a man purpose."

Zach was thrown off by the comment. "What gave you the impression that I was a Christian?"

"Oh, you're not?" Rob seemed surprised.

"Hell no! Don't you see what I'm like?" Zach wondered at himself. Why was he feeling so defensive about this?

"You mean the way you go out every night partying, picking up girls, and drinking yourself silly?"

"Exactly," said Zach.

"That's a show. I don't know you well, Zachary, but you are too good-natured for that to be the real you. I can see that at a glance. I'm sorry if I offended you. I usually assume all Gentiles are Christians. My mistake."

Zach was a little shaken by the whole conversation, and he hastily said goodbye. When he left, he decided to walk the ten blocks home instead of taking a cab or the subway. He had planned to go to a club, but now he wasn't in the mood. First, what the hell was Rob talking about? Zach hated God. Second, Zach would need to think good and hard about the fact that Rob is not a failed writer and loves his job so much that he doesn't plan to retire. Who does that?

What nagged him the whole way home was the contrast between Rob and Jennifer. Jennifer clearly regretted her life and seemed to want to live vicariously through Zach. He knew that if she could do it all over again, she would continue to pursue writing and would not have settled for the publishing gig. It wasn't hard for him to see himself in the same spot in twenty or thirty years. And then there was Rob. The guy was in love with publishing. That did not compute on any level in Zach's mind. There was obviously a fundamental difference between Zach and Rob. Zach was more like Jennifer.

He walked and pondered, and when he arrived home, it was midnight. Still early in Zach's world. He sat down at the kitchen table with a glass of water. He was hungry, so he looked in the fridge and found leftover Chinese food. When did he eat that? It passed the smell test, and there was no fuzz on it, so he heated it up in the container it was in and sat back down to think some more. As he sat, his mind wandered to the envelope from Hazel Grace. He looked to the drawer where he had left it, staring long and hard. At one a.m., Zach opened the envelope. At one fifteen, he opened his laptop.

Wilbur Lee was getting ready to go. "Wilbur, I don't like it," said Connie. They had been married now 5 years, and Wilbur was finishing seminary, welding on construction sites, and God had lately directed him to an abandoned mining town. Like many such towns, the place had a sad sense of what once was. There was once a glory in the constant production of energy. Men moved there and brought their families with them full of the hope of making a living and raising a family. In short order, there was a school, three churches; Baptist, Methodist, and Church of Christ, a small hospital, three stores, two cafes, a baseball field, and a multitude of home hairdressers, handymen, bakers, butchers, and whatever else grew out of the needs of the thriving mining community.

And then one day, a man in overalls, a helmet with a light on it, and a face covered in black soot, indistinguishable from the rest, cut out the last lump of coal that would come from that mine. It wasn't even that there was no more coal. But government regulations, environmental laws, and other such things added up to the conclusion that the mining company would be better off shutting it down. Now the only thing left in the town was a gas station, a nursing home, and a trailer park, which for the moment, just so happened to be largely occupied by a group of Hell's Angels.

Wilbur had been ministering at the nursing home for a few weeks, since starting construction work at a nearby town. Connie was increasingly concerned for his safety, having seen firsthand the rowdiness of the biker gang as they passed by the trailer park on their way to the nursing home. "I don't like it at all," she repeated.

"Pretty Connie, don't you worry about me. You know the Lord wouldn't have directed me to go there if he didn't have a plan to keep me safe," he comforted her. "Don't you think that maybe God wants to get at those Hell's Angels? Why don't you pray for

a door to open in the trailer park?" Connie was nervous, but she knew better than to try to stop him. If he thought God had told him to do it, there was no one who could get in his way.

Wilbur drove to the nursing home and as he passed by the trailer park, as usual, he saw the bikers outside, a fire built in a metal trash barrel, and it looked like, though it was only 2pm, the bikers were well into a case of beer. Wilbur prayed for them as he passed, just as he always did. When he got to the nursing home, he was greeted by the administrator, who was always happy to see him. She was clearly a believer and had told Wilbur when he first arrived that he had been an answer to her prayers of the last three years. She loved the residents and ran a nice old folk's home, considering the sadness surrounding the rest of the town and what few citizens were left in it.

Staff were wheeling and walking the residents to the cafeteria for their church service and Wilbur was getting out his Bible and his notes for his sermon. He was going to preach the Gospel, and then visit with many of the residents before driving the fifty miles to his class in Old Testament prophets at seminary school. As he shuffled his pages around, he looked up in time to see a large viking of a man leaving the room of one of the residents. He was mostly bald on top, but the back of his hair went all the way to the Hells Angels devil's head patch on the back of his leather vest. The man did not turn around and look at Wilbur, but Wilbur thought he'd be able to recognize him again by the gray-

blonde hair.

Wilbur preached as though he was preaching the last sermon on earth. He always preached this way with a keen sense of eternity and the knowledge that any one of his hearers could be hearing their last sermon. But it was especially true in this place. It seemed every time he showed up, there was someone missing who had been alive and listening the week before. God had given him a terrible burden for these old minors and their hacking, wheezing black lungs. He had prayed with dozens of them in the last month to accept Jesus. He knew his time in this place was growing short, and he prayed that God would give these folks a revival in his time remaining.

After he preached his sermon, he led them in four or five hymns. It was a joy for him to see some of their faces light up with the songs of their childhood. He had a hard time stopping once he'd got going, especially if the nurse was there who could play the piano. Today they got through seven songs before the director came and said it was time for the residents to go back to their rooms. One thing that had been nagging at Wilbur the whole afternoon was that open door which the hairy biker had come. He noticed that the door was still open and that whoever was in there did not come out for "church." He decided he would start his visits today with the occupant of that room.

"Praise God! How are you today?" Wilbur came in ready. A man was in his bed and the television was on a soap opera

of some kind. The man did not look like he was paying much attention to it. He seemed to stare through the TV to something beyond it. His mouth hung slightly open, and he did not look at Wilbur. Wilbur sat down in the chair next to the man's bed. He said, "My name is Wilbur Tucker. I'm here to tell you about Jesus Christ." The man did not respond. "He loves you very much and he died for your sins. If you would believe in him, he will give you everlasting life." The man continued to stare through the television. Wilbur looked up and saw two actors sharing a passionate kiss. This seemed inappropriate for the situation so, with his eyes on the man, he reached up and pressed the "off" button.

The man did not flinch. He did not look away from the TV. But it was quiet now. Wilbur continued. "I'd like to pray for you, sir." No response. "Lord, I pray for my brother here. He has lived a long life, and maybe it was a hard life. I pray that you will give him comfort. I pray that if he doesn't know you yet, that you would reveal yourself to him and save his soul. I pray that he would wake up one day from this state that he is in." Wilbur paused for a minute, attempting to listen to the Holy Ghost's prompting and nudging. Then he continued, "Yes, Lord, I pray that you would, WAKE HIM UP!" The man blinked. Wilbur felt the power of God running through his own body and he took the risk of putting both hands on the man.

"Father Almighty! I know you love this man! I pray that his mind would come awake and he would get to talk to his son,

and they could say all the things they've never said to each other before!" Wilbur, of course, had no way to know whether the biker was the son of this catatonic man, but something made him sure that this was what he was to pray. He continued, "Lord Jesus! Fill this man with your Holy Spirit and heal his mind! Heal him and save him!"

"What the hell do you think you're doing? Who the hell are you?" The voice behind Wilbur was yelling and Wilbur didn't need to turn around to know that the biker was in the doorway. He paused, prayed for God's continued help, stood up full of the Holy Ghost, and turned around to face whatever was coming next.

The men locked eyes. Wilbur saw a demon looking at him. This emboldened Wilbur. At once, he felt courage from God and an infusion of love for this poor man in front of him. He had no way of knowing the circumstances, but he knew enough. Here was a son of a man whose mind was gone and for who knew how long. The son was a Hells Angel, so probably a rough character, and yet he seemed to care for his father. Most of the people that Wilbur saw in the nursing home never ever received a visitor. This man was now here for at least the second time that day. Wilbur looked at the anger in the man's eyes and felt nothing but compassion.

The man repeated his question, "What the hell are you doing in here?" Wilbur could see that he was used to intimidating people with his bullhorn of a voice and his gargantuan size.

Wilbur did not have it in him to be intimidated. He looked the man in the eyes and said, "I was just praying for your father."

"Who told you he was my father?" Said the man, incredulous.

"It was just a guess. I was praying for him. That God would save his soul. I was also praying with faith that Jesus would wake him up and he would be able to talk to you again."

This seemed to have the effect of angering the man further. "He doesn't need to wake up. The bastard never said anything nice to me my whole life. You need to get yer Bible and get the hell out of here before I throw you out on your ass. Don't think I won't stab a preacher."

"Calm down. I will leave, but I am going to be back, and I am going to continue to pray for your dad. If you think you need to beat me up, go right ahead, but Jesus loves you, and I want you to know that I pray for you too."

This was too much for the man, and a change seemed to come over his face. Cold anger turned to blind fury. Something in Wilbur made him stand still for it. The biker closed the distance in half a second. He got in Wilbur's face with the intent of intimidating the smaller man. Wilbur was ordinarily a brave man, but his comportment at this moment was nothing short of supernatural. Everything in his spirit told him to stand still and take whatever comes. The verse that came to his heart was Isaiah

53:7, "he is brought as a lamb to the slaughter, and as a sheep before her shearers is dumb, so he openeth not his mouth." By this, he reasoned that if his Lord could take what his abusers gave before hanging him on the cross to die for Wilbur, and this man and his father, then he could take whatever this "Hell's Angel" had to dish out.

The man was inches away from his face. Wilbur did not flinch even once. What the man saw was the eyes of an angel bearing into him. It incensed whatever spirit was lurking inside the man, and his fury was elevated to a fever pitch. Seeing that Wilbur was not intimidated, he slapped the preacher across the face. Wilbur's head involuntarily whipped to the side. When he slowly raised it back up, he had the same tranquil look of gentleness in his eyes. The biker was even more furious and out of the corner of his eye, Wilbur could see that his hand had now closed into a fist. Just as Wilbur was praying for strength to take what was coming, a voice behind him said, "I wouldn't do that, son."

Chapter 13

"It says here you've worked in Jersey, but never here in the city?" The foreman was looking over Billy's application, and he was impressed. He did wonder if the man was too old to work this kind of job. He didn't need to worry. Billy Stone was as fit as ever and had more energy than most men half his age.

"No, never in the Big Apple," said Billy.

"You don't look much like a New Yorker," said the man, who both looked and sounded like he was born there and had never left the city in his life. "New Yorker," was said without the sound of either of the "R's" in "Yorker." The man looked back and forth from Billy to his resume and seemed to make up his mind. He pointed to an I-beam on the ground and said, "Grab that torch and mask, and finish that weld."

Billy calmly walked over, put on the face shield and a pair of gloves, and fired up the welding torch. He picked up the part that had obviously been prepared for torching to the beam and expertly welded them together. It was not a complicated job, but the foreman was impressed with the cleanness of it and the speed at which it was done. Ordinarily, he would have had more tests for an applicant, but this alone with Billy's resume was enough to show the foreman that he was lucky to get the yokel for the job if his age didn't become a factor. He needn't have worried about that, but he didn't know it yet.

"Can you start tomorrow?" Asked the foreman.

"I can start today," said Billy.

"Let's just say tomorrow. Be here at 7 am sharp."

"You got it," said Billy, as he shook the man's hand.

Billy got back in his truck and had to decide between finding Zach's place and securing a place of his own. He could try to find a motel with weekly rates, but that would be pricey in the city. He decided to put it off for a little while and focused on finding Zach. Getting an address from Steve was easy, as the former roommate was tasked with forwarding all of Zach's mail. Billy didn't know it at first, but the address was for Brad's place. Steve had not been notified of Zach's move, and Zach had gotten no important mail in Tulsa for some time.

After finding Brad's place, Billy ordered three hotdogs from an outside vendor on Bowery and Prince and walked a block until he found a park. He sat on a bench to consider his living situation. He had pretty much decided he would need to pony up for a hotel tonight, and then he could find something else after work the next day.

As Billy ate and contemplated his situation, he watched the people. This area of the city was on the edge of the bad part and the ok part, so there were all kinds. There were young professionals walking their dogs. There was a playground where moms, dads, grandmas, and Grandpa's played with children. There were hundreds of men and women, heads down, moving from place to place as though they were on a mission. He was amazed at the number of people who seemed to be from other countries. He had counted twenty or twenty-five in the ten minutes since he'd sat down.

Billy had always assumed New Yorkers were rude, but it wasn't that. It was that they were busy, some were lonely, and all seem to be in a hurry. If he stopped any of them, they were polite. He wondered how many of these people were born here. This was a place where people came to fulfill some dream or other. Is that what Zach was doing? Billy doubted it.

There were certainly the homeless. Billy had offered one of his hotdogs to a man who turned it down. He was portly and said he was waiting for the Bowery boys to come out.

"Who is that?" Asked Billy.

"The guys from the mission." He pointed his thumb up Bowery Street. Billy would find out later that this was one of the oldest streets in Manhattan, having been named by the Dutch in the sixteen hundreds. The Dutch word "Bowery" means *farm*. Bowery was first a footpath that connected several farms and spanned the whole of the island.

The Bowery Mission is on Bowery and Prince and had stood there since 1870. The homeless man was referring to the practice of some of the more senior residents to come into the park every day, feed the homeless from some pot of stew or other, and preach the gospel. In this manner, Billy would learn, they found new recruits for the mission. The Bowery was a men's mission, and the typical stay for someone who completed the program was six to nine months. The rules were fair but strict. In order to stay, you had to keep the rules, but those who did, were well set up to make it when they left. Most of them departed with a deeper faith and some new job skills. They were also clean and sober, and maybe had a G.E.D., and some new hope. Of course, not everyone was a total success story, and at least half of those who went in came back out prematurely, unwilling to follow the rules.

Just as Billy was about to ask when they were coming out, he saw a gang of men pull up in a van. Several of them jumped out of the van with tables, bowls, spoons, pots, and loaves and loaves of bread. Almost on cue, there were at least fifty people who crowded around from all over the park. Billy wasn't sure where they all came from so suddenly. A large black mustached man held up his hands and said, "Jesus told the people to get into order. He made them sit down in rows on the grass before he fed them the loaves and fishes. Nobody eats until you line up!" He said this good-naturedly. The crowd seemed to be used to it and quickly complied.

People began to move through the line and were getting their food. Billy thought if he hadn't just eaten three hotdogs, he might get in line too. Once most people started eating, the large man began to preach. He told them about Jesus and the cross, and he told them his personal story, how he had been homeless in this very park when the mission came to feed him. He told them how he had gone back to the mission to get a bed on a cold night and how he had decided to check into the mission's program. He said he met the Lord, got a G.E.D., and learned how to build websites. Now, he said, God had called him to work at the mission. There was room for them, he said. He finished by encouraging them to come and live there and change their life.

After his speech, most people dispersed, but there were a handful of men who stayed around to talk to the men. They spoke for a while, and Billy noticed that they prayed for several people in the park. The large man prayed for a young white man with long stringy hair, shabby clothes, and a guitar on his back. Billy imagined the young man had come to the city to be a rock star, but reality had driven him to the streets. He probably was one of the many who played on a street corner for loose change. The man's meaty hand was on the boy's shoulder, and his other one was in the sky. Billy wondered if this was for show. He discerned that the large man was genuine, and he joined in prayer for this boy in his mind.

When the young man and one or two others were helping to load the van, Billy decided to approach the large man.

"Hey brother, I appreciate what you said. Name's Billy."

"Hey Billy, I'm Cliff." Besides being large, Cliff had a perfectly trimmed mustache, and Billy placed him somewhere in his forties. Cliff continued, "Do you know

Jesus?"

Billy smiled, "Quite well." The men talked for a bit. The van left, and Cliff said he'd walk back. Billy had a way of becoming friends with people in a noticeably short time. It helped that he had the most trustworthy face on the planet. The two men walked down the road and talked about the mission. An idea was coming into focus for Billy. Perhaps he could make himself useful to the mission and then could stay there while he was in New York.

When they arrived at the front doors, Cliff said, "Hey Billy, man, you need to meet Terrence." Terrence was one of the seven pastors who worked at the mission. Six out of the seven had congregations, but Terrence worked full time for the mission. He was young, late twenties, handsome, and looked like he could have been the leader of one of the street gangs, which in fact, he had been. Cliff introduced Billy to him, and they sat together for a while in Terrence's office, talking. By the end, there was a plan in place.

"Ok, we have a bed for you. You can do handyman work from 5-8 each night. At six, we have chapel and dinner." Terrence liked the old man in front of him. He had been praying for a competent handyman. Usually, at least one of the residents was skilled enough to fill the role, but not lately. The ancient building that housed the mission had constant needs, and many of them had not been attended to for months.

Billy said, "I can start right now." He knew he'd have plenty of time to find Zach later. For now, Billy was amazed at the whirlwind of a day he'd had. He had only just arrived in the city, and he already had a job, a place to stay, and a Christian community full of his "type" of guys. He thanked God as he settled his stuff in the locker by his bed. He told Terrence that he'd need to go find a place to stash his truck. After paying extortionist rates for a month in a parking garage, he was ready to face his first task, a leaky toilet on the second floor of the Bowery Mission.

It would be hard to determine who was more surprised, Wilbur or the biker. They both turned to the man in the bed, who, if he hadn't been sitting up, would have looked like he'd been dead for a week.

"Daddy?" The biker lost all the color in his face as he moved past Wilbur to his father. The men looked at each other for what seemed like forever. Wilbur stepped back to the side of the room. He knew he must be witnessing something miraculous. He

began praying for the men. "How are you awake?"

What Wilbur would find out later is that the old man who had once mined coal in the town had been one of the few to stay around when they closed the mine. He figured he owned his house, and he had enough money to live on if he did odd jobs for people. He'd already raised his kids, including the biker, who turned out to be the leader of the state's chapter of the Hells Angels, who had taken up residence in the town for one sole purpose, so their leader could bury his dad.

Wilbur would learn later that the men hadn't spoken in fifteen years. By the time Mike came back to town with his hooligan friends, his father was lost to dementia. They never even had a real conversation. Soon after his arrival, his father drifted into semiconscious and then total unconsciousness. The doc who visited the nursing home once per week assured Mike that he'd be burying his father before the year's end.

Mike came every day, sometimes twice, while the Hell Angels practically built a commune in the trailer park. Members of the gang came and went, but there was a solid core around Mike, who were in it for the duration. Now, Mike and his father were going to reconnect and perhaps, get some forgiveness and closure in their relationship. As far as Wilbur could see, the old man's mind had come fully alive. Wilbur decided to sneak out and give them their privacy. As he was leaving the building, Mike came out after him, "Preacher!" Wilbur turned. "You coming back?"

"I'll be back tomorrow," assured *Wilbur.*

"I'll see you tomorrow," said *Mike as he turned back toward his father's room.*

Zach took a break. He was beginning to write furiously. He woke up in the morning and wrote until he absolutely had to appear at the office. He took sick days. He stayed in on the weekends. He shunned going out at night. He was locked in and driven to finish the book. From Friday to Monday morning, he didn't shower, and he barely ate. He refused to let himself think about what he would do when he was finished, but he knew without a doubt that he would indeed finish. Would Hazel Grace still want the novel after all this time? Had he forfeited the rest of the pay? He didn't care one way or another. This book had taken on significance for him, and it would be completed. *Wilbur* would exist, even if no one on the planet ever read it. He would create that book. What he would do after he was finished could be decided later.

Wilbur was as good as his word to Mike, and he returned the next day. When he got to the room, there was a commotion, and he could tell at once that the old man had passed. Mike was there along with a woman, similarly, decked out, and he seemed to be keeping it together, but Wilbur recognized pain when he saw it. Before Wilbur was sure what he'd say, Mike spotted him and came over to him.

"Preacher, we gotta talk." The Viking had an earnest look in his eyes. Wilbur knew God was up to something.

"Let's talk," said Wilbur.

"Not right now. Can you come to my house later?"

The men made an appointment for six o'clock, and Wilbur made his rounds, praying for Mike and for whatever God had in mind for him.

At five minutes until six, Wilbur drove up on quite a scene. The bikers were roasting what was probably a pig in a big pit in the ground. They were partying. Wilbur didn't know if this was in celebration of Mike's father or if this was a daily occurrence. There were motorcycles everywhere, and when one started up, it was deafening. When several started up, it sounded like the apocalypse had begun. Wilbur noticed that there were no Yamahas, Kawasaki's, or anything else but Harley Davidsons. There must have been fifty of them. This was triple the usual. This would be a grand finale to their time in the sleepy ghost town. Wilbur asked a man who he found out later was a "hang around" where he could *find Mike.*

A "*hang around*" was someone in the first phase of membership. If a prospect made it through that phase, he could become an "*associate*" for a couple of years. Next, he was reclassified as a "*prospect,*" after which he could become a full-fledged member, a "*full patch,*" if all the members voted him in. Wilbur would ask later what all a person would have to do to get to that point, and he was told, kindly, by Mike that it was better not to ask. There were various patches and ranks and a good bit of secrecy. Some of them left and worked jobs in various places periodically, but others seemed to be making some kind of living off their participation in the Hells Angels Motorcycle Club. Once, Wilbur had the poor taste to point out to Mike that they had left the apostrophe out of the name and shouldn't be Hell's Angels? Mike simply said it was deliberate.

That was all later after Wilbur and Mike had become friends. Today, Wilbur, usually a picture of peace under pressure, was on edge walking through the "*commune.*"

"*Hey preacher, over here.*" Mike was standing on the back porch of a little house that backed up to a two-street trailer park. It was his father's house. He had his own fire going and he pointed Wilbur to a chair. When they sat down, he held up a bottle of beer to Wilbur, who turned it down, and then he fixed his eyes on Wilbur and asked, "*What happened? How did you do that?*"

Wilbur let a moment go by. "*I didn't do anything. The*

person you need to ask is God," said Wilbur calmly.

"I don't believe in God. How did you do that?"

Again, Wilbur waited and prayed. Then he said, "Your father was unconscious, I prayed for him to wake up. He woke up. This is all I know. You know as much as I do."

"I don't! I don't know sh…" Mike was surprised at himself that he did not want to cuss in front of this preacher. He had once laid hands on a door-to-door preacher who woke him from a nap to share his "testimony" with him. He usually thought preachers were the scum of the earth. "I don't know anything about what happened, but I do know I haven't talked to that man in fifteen years. I know he hasn't spoken an intelligible word in at least two years. Yet, you came, and then he sat up and had a four-hour conversation with me." He continued to look at Wilbur with great suspicion. "The doctor said what happened was simply not possible. He said, that it had to be a miracle. I have no place in my mind for something like that. I'm not able to believe it, and yet, I know it happened."

"Mike, I have rarely seen such a powerful work of God, and I have been doing this a long time. But I know that this would have just been a typical day for Jesus of Nazareth. Do you know why Jesus healed the sick, kicked out demons, and raised the dead, and walked on water?"

"If," said Mike with a great emphasis on the "if." "If Jesus was real, and if he really did those things, I don't know why.

Just to show off?"

Wilbur thought Mike was trying to be offensive, but Wilbur was not offended. In fact, he went with it. "That is exactly what he was doing. He was showing off. Why do you think he was doing that?"

"Same reason I would be, so people would worship him," answered Mike.

"Well, Mike, you're right again," said Wilbur.

"And how does that make him so great?" challenged Mike.

"Because he is God, and we should worship him. It was kind of him to give folks a reason to believe what he was saying about himself and about God." Wilbur would find out in due course that Mike was rather intellectual and more philosophical than he looked. He was genuinely taking in what Wilbur said, and seeing the logic. "Do you know why else he did miracles?" asked Wilbur.

"Why?"

"So that they would kill him." Wilbur looked straight at him to watch it sink in.

"You're saying that Jesus knew they would kill him, and he wanted them to? Asked Mike. A woman, Mike's woman, came outside and asked if they wanted anything. Mike looked at Wilbur, who shook his head. The woman went back inside.

Wilbur answered his question. "Yes, it was the main

reason he had come." He went on from there to explain that Jesus had come to die for the sins of the world.

"I know all about that," said Mike. My old man believed it, and he told me so yesterday."

Wilbur changed course. "Mike, you know that Jesus did all those miracles so they would know he was who he said he was."

"I know that's what you said," said Mike, but with less rancor than before.

"He does the same thing today sometimes, two thousand years later. He must love you, and he must want you pretty bad to show you something like that." Wilbur could feel the power of God running through him as he spoke of God's love, as he told Mike how to be forgiven. Wilbur rightly assumed that there was much to forgive there. What he couldn't have guessed was that Mike was more powerfully impacted by the four-hour conversation with his father than he was with the miracle. He had truly hated the man, and yet, he had felt compelled to move to the town to be there when he died and to bury him. His father had been a nightmare to him growing up, but he had found faith sometime after Mike had last seen him. Mike didn't know that his father had used the last of his mental faculty to pray that God would reconcile him to Mike, and that he would save his son.

Zach had to stop. This was not even part of the story in Wilbur's sermon about the biker gang and the Hells Angel who became a pastor. Why was Zach making up this story about a father and his son? Why did his books always go there? Zach looked at the screen. Always before, when this happened, it would be a quick delete, but this time, Zach left it.

But something even more troubling to him was that he seemed to be writing stuff in the book more and more about the gospel. He almost convinced himself he must believe it or something. No matter what, he had to admit it was having an impact on him, and Wilbur Lee was having an impact on him. He successfully drove it from his mind and continued the story. Mike "got saved," and Wilbur also performed a wedding between Mike and his lady friend, who was only about a day behind Mike accepting Christ. One part of the story that was true was that, after leading the biker to Jesus, Wilbur helped Mike, or whatever his real name was, become a pastor, and the two of them had quite a harvest among the Hells Angels before Wilbur and his family moved out of the area.

Zach was happy to be done with that portion of the book. He thought if he'd written much more, he might start believing all of it. Did he want to believe it? Yeah, actually, he did want to believe it. Would he? For some twisted reason, he sort of hoped not.

"Hey Billy! Say it again. Say, "hi guys.""

Billy complied, and it sounded like "Hah-ee, gah-ees." The two men in the clothing distribution room, Hopeton and Maxwell, burst out laughing again as they engaged joyfully in their new favorite pastime, making fun of the good-natured southerner and his thick accent. Billy was happy to play along. He had lived in the Midwest for long enough that he could speak just fine without his southern accent, but he enjoyed laying it on thick, and he really loved these men.

Thomas Hopeton was an incredibly loving African American man in his thirties. He had been in prison, and one would not believe that this man had robbed a store and stabbed a clerk. God had radically transformed him in prison before he got out and came to the Bowery Mission, and now that he was here, he had finished his G.E.D. and was now learning the skills to become a paralegal.

Deon Maxwell was around the same age, but he came off ten years older. He was also African American and had been educated and had started a family before drugs took him out of his family, took his teaching job, and landed him alone on the streets. He had been six months at the Bowery and the staff was putting him to good use as a teacher and tutor. Billy could see that, while Deon had cleaned himself up, he was still bitter and not ready to "do his business" with God yet. Deon and Hopeton took shifts overseeing the clothing distribution room and all the volunteers who came there to help. The Bowery accepted donations all day every day, and these men folded and sorted the men's' clothes. They also had regular times each day when men came by referral for a new wardrobe that always included some kind of professional outfit for a job interview. Some left with suits, and others left in business casual, depending on the job they were going for.

Billy enjoyed almost all the men he'd met and spent time with in the mission. He worked every day on the construction site from 4am to 2pm and spent the rest of the afternoon at the Bowery. When evening came, he taught a Bible study in the cafeteria just before going into the gym for the dinner devotional, where at least once a week, he preached. Someone preached to these poor souls every day, usually twice. At lunchtime, they fed the homeless who dropped by but did not live there. To eat, they had to be preached to. This was often one of the staff, who did not seem to prepare much for the occasion, but it was just as often that some guest speaker would be allowed in.

These sermons were usually painful to listen to, and they were all the same. An out of touch white man would stand up, maybe after his overdone-up wife with a karaoke machine would have led them in outdated worship songs, and he would tell them that God could get them off drugs, God could get them their family back, God could get them a job. The men would barely stay awake as they did their time, patiently waiting for food. The person would then do an altar call, and the same man would come get saved every day, giving encouragement for the preacher to go on to the next mission and do it again.

One day, Billy was sitting in the back of the room with his Bible when Terrence came in to preach the evening message. He saw Billy and stopped. "You want to do it?"

"Do what?"

"Preach."

"When?"

"Five minutes."

After a two-second pause, Billy said, "Okay." Five minutes later, he was preaching. And that is how he came to be a part of the regular rotation.

If only Billy could find Zach. Brad had moved,

and Billy had been unsuccessful at getting a forwarding address from the building superintendent. Zach's sister didn't know what firm Zach was working for and so she was no help to Billy either. In fact, Zach and his sister had not been on speaking terms for months after her latest attempt to get Zach to forgive his father. Billy knew that his construction job was going to end soon, as the part of the project he was working on would soon be finished. They liked his work and had promised to try to find something for him on their next project, but the construction business was slowing down in the latest economic downturn, and Billy wasn't so sure.

Zach was looking at his laptop and getting ready to start writing. Yesterday's session had shaken him up. He woke this morning thinking about…God. Yes, he had to admit it. It was beginning to bother him that there may be a God. He decided he would have to think about that later. He was ready to deal with the missing pages and finish this book. He opened them up and began to read them. As he read, something in the pit of his stomach began to move and he felt himself getting lightheaded before he understood why.

Zach continued to read the missing pages until he came to a part that said…

I went back to construction work, where I was ministering, sowing seeds, and touching different lives on every job. My job was not just a paycheck or a dirty, nasty job as it was often referred to, but a wonderful challenge to get a job done, do it well, make a difference and by all possible means win some believers.

I was working on a job in Louisiana in an oil refinery. There was a young man on the job that had a bad attitude. He was mad at the world, he cursed and complained with every breath. One day he walked up beside me cussing and complaining. I looked at him and said, "well, praise the Lord anyhow."

Zach continued to read. He read about the man who was hated by everyone, who got drunk every night, and who had decided one day to kill the singing preacher. Before Zach even finished the section, he knew. He stopped a moment and thought he remembered something. He went back to the counter where he had left the envelope and shuffled through some pages until he found it. It was a note on the back. It said, "Wilbur, that's exactly how I remember it. Thanks, old friend, for the reminder of how faithful Jesus is to us. Please keep praying that she will let me see my kids. God bless you! B."

Zach looked at the pages now across the room.

He knew somehow that if he read those pages, it would change everything. He started toward them and then stopped. He sat down on a chair and willed himself to stay put. He looked out the window at absolutely nothing and just waited. He waited for thirty minutes, trying not to look at the pages on which the sermon was typed. He thought of leaving the apartment. He thought of throwing away the pages. Why didn't he want to just read the damn thing? *Stop being a wuss!* He told himself.

He walked over in somewhat of a trance, picked up the pages, and then set them down again. It had been a while since he'd had any coffee. He should make some. He took his time making the coffee and had determined that he would read the pages when he had had a cup. But suddenly, before the coffee was done brewing, he got up, went back to the pages and began reading.

He read about the man who hated everybody, who had a wife and kids at home, and he hated them too. He read about his plans to kill Wilbur Lee Tucker, and he read about how he stopped. He read about the fan and the voice, "I have never given up on you, and I never will."

Time slowed down to a tenth of regular speed as Zach read what happened next. When he got to the part where Wilbur and the man, obviously Billy Stone, talked about how he would go home and be there for his wife and his kids, Zach threw the pages down and ran for the kitchen garbage can where he threw up. Why did he throw up? He didn't quite know, but his whole body was in turmoil, and his mind had not caught up with it yet. There was a note in Wilbur's hand at the bottom of the section that said simply, "Billy's wife left him, and to this day, though he begs and begs, she won't let him see his kids, and he thinks she is probably lying to them about him. Dear Lord, help my friend Billy. Reconcile him with his children. Your Word says,

'And he will turn

The hearts of the fathers to the children,

And the hearts of the children to their fathers,

Lest I come and strike the earth with a curse' —
Malachi 4:6

Zach read this again and then set the papers down on the table. Did he even want this to be true? He put on his shoes, grabbed his keys, and left his apartment, with all the lights on. He needed to walk. He didn't know where he'd go, but he would walk until he had sorted out some things. He exited the building with no plan but was compelled to go right for some reason.

At first, he just walked. He knew that by the time he got back, he needed to have some things sorted, but he was attempting to put off the work. He focused on noticing the scene around him. Near his apartment, the scenes and even some of the faces were familiar. The stores, the restaurants, the homeless guy who seemed to live on his block. He decided to jump on the subway. He had a desire to go to Central Park, and it was too far for him to walk from his place. As he sat on the train, he began to work it out. He started by admitting that the man in the sermon had to be Billy, his father. The way he was described is exactly what he'd always heard about him from his mother and grandmother.

But obviously, there was more to the story. What Zach had been trying not to see was that, if what it looked like is what it was, Billy had been saved when Zach was five years old. Furthermore, he had been trying to get to him for twenty years. Was it true that his mom had known this, but in her understandable bitterness, she had never been able to forgive him? Zach thought of all the horrible things his mother had said about his father; how he didn't want anything to do with him, how he was the devil, how you can't trust any man, because they are all evil.

Zach suddenly thought of his sister. In hindsight, this was what she was trying to tell Zach for a while, but Zach would get so angry and blow up on her when she brought Billy up. Where had all this hatred for his father come from? Well, obviously, it came from his mother. Zach began to feel emotion coming on more powerful than the train he was riding. Still three stops from the park, he decided to get off the train before he lost it.

Walking now, he continued to think about his mom. He admitted that she must have…just simply lied. But why? This was something that he would never know, but right now, in this moment, his saint of a mother lost all her veneer. He thought now about how many times he had felt resentment towards her, even still after her death, and how he had hated and berated himself for thinking ill of her. Had he always known she had screwed him up?

He thought about his failures with women. He thought of how desperately he needed to please women but then would only end up hating them until recently. He thought about growing up without a father. He had always considered himself lucky. Why? The truth was that the way his mother and even his grandmother talked about men, especially about Billy, had left Zach completely confused. Zach realized in this moment that a driving motivation all his life was to not be like other guys or like *any* guys. He could see now how this had left him screwed up, and he could see now at least some of the reason for the course his life had taken.

And now, he had to grapple with the thing that he still didn't want to deal with. He had always wanted his father. Only now could he admit that from an early age, he longed for his dad. Even before Billy's transformation, a three- and four-year-old Zach would cry when the man went away. He would cry for his dad. This must-have driven his mother to rage. This must-have fueled some of her ambition to teach her son to hate the man, all men. Zach remembered now how he would dream of his father's return. How long had Zach felt this way? Maybe it was a good long while? But at some point, maybe ten, maybe eleven years old, the transformation was complete, and he had no longer wanted his dad to come home. The man he had learned to hate wasn't even his father, but the monster that his mother had created in his mind.

But how about now? Could things be different? Could his mind shift after all these years? He walked endlessly. Wilbur and Billy were friends. Wilbur had obviously wanted to help Billy reconcile with Zach, and that's why Zach's name was written on Wilbur's sermon for Hazel Grace to find him. And Billy. Billy not only wasn't the bastard that his mother had always said he was, but he was actually a good guy who had been trying for years to reconcile with him.

As he walked, Zach's desire to find Billy and talk to him grew until he knew that he *must* see him. He knew he could get an address from his sister, but how he longed to see him now, at this moment. But could he? He had been such an ass to Billy the last time he saw him. Did Billy get mad and give up? Had Zach finally pushed him to quit? There was even a fear that Billy might die before Zach could find him.

As he walked, he became more and more anxious. He knew that there were forces at work that he could not explain. It was all too weird. He also knew that he was going to have to deal with the fact of God before all this was through. He walked faster and faster, but with nowhere to go. Finally, feeling desperate and needing to engage in some kind of action, he found a clearing in the park and threw himself down on his face, and he did something he had not done since he was a little boy, praying for his dad who would not come home. He prayed. He wept, and he cried out to God.

"Lord, I don't know what to think about any of this. I want…I don't know what I want. But I can't deny that you have been after me. I can't deny that things unexplainable have been happening to me. Maybe I'm crazy. Maybe I'm losing my mind. Lord, help me. I need you. I…I want…You!

Zach heard a song in his head, and he struggled to make it out. As it came into focus, he recognized the words, but not the tune, and then he realized the song was not in his head but was coming from somewhere in the park. It was faint, but those words! He sat up and looked around, but he couldn't see anything. He got up and followed the sound down the trail. After a few moments, he rounded the corner and there, on a rock was man with a guitar. He was singing familiar words.

Grandpa's Last Gift

Oh, when I think of my life down here
I dreamed of wealth and fame
I worked so hard to gain it all
Just finding guilt and shame
But then I met this friend of mine
Yes, Jesus is His name. He filled my heart
With joy divine, then He called me by His name

Oh, since I met this friend of mine
It's never been the same, I found what
I was looking for, yes, Jesus is his name
Now I'm walking in the light of God
I have His peace within, this very
Special friend of mine, yes, Jesus in his name

Now he's walking with me day-by-day
Along life's narrow way. Oh, I'm so glad
This friend of mine is showing me the way
If I could work a million years
I never could repay, the debt I owe
This friend of mine, yes Jesus is His name

Oh, since I met this friend of mine
It's never been the same. I found what
I was looking for, yes, Jesus is his name

Zach watched him a good long time in total shock. If this was not a sign, he didn't know what was. His inner turmoil was at a fever pitch. The part of him that did not want to believe there was a God or that his father was good was fighting for its life inside of him, raining down blows on the newer part, which was just coming awake. The reality he was coming to terms with was that Zach did want God. He did want Billy, and he did want…a girl in Oklahoma who had prayed for him all along and who had loved him enough to reject him when he was not ready.

The new part of Zach put its foot on the throat of the part that was resisting. He walked quickly to the man. "Where did you learn that song?" Zach's tone was nearly accusing.

The man looked up at Zach and held his gaze for a moment before answering, "I learned it on the job sight."

"From who?"

"A welder," said the man, as if that was enough.

"What is his name?" Zach was overly patient, prolonging the moment now.

"I think it's Willy, or Bill, or something. We just call him the hick. Hell of a good guy, though. Sings all the time."

"Could you tell me where the construction site is?"

"It's down on 60th. New high-rise development. You can't miss it."

"Thanks," said Zach and turned to leave, but stopped himself, went back, and threw a twenty into the guy's guitar case.

"Thanks, dude! God bless you!" And he started back in on "Jesus is His Name."

"I don't want you to go, Billy." Hopeton was crying as Billy, Cliff, Terence, Deon, and a few others were gathered around a table in the cafeteria. Terence had the guys in the kitchen bake a cake when Billy said it was going to be his last day.

"Why are you leaving?" Asked another nearby.

"I just feel like the Lord is saying my time is up here. I got a job in Tulsa for the next couple of months. I can go only so long without making money." Billy said all this with a touch of sadness in his voice. The truth was that he had loved his time here. Since being laid off, he'd spent almost all his time at the mission, and he knew he could be happy here for what was left of his life. But

Billy did not live his life simply doing what he wanted. He looked to do what God wanted, and the more he prayed about it, the more he felt compelled to head out. All he could say was that his time was coming to an end there.

"What about your boy?" Asked Cliff.

"I guess I just need to trust God with that one," said Billy.

"Dawg, that's messed up," protested Hopeton, "You came all the way out here, and you didn't even get to see him. Why would God do that?"

"God can do whatever he wants to, Hopeton. I have peace because I always do what he says, even when I don't understand or like it."

"How do you know what he says?" Asked another. "Is it a voice? A thought in your head?"

"If it's a thought or a voice, it's not in my head. It's in my gut, my bones, somewhere deep down. It's a voiceless voice. I only ever really 'heard' his voice once," said Billy.

"Was that when he spoke through the fan?" Asked Cliff.

"You got it. A long time ago. Since then, I have wanted to hear it again, but he hasn't spoken that way. He speaks through his Word, and he speaks to me through my gut and through my peace. And I have peace about going home, even if it means going empty-handed."

"But why did he send you here then?" Asked Deon.

"That's easy to meet you fellers." They all smiled in agreement.

"Isn't your boy from Tulsa? It seems unfair that you are going there when he is here," said Hopeton.

"God is always fair, Hope, and he's got a plan. He'll let me know what it is when he's good and ready."

"I'm looking for Billy Stone, he's a welder."

"I know Billy. But you're too late. His job ended last week." The same foreman who hired Billy now spoke to Zach.

"He told me he had a son here. You have *got* to be him," said the foreman. The only person who had ever told Zach that he looked like his father was his mother, and that was only if she was furious with him. Zach had tried to imagine what Billy looked like, and he then did everything he could to look different. But now, he felt a certain sense of pride in the foreman's words. *Wow*, he thought, *this is new.*

"Do you know where he lives?" Zach was feeling a little panicked now.

"No, I don't."

Zach was feeling despondent when another nearby said, "I think Chuck knows. He was saying he just went and saw him yesterday. Said they were having a Bible study at some mission on Prince Street."

"Where's Chuck?" Asked the foreman.

The man looked around and was about to give up when he saw who he was looking for. They called Chuck over and learned that Billy was staying at the Bowery.

"Saint, that guy is. Holy shit, are you his kid?" Chuck obviously knew some details.

"Where is the mission?"

"Crap, uh, I think Billy's gettin ready to move. He's got a job somewhere southwest. Crap! You gotta go there right now. You might be too late!"

Zach thanked the men and bolted to the subway. He'd learned that the Bowery Mission was on Bowery and Prince, and there was a stop right near there.

Riding the subway, he caught himself watching a

man with his young son. Zach started getting upset, and then faced the sudden revelation that, no, he did not need to be upset at this scene and other such scenes before him. Had he always gotten mad at the sight of someone being a good dad? It was amazing to him to realize that not only had this been the case, but it no longer needed to be. This was simply too much to think about right now. The subway reached the stop, and he exited with the crowd that had packed the train car.

Zach was only about two blocks from the corner of Prince and Bowery, and he found the mission right away. He barely hesitated before going in the front doors, which led to a small room with a check-in security desk. There was a woman standing there who meekly informed him that she was a volunteer and didn't really know anyone, since it was her first day at the mission. She rang for a staff member, and Terrence emerged from a doorway.

"What can I do for you?" Asked the man.

The volunteer offered, "This gentleman is looking for someone who lives here. What was his name?" She asked Zach.

"Billy Stone." Terrence lit up at the name.

"Oh yeah, Billy. Who's asking?"

Zach's stomach flipped over as he said, "I'm his

son."

Terrence's face went through three stages at this news, thoughtfulness, surprise, and then a kind of anxiousness before saying, "Oh man! You look just like him! Okay, um," and then to the volunteer, "Do you know Cliff? Light skin, mustache?"

"Yes," she said because everybody knew Cliff, who conducted all the volunteer's orientation.

"Would you please go get him?" She disappeared through the same doorway Terrence had come from and returned one minute later with Cliff. She had obviously filled him in on the way down, and Cliff came out frantic.

"Oh, Lord! Oh, Lord! Praise GOD! Amen, amen!" Cliff was experiencing some kind of religious experience. "I heard that God answers prayers, but praise His Holy Name! Hallelujah!" And then Cliff became concerned at a sudden realization. Just then, Hopeton came in from outside and Cliff grabbed his arm. "Hope! Look here!" And he pointed to Zach. Hopeton saw the face and knew immediately who he was. "Hope!" Said Cliff, "When did Billy leave?" His voice was urgent.

"He left this morning, around 9." Hopeton looked at Zach. "He don't even carry a cell phone."

"Did he say where he was going?" Zach looked at the men, hopeful.

"He said he had a job in Tulsa. He was out of money," said Hopeton. "It don't cost nothing to live here, but he said he had a house in Illinois, and he had to pay for it. He also said God told him it was about time to leave."

Zach felt despondent. He knew he could make up with his sister, which he should anyway, and he could find out where Billy, that is, his *dad*, lives. It wasn't like he couldn't find him, but, man, he had felt so certain that today was going to be the day, that this was the moment.

"Young man, have faith, Amen. You need to have faith and, Amen, trust the Lord, Amen, and He will lift you up on Eagles wings!" Cliff was beginning to preach. Zach realized that the man used "Amen," where most men would use, "Um."

"Son, I know the Lord has a word for you, Amen. And He is going to bring you to your Promised Land! Amen!" Standing next to him, Hopeton began to hum the background as though he were the organist of a gospel choir behind a gospel preacher. As Cliff's voice would rise, the humming would rise, sprinkled by an occasional "Hallelujah!" Terrence got in on it too with a "Yes Lord" and a "praise Gawd" every time it was appropriate.

Cliff continued, "We got to pray! Amen, we got

to pray to your Father in heaven who sent His one and only Son! Amen, that whosoever…"

"ANYboday!" Hopeton shouted.

"WhosoEVer would believe, would not, Amen, would NOT perish, but have everlasting, Amen, everlasting life!"

"Praise Jesus!" Added Terrence.

"Lord, we ask you, Amen, to stop Billy Stone in his tracks, wherever he is, whatever he's doing, call him back to the Bowery Mission, Lord Jesus, the place, Amen, where You have shown Yourself, Amen. You have shown Yourself miraculous on ten thousand occasions! Lord, You are a God of miracles! You can, Amen, do ANYthing! Lord! Do this! Bring back this man with his daddy, Amen. Unite father and son as you are united, Amen, with Your precious Son at your right hand!" At this good preaching, Hopeton and Terrence were stomping and clapping now at each revelation. The volunteer was quietly into it as well. Zach noticed her lips were moving, her eyes were closed, and her hand was raised up.

For his part, Zach found himself agreeing with what was being prayed, even the part about Jesus dying for the world. He had some business to do with God, but he was beginning to consider himself one of these crazies who were praying for him now.

"Lord! You said, Amen, that you would 'turn the hearts of the fathers to the children, and the heart of children to their fathers, lest I come and smite the earth with a curse!'"

Hopeton sang out, "Malachi preached! Mmmm!"

"Lord! It is already a curse when the fathers and the sons don't know each other! Lord, we are all dying, Amen, for lack of our fathers! But You, Amen, You are a good, good Father!"

"Yes, Lord," was sung out again by the Hopeton.

"Amen! You are a good, good Father! Father God," continued Cliff, "Bring back this man's daddy!"

The prayer went on this way. There was a part of Zach that felt a little ridiculous, okay maybe a lot ridiculous, in the situation, but he realized at some point that he had started crying. When the prayers and the praises suddenly began to die down, Hopeton looked at Zach with a puzzled expression, and asked, how long you been a Christian? Zach looked puzzled. "We heard you was an unbeliever."

"Well, I…I guess, I don't know about that," said Zach.

"Oh, you've been born again. I can see that," said Cliff.

Terrence said, "Hold up now, hold up. Zach, have you ever put your trust in Jesus?"

"I don't know. I guess I'd say I'm starting to believe in Him." Zach was amazed at how sure he felt about it.

"Ok, then you need to repent," said Terrence.

Zach had read enough about this in Wilbur's book. In fact, the idea had already occurred to him, and he realized he had been recalling all day the sins he would need to confess if he was ever going to engage in such an exercise. There was a pause, all eyes on Zach, the lips of the volunteer still moving, and Zach said, "Okay."

"Praise Jesus!" Cliff jumped up and down. The others hooped and hollered and patted him on the back. Terrence got somber and said, why don't we go inside?

They went into a room with a couch. Terrence had led him in and intended to keep everyone else out for the sake of Zach's privacy, but Zach said, "No, they can stay." All but the volunteer followed him into the room. Zach asked, "How do I do this?"

"Just tell God that you believe in Him, that you want Him to forgive you for your sins. And if you want to, you can tell Him what some of them are."

"Doesn't he already know?" Asked Zach sincerely.

"Yes, but confessions are as much for us as it is for Him. If you say it out loud, it's easier to believe that He hears and forgives," counseled Terrence.

"Okay," said "Zach," here goes. "Um, Lord…I am sorry for my sins. I'm sorry I hated my dad. I'm sorry I hated my mom. I have been a womanizer. A liar. A jerk." Memories came flooding into Zach's mind, and he realized that he would not have the time to list all the things. He'd have to do this over time, but for now, he said, "forgive me for all of it, God, and I believe you died on the cross for me…I believe you are real. I believe Jesus is God. I want to be a Christian."

Terrence said, "Zach, let us pray for you." Zach agreed and kept his head bowed. Tears were streaming down his face now as he felt in greater and greater measure the power of God flooding through him, washing him clean. The men put their hands on his back and shoulders and began to cry out to God for him, thanking God for saving him. They prayed for his life, for his forgiveness, for his future, and they spent a good deal of time continuing to pray for his reconciliation with Billy.

This went on for ten minutes when Zach thought he noticed another hand on his back. He figured the volunteer had come in to join, and then one by one, the other hands removed themselves. Zach risked breaking the moment and opened an eye to the room. He had thought his tears were spent, but there seemed to be a fresh supply as he saw the eyes of his earthly father, Billy Stone, tears down his own face, looking at his beloved son. The day that he'd longed and prayed for twenty years had arrived in a room with Terrence, Cliff, Hopeton, Billy, Zach, and the Holy Spirit.

There were no dry eyes as the two Stone's embraced. Billy held his boy for a good long time, and Zach, intimacy issues aside, loved every second of it. So much happened in those sixty seconds. Something seemed to be oozing from father to son. It was the substance that made the universe right. It was the cure for the mad, mad world. It was powerful. Only the Father in heaven could have invented this. Zach was healing already. There was much to discuss. Much to work out and much to learn, but this was a jump start on the wholeness that Zach had not even known in the womb of his angry mother. This was home.

"Just another day at the Bowery!" Shouted Terrence, and Hopeton began to sing, "*Victory is mine!*" The others soon joined in, clapping on the upbeat in perfect time, "*Victory is mine; victory today is mine! I told Satan, get thee behind, victory today is mine.*"

"Joy is mine!"

"Joy is mine; joy is mine, joy today is mine. I told Satan, get thee behind, cuz joy today is mine!"

The men sang like this for a while, worshiping and celebrating the answers to their prayers. It was surreal for Zach and Billy. There are only a few moments in life when something like a twenty-year goal is reached. Both men had this goal, although only one of them had known it throughout the time. Life is a journey, but the best life journeys are really a series of journeys, of adventures. This was an amazing end to a long hard road. It was also a beginning, and hope and love hung in the air all around them.

Chapter 14

Hazel Grace was still valiantly trying to fall in love with a decent guy. *Here we are again*, she thought. It had been months since her heart was officially broken by Zach. She had continued to see the man she'd been dating for a while, and, to her dismay, she could not seem to fall in love with him. Truthfully, she could not even fall in serious "like" with him. *Why, why, why not!* If she had been born in another culture or another time, she might have been in an arranged marriage with this man. Wouldn't she have been able to learn to love him then? Maybe, but it was hard to imagine.

He checked all the boxes. He was handsome, smart, successful, dependable, seemed to love the Lord, or he at least valued church and the Bible. She would never know quite why he didn't check off the most important box, the chemistry box. She needed to feel *something* for the guy. She had not intended to do this. This was supposed to be a routine weekly date with him, but in the moment, she was certain.

"Brian, I think we should break up." She felt so

bad saying it. She felt bad for Brian, but she also felt bad for herself. Was she damaged? Was she one of those girls who only dated projects? Who knew?

"Yeah. It's not working," said Brian, with no feeling at all. *What the crap?* She had been expecting to break his heart. She felt a little hurt that her words didn't seem to impact him. In fact, if she didn't know better, she'd say he was relieved. *Oh, Hazel Grace, don't look a gift horse in the mouth!*

Five minutes later, the breakup was out of the way, the food arrived, and the two enjoyed a companionable meal together. Brian was a good guy, and maybe he'd remain a friend. When she left the restaurant, she felt a little lighter. Looking up into heaven, she didn't say the words, but her heart was telling her that she was content, and that she was thankful to God for all the good folks in her life. She would just have to be single if that's what he wanted.

Wilbur was feeling blessed. Lately, there had been less time for welding and more time for ministry. As he reflected on the past several months, he could not have been more grateful to God. It never ceased to amaze him that how Jesus always seemed to know

exactly where Wilbur and Connie were needed.

This season had been so special. Maybe it was because they had four children of their own now, but children's ministry was front and center of the work. It seemed that daily there was a child coming into the kingdom of God by faith. Often, the kids would go home to their parents so changed that the mothers and fathers would come to see what had changed their child so dramatically. Wilbur got to lead more than a few people to Jesus this way.

When the number of children needing to be picked up every week became greater than the number of cars and drivers available, Wilbur prayed for a solution. In answer to those prayers, a large and established church nearby reached out to ask if Wilbur's infant church plant needed anything. "We could use a bus," said Wilbur in reply. He thought that it had been a long shot, but he also thought, "Hey, you don't get what you don't ask for." Amazingly they agreed and provided a bus for the work!

Now, Wilbur was moved once again to pray. Connie had been picking up a mom with her four children each week, and lately, the father had also been coming. But the youngest, a boy of eighteen months, had several holes in his heart, and the poor family had been told by their doctor that if he didn't have surgery soon, then he would surely die.

"Pastor," said the mother one day when they were talking to Wilbur and Connie after the service, "We want to get Buddy baptized to the Lord, especially since..."

Wilbur understood and did not wait for her to say her worst fear. "Of course, we can do that. Why don't you come back tonight, and we'll dedicate him? We don't baptize infants. We believe that the Bible says baptism is for people who have decided to put their faith in Jesus. I hope and pray that Buddy chooses that as soon as he possibly can. But when people baptize their babies, they are really dedicating them to the Lord, and they are saying they want to raise him up to follow and worship Jesus. Isn't that what you're saying?"

The woman said, "Yes. That's what we mean. I want him to grow up, and…" she could not finish the sentence, at once overcome with the fear that Buddy would not grow up at all, and she quietly wept. One arm around Jenny, Connie put her other hand on Wilbur in this moment, and at the same time, the warmth that Wilbur had come to identify with the unction of the Holy Ghost came over him.

"Jenny, would it be ok with you if when we dedicate Buddy tonight, I also anoint him and pray over him for healing?"

The mother looked up, hopeful, and a world of meaning was in her eyes. "Do you think Jesus would heal my baby?"

"I don't know if he will," said Wilbur gently, "but I know that he can." Wilbur silently prayed even as he waited for an answer. It was true that in this fallen world, sometimes people did not get healed, and their healing was withheld until heaven, but Wilbur was feeling faith for this. He would have offered anyway,

but in this case, he felt power in the asking.

"We would like that," said Jenny, looking at her husband, who was also nodding in hopeful but sober agreement.

That night before the sermon, Wilbur invited the whole family down to the front of the church. "Folks, most of you know that Buddy Adams has been diagnosed with having holes in his heart and needs surgery or the doctors say the worst will happen." A look in his eye showed anyone paying attention that something had just occurred to Wilbur. "It crosses my mind that this boy's condition is not unlike many of yours. The holes in his heart are physical, but they are not worse than the holes in some of our hearts. What hole is in your heart that longs to be filled with the power and presence of Almighty God?

Zach was typing as fast as he possibly could now. He knew there would be many typos. He had not eaten for seven hours, and he didn't remember when he realized he needed to go to the bathroom. Afraid to break the spell, he crossed his legs and wrote with abandon. After what had happened to him, he was seeing all of this in a brand-new light. He found himself praying more and more for the writing he was doing. He caught himself thinking about who might read it, and how it might change them, or help them. He prayed that God would use it.

He could hardly believe the change in his life in

just a week. Billy had been staying with him, delaying his temporary move to Tulsa until this morning. It had been wonderful to get to know his dad. He still had to get used to the fact that much of what he thought he knew of him had simply been a lie. He had worked to forgive his mother, who, in her pain and brokenness, had lied to him his whole life.

Billy had just left that very morning, and Zach looked forward to seeing him again soon, but for now, he was a man with two obsessions; the first was to finish this book. The second was to put it in the hands of the woman he loved. He had tried calling her once, but she had not answered, and he didn't leave a message. Now, he had no way of knowing if she even knew he called. For all he knew, she might have completely moved on and was in some serious relationship, maybe even engaged.

He couldn't think about this right now. He trusted God with the whole situation, and that was an entirely new thing for him. Now, he just had to get words on paper. He went back to what he was writing, once again amazed at God and Wilbur Tucker.

"Some seek to fill that hole with drinking or drugs. Some go from relationship to relationship, looking to fill that hole. What about you? Maybe you are a workaholic, or maybe you are a

pleasure seeker. Brothers and sisters, there is nothing in this world that can fill that hole. That hole was not made for anything in this world. That hole is a God-shaped hole."

This part was not in the sermon that Hazel Grace had given Zach, but only the part about healing the sick baby. Zach added these words after hearing them at the Time Square Church in Manhattan, where Zach had attended two days prior with his dad, Hopeton, and Cliff. It did sound like something Wilbur would say. Zach felt like he knew this man well after writing his story. He continued to type.

"That hole can only be filled one way. Ask God to fill it with himself. Ask him to come into your life and change it and change you. Let him fill that hole and surrender to him forever. Tonight, Buddy Adams has literal holes in his heart. The Bible says to anoint the sick and pray for them."

Wilbur took a small jar from behind the podium. "Friends, there is nothing magical about this oil. It is olive oil, and you can eat it on your salad, but what oil represents throughout the Bible is the anointing of God by his Holy Ghost. In the name of Jesus Christ of Nazareth, who died for our sins and rose again, ascended into heaven and will return, I anoint this boy for the healing of his infirmity. In Jesus' name, I command the holes in his heart to be healed! I speak to them and I say, 'Mend!'"

There was a power in the room, and many began to weep

and say, "Yes Lord," and "Praise the Lord." Wilbur asked the mother and father of the boy to lay their hands on the boy and they all prayed for a good ten minutes, Wilbur doing the talking as the parents agreed.

After some time, it felt to Wilbur that they were done. He always seemed to just know when the prayer had been prayed, and God had nudged him to stop, trusting in the Lord for whatever the outcome would be. That night, Wilbur and Connie prayed together once more for the family and for Buddy.

The next day Buddy was scheduled for surgery. As they were prepping him, the doctor ordered one more Ultrasound to make sure he knew what to expect once he had gotten in there. They had to order a second one when the first seemed to show no holes. After the second one, the surgeon, a man of pure science, uttered a word he had never uttered to a patient before. That word was "miracle."

It had been a month since Hazel Grace had broken up with the last perfect guy who was not right for her. She had peace, but she was a little worried that the part of her that was even able to be attracted to someone in that way was just dead. Maybe this was an answer to her prayers. How many times had she asked God to take away her desires if he were calling her to a life of singleness? She knew her mom, dad, grandma, and even her Grandpa, if he was still alive, would tell her not to be so extreme about it. Maybe God would want singleness for her, or maybe he wouldn't. Did she have to know that now?

Still, the thought of never having a husband or a family made her sad. Family was so important in her life, and it was the source of the best parts of her memory. She thought of all this as she waited for Sarah to finish getting dressed. They were going to go shopping for some dress patterns or something. Hazel Grace had agreed to go along just to spend some time with her mom. Hazel Grace did not get the sewing gene but always loved the hobby store where her mom, grandma, and aunts got their supplies. It was neat to see all the raw materials of people's craftiness.

Her mom called downstairs and told her to be watching for Aunt Michelle, who had asked at the last minute to come along. Michelle had a new SUV and wanted to show it off to the ladies. Hazel Grace loved her aunt and looked forward to spending time with her.

She had finally decided to start graduate school in education administration and had been passing the time waiting for the semester to start by continuing to help her father at his law office, although only three days per week now, and helping with some stuff at church.

She was ready to go shopping and decided to go outside to wait for Michelle. It was a beautiful day for November. The leaves had mostly fallen, and it was just starting to get colder. The air had such a feeling of familiarity this morning. She realized as she breathed it in, sitting in her front porch swing, that it had been about two years since she'd met Zach and he had come over to her house. She wondered how he was, and she wished she could call him. But that was all behind her, and she didn't need to stir up old sad feelings.

Darn, she thought. She did have to admit she felt sad now thinking about him. Would he ever find his way to God? Was he happy? She really hoped so. Painful as it was, she was glad she had met him. She missed him, but she was content. She sat back in the swing and gazed down the road. Michelle would come over the hill any minute. *There she is*, thought Hazel as something came over the horizon. She thought her mom had said Michelle had bought a black SUV. Now she could tell she was wrong and that wasn't Michelle at all.

Rather than a black SUV, a red car was coming toward the house. Hazel Grace pretty much knew everyone in the neighborhood. This was some stranger. As she watched the car approach it seemed to be slowing down until it stopped in front of her house. There was a glare on the windshield, so she could not make out the figure in the car. She waited for someone to emerge before she would get up, but it was some time. Whoever it was seemed to be stalling.

After what seemed like a long time, the door opened, and a leg came out, followed by a familiar face. Zach Stone was standing in the street in front of her house in the same place she'd seen him two years ago. Though he was polished up, it was the same Zach in all the right ways. But there were differences besides the polished look. He had a different kind of confidence. In the way he stood looking at her. She could not have known it, but what delayed his emergence was that he was engaging in his new favorite pastime, prayer. She was seeing a Zach Stone she had never seen before. She didn't quite know it, but she was looking at a new creation, the real Zach Stone. He walked deliberately to her, and the closer he came, the more she felt she might faint. She didn't know when she had stood up, but she was walking toward him too.

Zach had not intended to go straight to her and pick her up as he did, but he could not stop himself. The relief he felt just in seeing her after the tension of the last few weeks leading up to this was powerful. He had stopped himself from contacting her a thousand times. He was anxious to make sure she would accept him, to make sure she wasn't with someone else, to make sure he had at least a chance to get her to love him, but something made him stop. Something knew it had to be like this, in person with a book in hand.

He put her down and looked into her brilliant brown eyes. What he saw there relieved all his fears. He had truly trusted God. He knew there was no guarantee of a good reception, and he would accept whatever God had, but what he saw now told him that there would be a happy ending. These were the eyes of a woman in love. These were the eyes of a woman who hadn't been sure she could love again but was now assured. He hoped and believed that these were the eyes of his wife. Everything in her face asked him to kiss her, and so he did.

Chapter 15

The church was completely packed. On one side was a herd of Jacksons, Tuckers, and the many people who loved them. On the other side was Zach's sister, and Steve, the ex-roommate and programmer, Cliff, Hopeton, Terrence, Deon, Matt, who ran the lawn crew, and John, Ern, and Thomas from Billy's house. Also on that same side was Brad, another senior editor, and the editor from the Christian book publishing company who had been working with Zach and Hazel Grace to publish *Wilbur*. It was coming out this month and advance sales had been better than expected. Zach was already under contract for another one.

Zach felt like he was floating a foot off the ground as he stood with the minister and with his best man, Billy Stone, next to him, and Jillian a few feet away as the Maid of Honor. The flower girl, Lucy, came down confidently and did her job well, followed by an even younger ring bearer who lost his nerve and had to be carried down by his mother, with his face hidden in her neck.

Then the music changed, and the double doors were opened by the ushers. Zach was completely breathless as his bride appeared in the doorway with her father, who had already become a good friend to Zach in the six months he'd been back in Tulsa. As they walked down the aisle toward them, Zach held Hazel Grace's eyes. *My Lord*, he thought, as he considered how perfect she looked. She was so beautiful! *Oh God, I don't know how I got here. I don't believe in luck. You are so good to me. Make me worthy of this woman you have given me. Thank you for saving me, for loving me, and for bringing my dad into my life. Lord, don't ever let me go. Thank you, thank you, thank you, Lord.*

"Who gives this bride?"

"Her mother and I."

The minister nodded, and Russel Jackson hugged his new son-in-law. He pulled back from the hug and gave one more sincere look at the young man that somehow said both, "I'm proud to have you in the family," and at the same time, "Don't hurt her. She is special to me." Zach nodded to him in answer to the unasked question. He then turned his attention to his bride, who was radiant with joy. They looked at each other for a good long moment, and Zach wondered how he had the power to refrain from grabbing her right then and there. Finally, they turned to the minister.

"Friends, this is such an exciting day." Pastor Tim spoke both to them and over their heads, to the witnesses in the room. "Zachary Stone and Hazel Grace Jackson have committed to one another for the rest of their lives until one of them passes or until Jesus Christ returns to take us home.

"I've known Hazel Grace and her sweet family for many years. Her grandfather was a mentor of mine in ministry, and I have enjoyed somewhere near two hundred thousand calories at the table of a Jackson or a Tucker in my time as pastor of this church. I could not be more thrilled to see how this little girl has grown up and to see the wise and loving young woman you see before you today."

On the bride's side, the tears were starting to fall steadily. Grandma Connie held the hand of her daughter, remembering the proud day Sarah had stood in the very same spot to be given to Russel Jackson. In fact, Connie had been in this room at the church a million times. Watching her grandchildren pass into these new stages of life was such a joy. She briefly felt a pang of, "If only Wilbur were here." She knew how proud he would be.

"Marriage is not easy, though there are many in this room who make it look easy, they will be the first to tell you that whatever they have came by hard work."

Heads nodded all around. The pastor went on to explain that the first conflict on earth was a marital conflict between the first man and his wife. He said that because of their conflict and the sin that came as a result, almost every marriage in history has suffered as a result.

"But God loves marriage. He sent His only begotten Son to redeem all things, especially marriage, which reflects Jesus and His bride, the church." Pastor Tim went on that way, skillfully and powerfully explaining how the gospel applies to this institution of marriage. Zach didn't know how he managed it, but he did manage to take it in, though he was anxious for it to be over.

Finally, the pastor asked for the rings, which Billy, decked out and looking surprisingly at home in his tuxedo, produced from his jacket pocket. Zach took the ring for Hazel Grace and recited the vows he'd written for her. "Hazel Grace Jackson, I consider you a gift from God that I don't deserve. When I think about the last two years, where we started, and where we've come, I can only thank God, who obviously loves me so much. You are a miracle. I promise to love you, to honor you as my wife, to lead our family closer and closer to Jesus, to care for you, and to put you first above all others as flesh of my flesh and bone of my bones. I give you this ring as a sign and token of my love and devotion to you and my promise to walk beside you until death or the return of Christ."

Zach never took his eyes off hers. Hazel Grace was beginning to tremble as Zach slipped the wedding band onto her finger. She risked looking away from his eyes and down at her finger. This was really happening. She quickly returned to his eyes. "Zachary Stone, I love you and have waited for you my whole life. It was you who my parents and grandparents prayed for. It was you who my grandfather led me to. It was you who I compared every other man to and found them wanting. I promise to be devoted to you, to follow you as you lead our family, to be a helpmeet for you in the calling that God has on your life. I will love and support you. This ring is a promise and sign of my commitment to God first and then to you, my beloved husband."

This is what she said, although it was hard to understand because of the effect the joy and emotion had on her voice. Tears were now flowing in a steady stream from Zach's face as he waited patiently and savored every word of promise. She slipped the wedding ring on his finger, and they held hands and looked at each other, neither willing to look away. The combination of laughter and tears in that moment was as close to bliss as is possible to imagine outside of heaven; as a boy and his bride were becoming one in the presence of their Lord and the best people they knew in the whole world.

Finally, the minister said, "Ladies and gentlemen, it is my profound honor to be the first to present to you Mr. and Mrs. Zachary Stone!" The packed room full of witnesses burst into applause and hollering. This was a happy day! "Zach, you may now kiss your bride!"

And this he did. They kissed long enough to make a few people giggle a bit before tearing themselves away as the music of celebration began, and they practically danced back down the aisle. They had come down as two, but they were leaving as one. As they left the room, Hazel Grace thought of Wilbur Lee Tucker and how he was making as much of an impact now as he always had. She smiled, looked heavenward and whispered, "You're right, Grandpa, God has a plan!"

Afterword

  While Zachary Stone and Hazel Grace's story is fiction, Wilbur Lee Tucker's life is true. Billy is a genuine guy that Wilbur met on a job and who never wavered in his belief that God spoke to him through the fan that Wilbur turned in his direction. The Hells Angel character? He is real and eventually became a preacher. The kid with a hole in his heart, the young Wilbur getting hit by a car, his healed toothache, the thimble story and the out of body experience, all happened. These amazing stories are just a few of the countless stories that were a part of Wilbur's daily life and ministry. The ones written in this novel were all included in the last sermon he was known to write. He didn't write the sermon so that everyone would be awed by his life, but so that maybe in death, he could continue to bring people to the Lord.

  That's where I come in, his daughter and co-writer of this book, Sonya Tucker-Poindexter. We found his last sermon just one day before he passed away. For the next six months, it was too painful to read or even think about. However, the Lord kept tugging on my heart to share these stories and do exactly what Dad wanted, bring people to the Lord. I pray that dad's stories have touched your life, and perhaps we can follow in his footsteps. As he wrote in this last sermon… "God fills us with His love so we can be like Jesus, looking out for broken lives, broken homes and see the need all around us."

Wilbur Tucker – Last Sermon
"By All Means"

To the weak I became weak, to win the weak. I have become all things to all people so that by all means I might save some. 1 Corinthians 9:22

God has a plan for every single life that is born into this world. We were born to serve him and to fulfill His plan for our life. If we fail to seek God's will, we miss the real meaning and purpose of life. Without God, there is something missing. There is an emptiness or void in our life. We can try to fill that void with material things, but they cannot satisfy. The only thing that can fill that emptiness is Jesus Christ.

They say that life is what happens while we are

busy making other plans. Sometimes life seems so haphazard doesn't it? But I assure you that God has a plan! He fills us with His love so we can be like Jesus, always looking out for broken lives, broken homes and using God's love to help those all around us. If we can share our lives with broken people, they too can find hope for eternity. I want to show you through my experiences how God is always there and always has a plan. His love, mercy and grace made something beautiful out of my life.

I was the youngest of 5 children. Our mother died when I was 4 years old. While my brothers and sisters were scattered to different homes of our mom's family, I stayed with my dad. During the day, he would often leave me with the bootlegger that lived next door. The man would give me a quarter and send me away. One day while making my way to the store, I got hit by a car. I got up and ran home.

(He doesn't expand on "I got hit by a car," and he never told us about it. I assume he had no one to tell or help him at the time, so he just got up and ran home. Since he mentions it here, I think he attributes it to God taking care of him when no one else would.)

My grandmother would pick me up and take me to church every time the doors were open for service. At an early age, I learned to pray. I learned to trust in God. I remember kneeling at the altar and praying sincerely, in confidence. When I was 7 years old, I was at my grandmother's for a week during the summer. I had a bad toothache, and she asked the pastor to come and pray for me. The tooth quit hurting instantly. I never forgot that experience. I felt the call to preach at that time. However, I thought it was the last thing I ever wanted to do.

At 8 years old, I worked in a gas station – fixing flats, pumping gas and whatever else needed to be done. I never met a stranger. They were all my friends. Many of them would give me a Christmas gift. I wasn't content until I gave them something back. God does have a plan!

In my teens, I was like everyone else. I went astray, did my own thing; whatever you might call it. I sinned against God, doing what I knew was wrong. At 22 years old, my cousin introduced me to the girl of my dreams. She was the most beautiful thing I had ever seen in my life. I was hooked and loving every minute of it. Soon, we were married. I went to church with her and her family on Sunday mornings, Sunday nights and Wednesday nights. They were a large family and committed to God. Her dad and mom were a great influence and witness in my life.

(Large family is an understatement. Connie is one of 19 children.)

I got certified as a welder and started working construction jobs around the country. I was going to a job in New Mexico when I turned to Jesus and asked for forgiveness of my sins and for Him to come into my life. Wow! What a change! I became hungry for the word of God. I called my wife immediately to tell her and I couldn't wait to tell others. One of the fellows I was working with was always singing and I would join in. He asked me one day if I was a Christian. I said yes, and asked what made him think that? He said he could tell by the kind of cigarette I smoked. Since I couldn't see Jesus walking down the street smoking a Winston, I put my cigarettes on the altar and God set me free from not only cigarettes but my temper and language problems. He gave me a peace, power and joy that I had never known before. God has a plan and I am so glad to be a part of it.

It wasn't too long after that job that I felt the call to ministry.

(The next few paragraphs are an insert from my uncle Bill about dad's call to ministry. It was not included in the final sermon but told the day before dad died as we sang and prayed around his bed.)

"One time, Wilbur and I were fishing and talking about what the Lord had done in our lives. Wilbur was telling me about his decision to go to Colorado Springs to seminary school.

His story began with much prayer; he needed the Lord's help. Wilbur turned to scripture and was led to the story of Gideon and the fleece. He said he went to prayer again. After a while, the Lord told him to do a fleece (clarification of God's plan). He asked Mom Butcher, his mother-in-law, if he could use her thimble for a couple of days. That night, he went outside to his car and placed the thimble on top…then went to prayer again. Wilbur asked the Lord that in the morning, to have the top of the car wet and the thimble dry. The next morning, Wilbur found the top of the car wet, and the thimble completely dry.

At this point, I asked - weren't you afraid the thimble would blow away? Wilbur said, no…this is in God's hands, His plan.

Wilbur continued…he explained that, like Gideon, he wanted further clarification. This time, he prayed that in the morning, the top of the car would be dry and the thimble be filled with water. The next morning, sure enough…the car was dry, and he poured water out of the thimble. Wilbur knew what he had to

324

do. He and his family set out for seminary school in Colorado Springs. He said he found a job and a place to live…all with God's help."

(The sermon continues…)

I loaded the car with my wife and 2 baby girls and left home for seminary school. I had no job and no money to live on. I didn't know how we would make it work but I knew I needed to study and learn. One day, I went behind the garage, knelt down and prayed. God told me, as clear as if He was standing beside me, "fear not, for I am with you." I trusted him. I enrolled in college, got a call to a work on a job in Iowa, and made enough money to pay rent, get groceries and start school. I was driving over 100 miles away from home to work and then going to school 4 hours, 4 nights a week. Anything God calls us to do, He will make a way to get it done.

One night in college, I remember vividly we had a chapel service, and the altar was open for anyone who wanted to come. I was praying that God would bless and really touch the lives and needs there in the service. While I was praying, I had a vision. I saw Jesus carrying the cross up the mountain. He was looking back over His shoulder into that chapel where altars were full and others were making their way to the altar. I opened my eyes, stood up and saw the same thing Jesus was seeing. It was happening right before my eyes. The words came to me, "this is what it's all about." God has a plan!

While I was in college, I started ministering in a nursing home and an abandoned mining town. I was helping in a mission's church in an area of poor and struggling people. Some of the members of the Hell's Angels were living there. We visited their homes and invited them to come to our service. We saw the change God made in their lives. One of them became a preacher. God has a plan!

After graduating from college, I went to a job in Wyoming. We were living in a desert area in a homemade trailer. My wife and I now had four children. With the help of materials from my company, I started having brush arbor meetings where we were camping. We invited other campers to come, and the Lord was blessing us. One day, on my way home from work, I saw a woman with a baby in her arms and two more small children walking down the road. I asked on the job if anyone knew about the woman and children. Someone said that her husband had a tent home in the hills. That evening after work I went looking and found the family. They had no food or even milk for the baby. I invited them to come home with me. In Wyoming, at night, even in the summer, it gets very cold. They loaded everything they had into my car and went with me, not knowing I had a wife and four children living in an 8X20 homemade trailer. But we had lights, heat and food! We were very, very warm and cozy with eleven people inside. I was able to get the man a job at the plant where I was working, and eventually, he found another job and a home for his family. God really blessed them.

I left that job to go to my first pastorate. When we began, there were about 18 people attending services. We started picking up children and bringing them to Sunday school. We started growing. One Christmas, a larger church adopted my family and asked what we needed. I told him that I had been praying for a bus. That church gave us a bus! All fixed up and delivered. We started a bus ministry and a vacation bible school. We were soon picking up 47 children and taking them to and from vacation bible school. On the last day of bible school, we had 47 children at the altar to accept Jesus as their Savior. God has a plan!

One of the fathers of the children started coming to every service. He wanted to know what had changed his son's life. One Sunday night, he went to the altar. After the service, I met him at the door. He told me he thought he had a heart attack and that his wife was on his way to take him to the hospital. He was on disability from the military. The next morning, I went to visit him in the hospital. He was doing well. I told him that I thought his heart attack might have just been good old-fashioned conviction. He asked, what is that? I told him I could remember when I went to revival, and the altar was open, I felt like I was going to have a heart attack. My heart was beating and thumping so hard. But, after the service was over, I felt fine. I told him about Jesus saying, "Behold, I stand at the door and knock, if any man hears my voice and opens the door, I will come in." That may have been Jesus knocking at your door. Do you want to open that door to your heart and let Jesus come in? He said yes and he did. That man became the bus minister of that church. By then, we were running over 100 children in our Sunday school program.

My wife started picking up a mom and her four children and bringing them to Sunday school. Soon, the dad also started coming. They had an 18-month-old baby with holes in his heart and had to have surgery. They didn't know if he would survive or not, but without the surgery, he had no chance. They asked me if I would dedicate him to the Lord. I said I would be glad to. I felt led to anoint him for healing and asked them if they wanted to do that. They said, yes. On Sunday night, they brought the baby to service. I dedicated him and anointed him for healing. On Monday morning, they took him to the hospital to get ready for surgery. The holes in his heart were gone. There was no sign of them. The baby boy started growing and playing like a regular child. To God be the glory, great things He has done and continues doing every day. What a joy it is to be a part of it!

I received a call from another church and felt that was where God was leading me. The church was running about 12-20 people in the services. We started reaching out, picking up children, and bringing them to Sunday school. I told the people in the church if we had 100 people in our Easter service that I would sing a song from the roof of the church. On Easter Sunday, I sang "I'm So Glad I'm A Part of the Family of God" from the roof of the church...in the rain. We had 117 people in that service. Praise God for his plan.

I heard about a nursing home nearby and felt the need to go minister there. I went to visit and asked if I could come once a week and minister. They allowed me to come one time, the following Tuesday. When I got there, the people looked depressed. Their faces were sagging like they were just waiting to die. We started singing some old hymns, and I watched them come alive.

I shared the word of God and got a few smiles, several "Amen's," and even a "Praise God." On Friday, I got a call from that nursing home. They said all they heard all week was about that service. They wanted me to come back every week. It was so beautiful to see them waiting for me each Tuesday and praising the Lord with happiness in their hearts. His plan works!

While working on a job, I often sing a lot. On one job, a foreman told me I had to quit singing so much. I asked him if that meant I also had to stop breathing. I love the song, Redeemed! I sing, for I cannot be silent. His love is the theme of my song. Praise God for the song that He gives us.

Many times, I would hear people holler out, "sing Rock of Ages or sing Old Rugged Cross." On one job, I was working with a helper. The other men asked him if he was learning any new songs. He told them, no, but I learned that Jesus loves me because Preacher Tucker told me so. Another time, I was working with a young man and had the opportunity to share about the coming of Christ, and in the twinkle of an eye, we'll be gone. I was singing songs like Jesus is Coming Soon and What a Day That Will Be When My Jesus I Shall See. We were working in an area where there was only one way out. I would work and do my part, then I would come out, and he would go in and do his part. One day, I needed another tool, and found that I could squeeze and go out another hole. While I was gone, he realized that I was not there. It scared him. He thought he had gone and missed the coming of Christ! When I got back, I stuck my head into the hole. He had a million-dollar smile! He said he was never so glad to see anyone in his whole life. Before the job ended, we prayed together for him to be ready. God works in mysterious ways, doesn't he? His wonders to perform!

Another time, I was working with a man out in the field on some duct-work, and it started pouring down rain. We had to get inside the duct to get out of the rain. We had talked before, and he told me he was ready for something better, a better way to live. I told him Jesus is the way. He asked me to pray for him. I did, and the rain stopped. We went back to work. I was thinking about what had just happened. I thought he is the one who needs to pray. The rain started pouring down again. We went back inside, and I told him what I was thinking. He prayed a sinner's prayer. The rain stopped, and the peace of God took over, and he knew it. He later said he could see life in a whole new way. "I once was lost, but now I am found, was blind, but now I see." Praise God for his wonderful plan.

I returned to Oklahoma for a job and had to go to a welding school to take a test. I had never done that before. The inspector told me what he expected, and I ran the test. The inspector liked my work and told me I needed to come teach at the school. I went back to my current job, completed it, and then went back to the school to check on teaching. I started running different tests to qualify and soon was teaching. I moved to an evening shift to be a supervisor and teach blueprint class and all phases of welding.

I started Bible study with some of my students on Wednesday nights. We averaged over a dozen people every week. Some of them started coming with me to church on Sunday mornings. I think they came for my mother-in-law's cooking. We went to her house for dinner, and she treated all of them like one of her own. There was always plenty to eat with all the covered dishes everybody brought. It was a great family time, and that should be important for all of us. Over the years, I have received letters from some of those students. They thanked me for showing them a way to live while teaching them how to make a living.

On the evening shift, we usually stopped at 11:30pm, cleaned up, locked up and got out by midnight. One Friday night, everyone finished their work, and we were able to leave by 11:45pm. One the way home a drunk driver ran a stop sign and hit me. We were both pronounced dead at the scene. The medics called the coroner out to examine the body, and during his exam, I moaned. They rushed me to the hospital. They said my head was the size of a watermelon. I still don't remember anything about the wreck. I woke up in the hospital with part of a scripture running through my mind. "The angels of the Lord encampeth around them that trust in Him." One of my brother-in-law's told me he visited me at the hospital. He said about all I had done was quote scriptures to him. I did not remember even seeing him. There is power in the word of God. It changes things like attitudes and situations. With God all things are possible!

When I got out of the hospital, I went back to the school to pick up my paycheck. They told me I was terminated for quitting early on that Friday night. That was a big shock. I was going to miss the bible study opportunity. Despite my faith, I was worried. I said out loud, "Lord, it is sure going to be interesting to see how you work this out for my good." All along, I knew God had something better for me. I'm glad He knows His business a whole lot better than we do. He has been doing it for a long time and He never fails. Praise His holy name!

I went back to construction work, where I was ministering, sowing seeds and touching different lives on every job. My job was not just a paycheck or a dirty, nasty job as it was often referred to but a wonderful challenge to get a job done, do it well, make a difference, and, by all means, win some believers.

I was working on a job in Louisiana in an oil refinery. There was a young man on the job that had a terrible attitude. He was mad at the world. He cursed and complained with every breath. One day, he walked up beside me, cussing and complaining. I looked at him and said, "well, praise the Lord anyhow." He looked back at me and shook his head, not knowing what to say. I told him I'm thankful to have a job, an opportunity to provide for my family. The more you complain, the more miserable you are going to be. And, probably whoever is working around you. His lousy attitude continued, but he started coming around me more often, asking questions and telling me about his life. He had two children. I said they were his greatest responsibility. The bible says, "Train up a child in the way he should go, and when he is old, he will not depart from it." I asked him that if he doesn't set a good example for them, who will? The last 2 or 3 days on the job, he and I were the only two people working inside the cat cracker. I was finishing up some welding, and he was over grinding on something, and I could hear him complaining. I could also hear some air blowing over by where he was working. I stopped what I was doing and went over and turned the air, so it was blowing directly on him. I went back and finished my welding job. The following day he walked up to me and asked, do you know when you turned that air on me yesterday? I said yes. He said God told me through that air that he had not given up on me yet. I said, well, praise the Lord. He said, oh, that's not all. I got down on my knees last night and made peace with God. When Christ makes us free, we are free indeed. He was a new creation in Christ Jesus. Old things were passed away, and all things became new. We worked together that last day of the job. He never cursed or complained. To God be the glory! I went back to that same plant the next year. He came up to me and said he's never been the same. Thanks to Calvary, things are different than before.

I went to a job in Springfield, Illinois, and visited a church there. One of the families invited me over for dinner. They had 8 children. After dinner, I told the children a couple of stories and did some tricks with a rope and a piece of paper. I went back to my motel for the afternoon then returned for the evening service. The mom came up to me and said her children thought I was an angel. She assured them that I was not an angel. They asked how she knew – she said no angel ever had 5 kids! Those children will never forget those stories. With God all things are possible. Without Him, I would be nothing. Without Him, I would be enslaved. Without Him, life would be hopeless. With Jesus, thank God I am saved.

My oldest daughter was playing basketball, and her team was in the state finals. One of the girls hurt her ankle and the team came to ask me to pray for her. I was blessed and praising God for the faith of those girls. We all gathered around the injured girl and prayed for her. The next day, she was able to play the whole game. They ended up winning 2nd in the state championship and went back and won 1st the following year. The team coach who won 2nd told our coach that they had everything planned on how they were going to beat us. However, they didn't plan on the little blonde-headed girl who wouldn't let them get the inside shot. That little blonde girl was my daughter. Ha! That didn't cost any extra.

After praying with the injured player, I went back to my room and could not get it off my mind. I had a song started and it kept running through my mind. The words finally came to me:

Oh, when I think of my life down here
I dreamed of wealth and fame
I worked so hard to gain it all
Just finding guilt and shame
But then I met this friend of mine
Yes, Jesus is His name. He filled my heart
With joy divine, then He called me by His name

Oh, since I met this friend of mine
It's never been the same, I found what
I was looking for, yes, Jesus is his name
Now I'm walking in the light of God
I have His peace within, this very
Special friend of mine, yes, Jesus in his name

Now he's walking with me day-by-day
Along life's narrow way. Oh, I'm so glad
This friend of mine is showing me the way
If I could work a million years
I never could repay, the debt I owe
This friend of mine, yes Jesus is His name

Oh, since I met this friend of mine
It's never been the same. I found what
I was looking for, yes, Jesus is his name

This is the end of his sermon. But not the end of his story. He wrote this sermon not too long after one of his most remarkable events. A doctor's visit that turned into a near-death/out-of-body experience. As I said before, books and movies have been written about these kinds of events. Dad's remarks: "I guess God isn't finished with me yet."

Dad went to see his doctor for a routine check-up. After multiple tests, he was sent directly to the hospital to have his heart checked. Long story short, he ended up having quadruple by-pass surgery. After the surgery, the doctor told us that dad's heart had stopped beating and had lost oxygen to the brain for more than 2 minutes. And that while dad was alive, he didn't think he had any brain function and he probably would not make it through the night. We all gathered in a circle in the waiting room, held hands and prayed. And we prayed and we prayed! The next morning, Dad woke up. He was hurting but he was alive and miraculously had full brain function. The doctor came into the room and after doing his checks, he told dad how remarkable it was that he was alive and well. Dad responded by telling him how thankful he was that he could grab ahold of his heart and bring him back to life. He went on to describe seeing the doctor holding his heart in his bare hands and squeezing over and over until his heart began to beat again. The doctor's face was priceless. That was precisely what happened. He said Wilbur, there is no way you could have seen that; you were under anesthesia, your chest was wide open. Dad said, I saw all of it. That was something, wasn't it? He looked over at us and said I also really appreciate you guys holding hands and praying for me.

There were 12 of us holding hands and praying. When we questioned him later, he named all 12 of us in the room. We have a large family, and throughout the day, people had come and gone. The only way to know which 12 were there at the time would have been to see us in person. I said, Dad, you had an out-of-body experience. He said "well, I don't know about all that but I guess God isn't finished with me yet." We never talked about his out-of-body experience again. For us, it was just another remarkable story in my dad's life of remarkable stories.

The last few years of his life were very tough. He suffered from anxiety and dementia. In the worst of times, our saving grace was to ask him to tell us his favorite scripture or sing a hymn. While he didn't know where he was or who we were, he never forgot scripture or hymns. It calmed him greatly. The last week of his life, while in and out of consciousness, he kept saying that he had been washed in the blood. I am comforted by this statement. It makes me think that he had already visited God, and he was telling us that it will be okay, he is ready and more importantly, God is ready and waiting for him. On his final 2 days, we all gathered around his bed and sang him home. Literally! We sang to him for hours; we covered every song we learned in Sunday school and every hymn he had taught us through the years. Just like his life, his departure was equally remarkable. After being unconscious for 2 dreary days, he opened his eyes, squeezed Mom's hand, and smiled. At that moment, his dog, who stayed outside but never left his bedroom window during these last few days, got up and put his face up against the glass. A big wind gust blew, the wind chimes sounded, a ray of light broke brightly through the clouds, and dad took his final breath.

It sounds dramatic, right? I think so, too, but that's exactly what happened. We have talked about it many times. He lived and died with the most remarkable stories. Made more so because they were never about him but always about the glory of God.

Made in the USA
Coppell, TX
01 April 2021

52800153R00201